# GATHER, DARKNESS!

Here is a classic of science-fiction, published in Great Britain for the first time. The author, Fritz Leiber, was awarded the coveted "Hugo" for the best science-fiction novel of 1965, and for over twenty years he has been in the forefront of the sf field. Few can rival his imagination and sheer powers of telling a story that grips the reader from the first page.

We are taken into the world of the second atomic age that is also a new Dark Age where religion and magic are the rule of the day, and a self-perpetuating heirarchy of priests governs a population that exists in the shackles of slaves. But, as has happened so often in human history, it takes only one man, of principle, to upset a dictatorial oligarchy.

That man is Brother Jarles, an honest, if naïve, priest, who dares to question the established order. He believes the ruling clique is despotic and corrupt, and does not believe in the mysticism that he has been taught. And because he dares to speak out, he becomes the pawn in a power struggle that masquerades as black and white magic; masquerades as the choice between Good and Evil.

*Gather, Darkness!* was first published in the golden age of science-fiction; today it still stands out as a chilling and convincing novel, a "must" for every sf addict!

TOM BOARDMAN JR.

# Gather, Darkness!

## Fritz Leiber

NEW ENGLISH LIBRARY/TIMES MIRROR

FOR JONQUIL, MY WIFE

First published in the United States of America

*Gather, Darkness!* by Fritz Leiber, copyright, 1943,
by Street & Smith Publications, Inc.,
for *Astounding Science-Fiction*, May-July, 1943
First published in Great Britain in 1966
by New English Library

© 1950 by Fritz Leiber

First Four Square edition June 1966
Reissued in this NEL edition August 1979

NEL Books are published by
New English Library from
Barnard's Inn, Holborn,
London EC1N 2JR.
Made and printed in Great Britain by
C. Nicholls and Co. Ltd,
The Philips Park Press, Manchester.

45004 349 5

# CHAPTER ONE

BROTHER JARLES, priest of the First and Outermost Circle, novice in the Hierarchy, swallowed hard against his churning anger; bent every effort to make his face a mask – not only to the commoners, for that was something every member of the Hierarchy was taught to do, but to his brother priests as well.

Any priest who hated the Hierarchy as he did during these frightening spasms of rage must be mad.

But priests could not go mad – at least, not without the Hierarchy knowing of it, as it knew of everything else.

A misfit then? But a priest was fitted to his job with infinite precision and foresight, the very outlines of his personality measured as if with an atomic probe. A priest could not hate his work.

No, he must be mad. And the Hierarchy must be concealing the fact from him for its own inscrutable purposes.

Or else – everything to the contrary – he was right.

At the touch of that sickening thought, the Great Square of Megatheopolis seemed to haze and bloat before his eyes. The commoners became drab blurs; the priests here and there, scarlet ones, topped with the healthy pink of well-fed faces.

Fighting for composure and vision itself, he forced himself to focus on the year-stone of a recently-built dwelling in the commoner's section. The inscription read, "139 G. G."

He sought to maintain calm by a calculation. The year 139 of the Great God would be the year 206 of the Golden Age, except that Golden Age dates were not recognized. It would also be the year 360 of the Atomic Age. And finally the year 2305 of the Dawn Civilization and – what was the god called? – Christ.

"Hamser Chohn, Commoner of the Fifth Ward! Stand forward, my son."

Brother Jarles winced. In moods like this, that reedy voice grated unendurably on him. Why had he been paired with Brother Chulian! Why, for that matter, must priests never work alone, but always by twos!

But he knew the reason. It was so they might spy on each other, make detailed reports on each other. So that the Hierarchy would know of everything.

Fighting every instant to maintain the mask, he turned back. His eyes automatically dodged the fourth face in the queue of commoners lined up before himself and Brother Chulian.

That fat, blue-eyed, soft-cheeked, shaven priest was consulting the work lists, which were printed in primitive style for the benefit of the commoners, who did not know – and were not supposed to know – anything of reading tapes. Really, there was no reason to hate Brother Chulian especially. Just a rank-and-file priest of the Second Circle. Just a bloated baby.

But you could hate a bloated baby when he exercised over adult commoners the powers of schoolmaster, minister, and parent.

Only one good thing – this particular job, so distasteful to Jarles, tickled Brother Chulian's sense of self-importance so much that he was willing to do it all by himself.

The little fat priest looked up from the work lists at the stalwart young commoner nervously twisting a shapeless hat in big, horny hands, pausing every second to wipe one of them against a home-woven smock.

"My son," he piped benignly, "you are to work for the next three months in the mines. That will reduce your contribution to the Hierarchy to a mere half of your private earnings. You will report here to the appropriate deacon at dawn tomorrow. Hamser Dom!"

The young commoner gulped, nodded twice, and quickly stepped aside.

Jarles' anger flared anew. The mines! Worse than the fields, or even the roads! Surely the man must know. And yet, when he had heard, he had looked grateful – that same fawning look the old books were always attributing to a faithful domestic animal of the genus Canis, now extinct.

Jarles wrenched his gaze away, again skipping the same face, now third in line. It was that of a woman.

The sinking sun sent rich shadows across the Great Square. The crowd was thinning. Only the tail-ends of a few wards were still waiting to hear what the work lists held in store. Here and there smocked or bloused commoners – the men in clumsy leggings, the women in heavy skirts – were gathering up the leftovers of homemade goods they had brought to barter or sell, loading them onto their own backs or those of small, burly mules, then trailing off into the narrow, cobbled streets of the commoner's section. Some wore broad-brimmed hats of a coarse felt. Others had already pulled up their hoods, although the chill of evening had not yet arrived.

Looking towards the commoners' section of Megatheopolis, Jarles was reminded of pictures he had seen of the cities of the Black Ages, or Middle Ages – or whatever that period of the Dawn Civilization had been called. Except that the houses here were mostly one-storey and windowless, and everything was very neat and clean. Although he was only a priest of the First Circle, he knew that the resemblance was no coincidence. The Hierarchy did not tolerate coincidence. It had a reason for everything.

An old crone in ragged garments and a peaked hat hobbled past. The other commoners drew away from her. A small boy yelled, "Mother Jujy! Witch! Witch!" shied a stone at her and raced off. But Jarles smiled at her faintly. And she smiled back – an unpleasant grimacing of wrinkled lips over toothless gums during which her hooked nose and jutting chin seemed about to meet. Then she was on her way again, feeling with her cane for secure places between the cobbles.

In the other direction, Megatheopolis was magically different. For there rose the gleaming buildings of the Sanctuary, topped by the incredible structure of the Cathedral, which fronted the Great Square.

Jarles looked up at the Great God, and for a moment felt fingering through his anger a touch of the same pious fear that vast idol had awakened in him when he was only a commoner's child – long before he had passed the tests and begun to learn the secrets of the priests. Could the Great God see his blasphemous rage, with those huge, searching, slightly frowning eyes? But such a superstitious fancy was unworthy even of a novice in the Hierarchy.

Without the Great God, the cathedral was still a mighty structure of soaring columns and peaked windows tall as pine trees. But where one might expect a steeple or a pair of towers, began the figure of the Great God – the upper half of a gigantic human form, terrible in its dignity and serenity. It did not clash with the structure below. The heavy folds of its drapery became the columns of the Cathedral, and it was built of the same grey plastic.

It dominated all Megatheopolis, like some unbelievable centaur. There was hardly an alley from which one could not glimpse the stern yet benignant face with the glowing nimbus of blue light.

One felt that the Great God was minutely studying every pygmy creature that crossed the Great Square, as if he could at any moment reach down and pick one up for a closer scrutiny.

As if? Every commoner knew there was no "as if" about it!

But that massive figure did not rouse in Jarles one atom of pride at the glory and grandeur of the Hierarchy and his great good fortune in having been chosen to become part of it. Instead, his anger thickened and tightened, becoming an intolerable shell about his emotions – as red and oppressive as the scarlet robe he wore.

"Sharlson Naurya!"

Jarles flinched at the name chirruped by Brother Chulian. But now the moment had arrived; he realized he would have to look at her. Not to, would be cowardly. Every novice priest experienced great difficulties before he finally succeeded in breaking all emotional ties that linked him to the commoners – to family and friends, and more than friends. Face the fact: Naurya could never mean anything to him.

Nor to her, he realized with something of a shock as he quickly slewed his head around so that he was looking up into her face. For she did not seem to recognize him or take note of him, although save for his robe and shaven pate, he was the same as ever. She stood there quietly, showing none of the cringing nervousness of the men. Her minds, calloused by the loom, were folded at her waist. Her face, paler for the masses of dark hair, was without emotion – or else a better mask than his own.

Something – the way she threw her shoulders back – the air of hidden purpose sunk deep, deep in her green eyes – thrust through the shell of his anger and prodded his heart.

"My little daughter, Naurya," Chulian cooed importantly, "I have good news for you. A great honour is yours. For the next six months you are to serve in the Sanctuary."

There was no change in her expression, no outward indication of her reaction, but it was a few seconds before she replied.

"It is too great an honour. I am unworthy. Such holy work is not for the likes of a simple weaver."

"That is true," said Chulian judiciously, bobbing his chubby hairless head up and down within the stiff funnel of his collar. "But the Hierarchy may lift up whom it will, even from the ranks of the most humble. It has deemed you worthy for the holy work. Rejoice, my daughter. Rejoice."

Her voice was as quiet and grave as when she first replied. "But I am still unworthy. I know it in my heart. I cannot do it."

"Cannot, my daughter?" Abruptly Chulian's voice became querulously stern. "Do you mean 'will not'?"

Almost imperceptibly, Naurya nodded. The eyes of the commoners behind her grew wide, and they stopped their nervous fumblings.

Brother Chulian's soft little mouth set in an implacable pout. The work lists crackled loudly as he clenched them in his red-gloved hand.

"You understand what you are doing, daughter? You understand that you are disobeying a command of the Hierarchy, and of the Great God the Hierarchy serves?"

"I know in my heart that I am unworthy. I cannot."

But this time the nod was very definite. Again Jarles felt something thrusting at his ribs.

Chulian bounced up from the bench he shared with Jarles. "No commoner may question the judgements of the

Hierarchy, for they are right! I sense more here than simple stubbornness, more even than sinful obstinacy. There is only one sort of commoner who would fear to enter the Sanctuary when bidden. I sense – witchcraft," he announced dramatically, and struck his chest with the flat of his hand. Instantly his scarlet robe ballooned out tautly, until it stood a handbreadth away from his body at every point. The effect was frighteningly grotesque, like a scarlet pouter pigeon. And above his shaven head a violet halo glowed.

The faces of the commoners grew more pale. But Naurya only smiled very faintly, and her green eyes seemed to bore into Chulian.

"And that, once sensed, is easily discovered!" the swollen little priest continued triumphantly.

He stepped quickly forward. His puffy scarlet glove clutched at her shoulder without seeming quite to touch it, yet Jarles saw her bite her lips against sudden hurt. Then the scarlet glove flirted downward, ripping the heavy smock, so that the shoulder was uncovered.

There were three circular marks on the white skin. One burned angry red. The others were rapidly becoming so.

Jarles thought that Chulian hesitated a moment and stared puzzledly at them, before gathering himself and shrilling out, "Witchmarks! Proof!"

Unsteadily Jarles got to his feet. His anger made him retch, a nauseating force. He slapped his own chest, felt the uniform inward pressure of the field at every point of his body, like a bath of warm wax; saw from the corner of his eye the gleam of his halo. Then he launched his fist at Chulian's neck.

The slow-looking blow did not seem to reach its mark, but Chulian tumbled down and rolled over twice. Even as he rolled, his robes stood out between him and the ground, as if he were inside a red rubber ball.

Again Jarles slapped his own chest. His robe went limp and his halo vanished. And in that instant his anger exploded hotly, burning the mask of hyprocrisy from his face.

Let them blast him! Let them blind and deafen him with excommunication! Let them drag him screaming to the crypts below the Sanctuary! The Hierarchy had seen fit to let him go mad without interfering. Very well, then! They would have a taste of his madness!

He sprang onto the bench and held up his hands for attention.

"Commoners of Megatheopolis!"

That checked the beginnings of a panicky flight. Eyes turned to stare at him stupidly. They had not yet begun to comprehend what had happened. But when a priest spoke, one listened.

"You have been taught that ignorance is good. I tell you it is evil!

"You have been taught that to think is evil. I tell you it is good!

"You have been told that it is your destiny to toil night and day, until your backs ache to breaking and your hands blister under the callouses. I tell you it is the destiny of all men to look for easier ways!

"You have let the priests rule your lives. I tell you that you must rule yourselves!

"You believe that the priests have supernatural powers. I tell you they have no powers you could not wield yourselves!

"You believe that the priests are chosen to serve the Great God and transmit his commands. But – if there is a god anywhere – each one of you, in his ignorant heart, knows more of him than the mightiest archpriest.

"You have been told that the Great God rules the universe – earth and sky. I tell you the Great God is a fake!"

Like whiplashes, the short, sharp sentences flicked into the corners of the Great Square, turned all eyes towards him. The words were not understood, except that they were very different from what the priests ever said. They frightened. They almost hurt. But they tugged irresistibly. Everywhere – even in the work queues – commoners looked at the nearest priest, and getting no contradictory order, trotted over towards Jarles.

And Jarles now looked around him in bewilderment. He had expected to be silenced almost at once. His sole object had been to say as much as he could, or rather to let his

11

anger say whatever it wanted to in its brief moment of freedom.

But the blow did not fall. No priest made a move towards him, or acted as if anything out of the ordinary were happening. And his unquenched anger continued to speak for him.

"Commoners of Megatheopolis, what I am going to ask you to do is hard. Harder than work in the mines, though I won't ask you to lift a finger. I want you to listen to what I say, to weigh my words for truth, to make a judgement as to the worth of what I tell you, and then to act on that judgement. You hardly know what all that means, but you must try to do it, nevertheless! To weigh my words for truth? That's to see how they square with what you've seen happen in your private lives – not what you've been told. To make a judgement? That's to decide whether or not you want something, after you've learned what it is. I know the priests have told you all that is wrong. Forget the priests! Forget I wear the scarlet robe. And listen, listen!"

Now surely the blow must fall! They wouldn't let him say any more! Involuntarily he looked up at the form of the Great God. But that serene idol was taking no more notice of what was happening in the square than a human being might take of a swarming of ants around a bit of sugar.

"You all know the story of the Golden Age," he was already saying, his voice now richly vibrant with secrets to unfold. "You hear it every time you go to the Cathedral. How the Great God gave divine powers to all men, so that they lived as in paradise, without toil or sorrow. How men grew restless and dissatisfied, wanting still more, and sinned in all manner of ways, and lived in vice and lechery. How the Great God in mercy restrained his anger, hoping that they would reform. How, in all their evil pride, they finally sought to storm heaven itself and all its stars. Then, as the priests never weary of telling you, the Great God rose up in his wisdom and wrath, and winnowed out the few men who had not sinned against him and were still obedient to his holy laws. Them he made into his Hierarchy and gave them supernatural powers even greater than before. The rest – the sinful ones – he cast down and ground into the dust, and gave his Hierarchy power over them, so that those who had not of their own free wills lived virtuously would be made to do so by force! Then he further decreed that his Hierarchy select from each generation of men the naturally virtuous to be priests, and reject the rest, to toil in blissful ignorance under the gentle but inflexible guidance of the priests, who are the Hierarchy."

He paused, looked searchingly into the staring faces.

"That much, all of you know by heart. But not one of you dreams of the truth behind the story!"

Without anger whipping him on, Jarles might have stopped then and there and walked into the Sanctuary and down into the crypts, so stupid and uncomprehending were the commoners' reactions, so obviously did they misinterpret every word. At first they had seemed only shocked and bewildered, though attentive as always. Then – when he had called upon them to think and judge – they had looked vaguely apprehensive, as if all this rigmarole were merely the introduction to some assignment of physical labour, literally harder than work in the mines. The story of the Golden Age had lulled them. It was something familiar. His last sentence had shattered the lull and brought them again into that state of stupid, anxious gawking.

But what else could he expect? If he could only manage to plant the seeds of questioning in just one commoner!

"There was a Golden Age. That much is true. Though as far as I know there was plenty of toil and sorrow in it. But at least all men had a little freedom and were getting more. The getting of it meant trouble – lots of it – and at one point the scientists became frightened and ... but you don't even know what a scientist is, do you? Any more than you know what a doctor is, or a lawyer, or a judge, or a teacher, or a scholar, or a statesman, or an executive, or, so help me, an artist. Because the priests are all of those things. They've rolled all the professions, all the privileged classes into one. You don't rightly know even what a priest is! There were religions in those days, you see, and worship of a god – in the Golden Age and the long ages before it, ever since man fought his way up, with hands and brain, to mastery of this planet. But the priests of those religions dealt only in

13

spiritual and moral matters – at least at such times as they were wise and good. Other work they left for other professions. And they didn't use force.

"But that's getting ahead of my story. I want to tell you about the scientists, and how the Golden Age ended. A scientist is a thinker. He's a thinker about how things happen. He watches things happen. Then if he knows a thing can happen, and if it's a thing men want, maybe he can figure out – by thinking and hard work – how to help it happen. No magic, see? No supernatural powers. Just watching, and thinking, and working."

He had forgotten to wonder why he had not been silenced. He thought only of how to choose the right words, how to hammer or ease them home – anything to get a flicker out of those faces!

"The scientists of the Golden Age became afraid that mankind was slipping back into barbarism and ignorance. Their position as members of a privileged profession was threatened. They decided that, for a time, they must take control of the world. They were not strong enough to do it directly. They weren't fighters. So they got the idea of establishing a new religion, modelled on the old religions, but powered *by science*. In the old religions, blessings and cursings worked through men's minds. In the religion the scientists established, blessings and cursings worked directly, by force!

"You want proof? You should want proof. Here it is!"

His hand whipped downward from collar to hem of his heavy, scarlet robe. A metal-edged slit appeared. He quickly stepped through it, bare except for a pair of scarlet trunks. Many of the commoners shuddered and shrank back, wincing. To see a priest unrobed was blasphemous. True, the priest had done it himself. But somehow they might be to blame.

"You have been taught that inviolability proceeds from the priest, a divine aura projected by his holy flesh and controlled by his will power. Watch!"

He slapped the breast of the empty robe smartly. Instantly it mushroomed outward. He pushed it away from him. It floated out and down from the bench. Commoners shoved wildly and clawed at each other, in their desire to avoid being touched by it.

It came to rest about two feet from the ground, jogging up and down gently, for all the world like a recumbent priest, complete even to the puffed scarlet gloves – except that there was no gleaming shaven head under the eerily glowing violet halo which all men knew to be an outward sign of the priest's holy thoughts.

The panic-stricken ones regathered in a circle around it, at what they hoped was a safe and reverent distance.

Jarles' voice was bitter as medicine. "Maybe you can get to the Hierarchy's heaven the way that robe's trying to. I know of no other. Can't you see it's a trick? Rip open that robe" – a commoner gasped horrifiedly at him for a moment, thinking the words a command – "and you'll find a network of fine wires. What does the Great God need with wires? They make what's called a bilateral, short-range, multi-purpose repulsor field. Something that pushes, see? Something very useful for protecting a priest from injury and powering his flabby fingers so that they're stronger than those of a smith's. And it props up his halo! Stop gawking at it, you fools! It's just a trick, I tell you!

"How do I know all this?" he fairly bellowed at them. "You *ought* to ask that question. Well – the priests told me! Yes, the priests! Do you know what happens to a young man when he passes the tests and is admitted to the Hierarchy as a novice?" That got them, he could tell. It took a racy question like that to whet their dull curiosity. "A lot of things happen to him you don't know about. I'm just going to tell you one. He's told, gradually, in small doses – but unmistakably – that there is no Great God. That there are no supernatural powers. That the priests are scientists ruling the world for its own good. That it's his duty to help them and his good fortune to share in the benefits.

"Don't you see? The scheme of the Golden Age scientists worked. Their new religion swept the world. And as soon as they got the world firmly by the throat, they were able to mould it just the way they wanted. For themselves, they made a regimented, monastic paradise. To find a model for the commoners' world, they went back to a time called the

15

Middle Ages and dug up a nice little thing called serfdom. Oh, they cleaned it up a bit, made it orderly and healthy, and added a few touches of downright slavery. But otherwise they didn't change it one jot. It was just the thing to keep a whole world in a state of frightened, ignorant, back-broken, grateful servitude.

"Surely, they averted barbarism. By establishing it!

"There was one very special wrinkle about the Middle Ages that you got a taste of today. My priestly educators haven't got around to telling me about it, but I can see the why and wherefore of it all right. Witchcraft! Don't cringe, you idiots! It's just another of their tricks, we can be sure. Some of the old religions had witchcraft mixed up with them, catering to the cheapest superstitions and fears. The scientists decided their religion ought to have a witchcraft, too. So they let scatterbrained old women like Mother Jujy go around pretending to tell fortunes, cast spells, and brew love potions. Just the thing to strengthen superstition and give commoners a bit of an outlet. And a marvellous straw man to knock down with their scientific exorcisms. Besides providing a neat excuse for getting at people they don't like, such as that girl you saw accused today."

He looked around for Sharlson Naurya, but could not find her in the crowd or Brother Chulian. It was getting dim. The small white sea of faces was beginning to smudge a little. He realized, with a start, that the sun had set. A chill breeze was trickling down from the hillside farmlands, making him shiver in his nakedness.

And still the Hierarchy held its hand. Round about the Square priests stood by twos, watching, doing nothing – wine-dark shadows.

But he fancied he saw a trace of something more than ignorant curiosity and bewildered awe in two or three of the white faces spread out before him. And, as a man in polar snows nurses the tiny flame that is all that stands between him and death by cold – cupping his hands around it, breathing upon it with infinite gentleness, shredding upon it tiny crumbs of tinder – so Jarles nursed that trace of genuine understanding he fancied he saw, but which might be only a trick of the shadows.

16

"Some of you heard why Sharlson Naurya was accused of witchcraft. She was ordered to serve in the Sanctuary and refused. Refused with courage and simple decency. So a priest of the Great God reached forward those chubby, uncalloused fingers stronger than a smith's and made witchmarks on her shoulder before he ripped down her smock.

"All of you must guess why Sharlson Naurya refused. All of you know who lives there." He pointed down a dark little street next to the Sanctuary. Eyes followed his finger. "Fallen sisters, they're called. Girls chosen by the Hierarchy for the holy sisterhoods, who then so sinned against the Great God that they could neither be suffered to remain in the Sanctuary nor permitted to return home to infect the innocent. So the Great God in his infinite mercy gives them a place where they may live apart." His voice was thick with irony. "You know! Some of you have been there yourselves, when the priests would tolerate it."

At that, the faintest of murmurings came from the crowd.

"Who takes your sweetest daughters for the sisterhoods, Commoners of Megatheopolis?

"Who sends you to the fields, the roads, the mines, to waste your years and break your backs?

"Who gives you fake thrills to deaden the pain?"

And now the muttering had become an angry murmuring. Stone-blind resentment, except perhaps in two or three cases, but dangerous. Around the edges of the square, violet will-o'-the-wisps began to glow, and there was a slight bulging of the wine-dark shadows. Jarles instantly caught at it.

"See them switch on their inviolability! Puff themselves up for safety. They're afraid of you, Commoners of Megatheopolis. Deadly afraid.

"With their holy gadgets the priests could farm the whole world, web it with perfect roads, honeycomb it with mines. And not one man lift pick or spade.

"There's another story you're told. How, when the Hierarchy has finally purified all mankind, the Great God will usher in another Golden Age, the New Golden Age, the Golden Age without Dross.

"I ask you – and especially the old ones among you – doesn't the New Golden Age get further and further away

17

every year? Don't the priests keep pushing it further and further into the future? Until now it's only a hazy dream, something to lull your little children to sleep with when they're half dead from their first day's work and crying?

"Maybe those Golden Age scientists did intend to restore mankind, when the threat of barbarism was finally past. I guess they did.

"But now the priests think only one thing. How to hold on to their power as long as mankind lasts – until the sun darkens and the earth freezes!"

Then he realized that the muttering had died and that the commoners were no longer looking at him, but upward. An eerie, leaden blue light was illuminating their faces, until they looked like a crowd of drowned men. And this time his eyes followed theirs.

The Great God had leaned forward, blotting out the first, faint evening stars, until his gigantic face was peering straight down at them, his blue nimbus blazing in all its deathly glory.

"Behold their greatest trick!" Jarles shouted. "The Incarnate God The Almighty Automaton!"

But they were not listening to him, and now that he had stopped speaking, his teeth were chattering from the cold. He hugged his arms to stop the shivering, alone on his little bench that now seemed very low.

"It has come," the commoners were thinking. "It was all a test, as we might have known. Unfair – except the priests are never, never unfair. We should not have listened. We should not have moved. And now we are to be blasted for our sin, for the greatest sin – to think a thought against the Hierarchy."

The hand of the Great God thrust downward, like a falling steeple checked in mid-air. The extended index finger, thick as a tree trunk, pointed at the puffed robe Jarles had cast aside, and which still hung two feet above the ground.

Crackling, coruscating blue light snaked from nimbus to mountainous shoulder and down the arm, spat like lightning from the fingertip. The empty robe glowed, frizzled, puffed a little more, then burst with a hollow pop, like a seaweed bladder in a fire.

That sound, and the spatter of red-hot fragments, thawed the frozen panic. The crowd broke, began to race towards the narrow, dark mouths of the streets – any street, it made no difference, so long as they got out of the square.

The crackling beam moved slowly towards the bench on which Jarles still stood, fusing the cobblestones, leaving a red-hot trough in its wake – a sign and mark for all times to come of the Great God's divine wrath.

He waited for it.

There was a swooping of blackness, a beat as of gigantic shadowy wings. And then around the renegade priest had closed an irregular sphere – mottled with blackness, inkily smeared, so that through it his naked body was still vaguely visible.

And the irregular sphere had the form of two great clawed hands, cupped together.

The blue beam from the Great God's finger moved swiftly then, impinged upon the sphere, crackled against it, showering blue sparks.

The sphere drank the beam and grew not one whit less black.

The beam thickened to a writhing pillar of blue light, turning the square to day and driving back the air in hot waves.

And still it only spattered harmlessly against the black-streaked, irregular sphere of the cupped hands.

It was still possible to glimpse the form of the renegade priest inside them, like an insect miraculously alive in the heart of a flame.

Then a great, evilly mirthful voice that seemed to blow the hot air from the square in one breath, that stopped every fleeing commoner in his tracks and turned him around to stare in paralysed terror at the black and flaming spectacle.

"The Lord of Evil defies the Great God!

"The Lord of Evil takes this man for his own."

The cupped hands jerked away, upward, off, and out of sight.

Then gales of satanic laughter that seemed to rock the Sanctuary itself.

# CHAPTER TWO

"BROTHER JARLES has begun to harangue the crowd in the Great Square, your resplendent archpriestship."

"Good! Send the reports in to me at the Apex Council as soon as he is finished."

Brother Goniface, priest of the Seventh Circle, archpriest, chief voice of the Realists in the Apex Council, smiled – but the smile was not apparent in the pale, lion-like mask of his face. He had touched off a bomb that would blast the Apex Council out of its complacency – both the Moderates, with their flabby compromises, and his own Realists, with their mulish conservatism.

His dangerous little experiment was running now and couldn't very well be stopped, let Brother Frejeris and the rest of the Moderates yelp as much as they wanted to – afterwards.

For afterwards everything would be neatly rounded off. Brother Jarles would be dead, frizzled by the Great God's wrath – an instructive example for the commoners and any other dissatisfied young priest. And Goniface would be able to explain at leisure to the Apex Council just how much vital information had been gained by study of the artificial crisis he had fomented.

Only at times like this did a man really live! To have power was good. To use it dangerously was better.

But to use it in fighting an enemy perhaps as strong as yourself was best of all.

He adjusted his gold-worked scarlet robe, commanded the great doors to open, and strode into the Council Chamber.

At the far end of the vast, pearly room, on an extensive dais, was a long table, with every seat behind it occupied by a gorgeous robed archpriest – every seat save one.

Goniface relished that long walk the length of the Council Chamber, with all the rest of them already in place. He liked to know that they were watching him every step of the way, hoping he would stumble slightly or scuff the floor, just once. Liked to think how they would spring on him like famished cats if they had the slightest inkling of the secret of his past, the darkest of dark jests.

Liked to know it, and then forget it!

For that long walk across the Council Chamber under those critical eyes gave Goniface something that no other archpriest seemed quite to understand. Something that he would not have allowed excitement over a dozen Jarleses to rob him of. An opportunity to drink in, at its richest and most tense, the power and glory of the Hierarchy – stablest government the world had ever known. The only government fully worth a strong man's effort to maintain and to dominate it. Built on a thousand lies – like all governments, thought Goniface – yet perfectly adapted to solve the intricate problems of human society. And so constituted, by virtue of its rigid social stratification, that the more a member of the priestly elite struggled for power in it, the more closely did he identify himself with the aims and welfare of that elite.

At times like these Brother Goniface became a visionary. He could look through the soaring, softly pearl-grey walls of the Council Chamber, and watch the busy, efficient working of the Sanctuary – sense its uninterrupted hum of intellectual and executive activity, its subtle pleasures. Then outward, past the limits of the Sanctuary, across the checkerboard of neatly tilled fields, around the curve of the earth, to the gleaming walls of other sanctuaries – the rural ones simple and modest hermitages, the urban ones each with its cathedral and Almighty Automaton brooding over a great square. And still farther than that, across blue oceans, to other continents and gorgeous tropical islands. And everywhere to see in vision and sense with a pleasure-beyond-pleasure the workings of the scarlet robe – from the lamaseries clinging unshakably to the titan Himalaya, to the snug stations buried deep in Antarctica. Everywhere the sanctuaries, webbing the whole world, like the ganglia of some globular marine organism, floating in the sea of space.

And then even beyond that – to heaven itself!

After he had walked a little more than halfway, his imagination began its return journey. And now it followed the lines of the social pyramid, or cone. First the broad base of commoners – that necessary, bestial, almost mindless substratum. Then a thin layer of deacons – insulation. Then the novices and rank and file of the first two circles of the priesthood, accounting for more than seven-eighths of the scarlet robes. Then, the cone swiftly narrowing, the various higher circles, each with its special domain of interest and endeavour, until the small Seventh Circle of major executives was reached.

And, on top of all, the archpriests and the Apex Council.

And, whether or not they knew it, whether or not they unconsciously feared or desired it, himself on top of that!

He slipped into his seat and asked, although he knew the answer, "What business today?"

"That, so please your archpriestships," came the well-modulated voice of a Second Circle clerk, "which you have asked me to refer to as the Matter of the Frightened Priests."

Goniface sensed a reaction of annoyance ripple along the Council Table. This was one of those fantastic matters that refused to adjust themselves to established procedures, and were, therefore, exceedingly vexing to conservative mentalities. For two days running the Apex Council had postponed dealing with it.

"What do you say, Brothers?" he proposed in easy, casual tones. "Shall we have all our country relations in together? Shame them by making them listen to each others' childish-seeming tales?"

"That is hardly in accord with the best psychological practices," observed Brother Frejeris, his voice like the middle notes of an organ for beauty and strength. "We then encourage mass hysteria."

Goniface nodded politely, remarking, "You dignify their condition, Brother, with a high-sounding term," and again looked up and down the table questioningly.

"Have them in together," urged Goniface's fellow Realist Jomald. "Else we'll be here all night."

Goniface glanced towards the senior member, lean Brother Sercival, whose white hair, shaven perhaps yesterday, still gave a silvery tint to his parchment skull.

"Together!" voted Brother Sercival through thin lips, ever stingy with words, the old Fanatic!

22

At that there was general agreement.

"A trifle of no importance," murmured Brother Frejeris, waving the matter aside with a sculpturesque white hand. "I merely sought to avoid a situation which may prove confusing to those of you who are not trained psychologists."

A clerk transmitted the necessary orders.

As they waited, Brother Frejeris glanced down into his lap. "I am informed," he said, very casually, "that there is a disturbance in the Great Square."

Goniface did not look at him.

"If it is of any consequence," he remarked smoothly, "our servant Cousin Deth will inform us."

"Your servant, Brother," Frejeris corrected, with equal smoothness.

Goniface made no reply.

A score of priests were ushered in through the side door. Superficially they seemed identical with the priests of the Megatheopolis Sanctuary, but to the members of the Apex Council, their every mannerism and gesture, the way they wore their robes and the precise cut of those robes, spelled "country."

They stood before the council table, an abashed and very much impressed clump of men.

Their numbers merely emphasized the lustrous grey vastness of the Council Chamber.

"Your reverend archpriestships," began a gnarly fellow, who seemed to have absorbed something of the earthiness of the endless tilled fields, without working in them. "I know what I'm going to say must seem very unreal here at Megatheopolis," he continued haltingly, his eyes tracing upward the vaulting of the walls until it was lost in the misty ceiling, " – here at Megatheopolis, where you can turn night into day if you want to. It's different where we come from, where night edges up and clamps down, and you feel the silence creep in from the fields and grab the town – "

"No atmosphere, man! The story!" interjected Frejeris.

"Story!" snapped Sercival.

"Well, it's ... it's wolves," the gnarly fellow said, with almost a touch of defiance. "I know there aren't any such

23

things, except in the old books. But at night, we see them. Grey, smoky ones, coloured like these walls, big as horses, with red eyes. They come loping, packs of them, like banks of mist over the fields, and come skulking into town, circling around the sanctuary. And whenever a pair of us must go out at night, they follow. The Finger of Wrath can't hurt them – or the Rod! They just back away from the light it makes and skulk in the shadows. I tell you, your reverences, our commoners are crazy with fear, and the novices are almost as bad. And then, at night, in the cells, something squats on our chests!"

"I know!" interrupted another country priest excitedly. "Cold furry things that twitch at the clothes and softly feel your face. And they squat there, light as down, while you don't know whether you're waking or dreaming, and they nuzzle you and chatter at you in their thin high voices, saying things you hardly dare repeat. But when the light's on, or when you try to clutch at them, they're never there. Yet you can feel them as they touch you and squat on you. Cold, skinny things, covered with a fine fur or hair – human hair!"

A third country priest, a sallow, high-foreheaded fellow with the look of a schoolmaster, had grown yet more pale at this last recital. "That's exactly how I felt!" he cried out nervously, his eyes fixed on something far away. "Brother Galjwin and I had gone to search the house of a commoner whom we suspected of having concealed a portion of his weavings, on which tithes were due the Hierarchy. They were a bad lot, the daughter the worst – a shameless hussy! But I was on to their tricks, and pretty soon I spotted a loose board in the wall. I pulled it out, and stuck my arm through and felt around behind. That red-haired hussy was grinning at me in the nastiest, most disrespectful way. I felt a roll of cloth with a heavy nap, and reached in farther, so I could get my fingers around it and pull it out. And then it came alive! It moved. It wriggled! Cold, furry, but human feeling, just like he said – though the space back there wasn't four inches wide! We had that inside wall torn down, and we watched the crack all the while. Nothing came out. But we found nothing. We gave the household an extra stint of weaving, as penance. We found witchmarks on the daughter, got a special dispensation, and had her sent to the mines with the men.

"One thing I'll never forget. When I jerked my hand out, there were two tiny hairs caught in the jag of a nail – two tiny hairs of the same angry copper shade as the girl's!

"And now, when I sleep badly, I keep feeling the thing. Thin spidery arms against my palm – wriggling!"

And now all tongues were unloosed, and there was a frightened babble. One voice, louder than the rest, exclaimed, "They say it's those things that make the witchmarks!"

A gorgeously robed archpriest laughed melodiously, contemptuously. But there was something a little hollow about the laughter.

Brother Frejeris smiled and arched his eyebrows eloquently, as if to say, "Mass hysteria. I warned you."

"I said it would all seem very unreal here at Megatheopolis," asserted the first rural speaker, apologetically, yet still with a shade of stubborn defiance. "But there was a Fifth Circle priest sent down to investigate when we made our first reports. He saw what we saw. He didn't say anything. Next day he went away. If he found out anything, we haven't heard about it."

"We expect the Hierarchy to protect us!"

"We want to know what the Hierarchy's going to do!"

"They say," broke in the fellow who had mentioned witchmarks, "that there's a Black Apex, just as there's an Apex Council, so please your reverences! And a Black Hierarchy, organized as we are, but serving Cathanas, Lord of Evil!"

"Yes," echoed the first speaker, the gnarly one. "And I want to know this! What if our centuries of pretending that there's a real god have somehow – I don't know how – awakened a real devil? What then?"

Goniface sat up and spoke into the shiver that followed those words. His voice lacked Frejeris' music, but it had its own stony compellingness.

"Silence! Or you *will* wake a real devil. The devil of our wrath!"

He looked up and down the table. "What to do with these fools?" he asked lightly.

"Whip them!" snapped Sercival, lean jaw like a trap, small eyes glittering in their leathery sockets. "Whip them! For being such cowards in the face of the wiles and threats of Sathanas!"

The country priests stirred uneasily. Frejeris rolled his eyes upward, as if such a statement were almost unbearably barbarous. But Goniface nodded politely, though not indicating agreement. He casually wondered to what degree old Sercival and the other Fanatics actually believed in the real existence of the Great God and his eternal adversary, Sathanas, Lord of Evil. Largely a pose, of course, but there was probably a substratum of genuineness. Not stemming from the ignorant superstitions of the commoners – those were wiped out in the First and Second Circle, or else a priest got no further – but from a kind of self-hypnosis induced by years of contemplating the stupendous powers of the Hierarchy, until those powers actually took on a supernatural tinge. Luckily, Fanatics were very rare – hardly worth calling a party. Only one on the Apex Council, and he only became one in his senility. Even at that, the old fool might some day prove useful. He was grim and bloody-minded enough, and would serve as a convenient scapegoat if it were ever necessary to employ extreme violence. The Fanatic Party, for that matter, was useful in counterbalancing the more numerous minority of Moderates, leaving Goniface's Realists in almost complete control.

But these poor country priests were not Fanatics. Far from it. If they had even a shadow of belief in the Great God – in any god – they wouldn't be so frightened. Goniface rose to reprimand them.

But there was an interruption. The high doors at the other end of the Chamber opened. A priest darted in. Goniface recognized one of Frejeris' Moderates.

The newcomer's progress towards the Council Table was nothing stately. He was almost running.

Goniface waited coolly.

The newcomer, breathing a little hard from the unac-

26

customed exertion, handed something to Frejeris which the latter quickly scanned.

Frejeris rose and spoke to Goniface directly, for the whole table to hear.

"I am informed that a First Circle priest is blaspheming the Hierarchy before a large crowd in the Great Square. Your servant Cousin Deth has taken charge and forbids interference. I demand you instantly explain to the Council what this madness means!"

"Who fosters mass hysteria now, Brother?" Goniface countered quickly. "Your information is incomplete. Shall I explain a subtle stratagem before those who would not understand it?" He indicated the country priests. "Or shall I finish the business before the Council?"

And before the Council had recovered from its first surprise, he was talking.

"Priests of the rural sanctuaries: You have said that your stories would seem unreal here. That is untrue. For the unreal is not, at Megatheopolis or anywhere else in the cosmos.

"The supernatural is unreal, and therefore is not.

"Have you forgotten the basic truth you learned in the First Circle? That there is only the cosmos and the electronic entities that constitute it, without soul or purpose, save so far as neuronic minds impose purpose upon it?

"No, your stories refer to real entities – if only to the imagery of your neuronic minds.

"There are many real entities which the Finger of Wrath cannot burn. I mention only solidographs, and remind you of the shadowiness of the wolves and other creatures you claim to fear. As for mental imagery, you cannot burn that except by turning the Finger of Wrath against your own skulls.

"One of you mentioned the Witchcraft. Has that one forgotten that the Witchcraft is our fosterling?

"I should not be telling you this. You should be telling it to your novices!

"Has the Hierarchy ever failed you? Yet now do you want the Hierarchy to drop all other business and, with much outward fuss and flourishing, attend only to you, because you are frightened – not hurt, merely frightened?

"How do you know that all this is not a test, imposed upon you by us, to determine your courage and resourcefulness? If it is a test, think how pitifully, thus far, you have failed!

"It may be also that some alien agency is striking at the Hierarchy, perhaps under cover of our fosterling the Witchcraft. And that we are holding our hand, to draw them out and learn all, before we strike in return. For the Hierarchy never strikes twice.

"If that is the case, elementary strategy forbids your being told anything, for fear of scaring off the enemy.

"This much I will tell you. The Hierarchy knew of the disturbances in your region long before you did. And it has concerned itself deeply with them.

"That is all you need to know. And you should have known it without asking!"

With cold gratification, Goniface noted that the last traces of panic had quite evaporated. The country priests stood straighter now, looked more like men. Still frightened – but only of their superiors. As they should be.

"Priests of the rural sanctuaries, you have grievously failed the Hierarchy. Our reports show that, since the beginning of the disturbances – or the test – in your region, you have done little but cry to the Hierarchy for help. It has been suggested that you be whipped. I am inclined to agree. Except that I believe you have enough iron in you not to fail again.

"The Hierarchy grips the globed earth like a hand. Will it be your eternal disgrace to be remembered as the ones who sought to loosen, infinitesimally, one fingertip? I say 'sought' advisedly, because we watch over you more closely than you think, and stand ever ready if even the least of you should fail.

"Not to fail, is your affair!

"Go back to your sanctuaries.

"Do what you should have done long ago.

"Call upon your courage and resourcefulness.

"Fear is a weapon – for you to use, not others to use against you.

"You have been trained in its use.

"Use it!

"And as for Sathanas, also our fosterling, our Lord of Evil, our black counterpart to our Great God" – he stole an ironic sidewise glance at Sercival, to see how the old Fanatic was taking this – "use him, too. Whip him from your towns if that seems expedient. But never, never again, stoop so low – low even as commoners! – as to believe in him!"

It was then – just as Goniface could see that the country priests had taken fire from his words and were beginning to burn with a desire to redeem themselves – that the laughter came. The walls of the Council Chamber were thick and proof against ordinary sound, yet still it came – evilly mirthful, uncanny peals.

It seemed to laugh at the Hierarchy – and at anyone who dared to decree what is and what is not.

The country priests paled and edged closer together. The haughty faces of the archpriests more or less successfully masked shock, apprehension, and a furious thinking as to what that noise might be and what it might portend. Frejeris looked suddenly at Goniface. Old Sercival began to tremble with what seemed a queer sort of fear and a queerer satisfaction.

But it was in Goniface's ears that the laughter thundered most shakingly and dismayingly. Thoughts flickered like wildfire across his mind.

But all the while he imperturbably fought to hold the eyes of the country priests, to oppose the influence of that unnerving laughter. And he succeeded, although the eyes grew wide with doubt.

The laughter echoed off, shudderingly.

"Your audience is at an end," Goniface declared harshly. "Leave us!"

The country priests hurried off. It was only the swishing of their robes, but it sounded as if they were already whispering.

Old Sercival rose up like some ancient prophet, hand shakily extended towards Goniface. "That was the laughter of Sathanas! It is a judgment of the Great God upon you

29

and the whole Hierarchy for centuries of hypocrisy and pretence! The Great God looses against the world his black dog Sathanas!"

And he sank back into his seat, trembling.

The Council shifted restlessly. Someone tittered contemptuously.

Goniface felt throbbing through him the same strange, intoxicating pulsation he had felt years ago when the secret of his past had been within a hairbreadth of discovery.

A fat little priest pressed through the tail end of the country delegation as it left the Chamber, and fairly scampered towards Goniface.

Goniface stopped him. "Make your report to the assembled Apex Council, Brother Chulian!"

The fat little priest's cherubic mouth gasped like that of a fish. "The likeness of great hands cupped around Brother Jarles and carried him off! Sathanas spoke!"

"*Your* report!" Goniface commanded harshly. "The rest we can hear from others better able to tell it."

The fat little priest dodged back as though water had been thrown in his face. He seemed for the first time to realize the presence of the Council. His piping voice grew subservient, his words terse.

"As instructed, I provoked the First Circle priest Brother Jarles to anger. I did this by ordering the Commoner Sharlson Naurya, whom Brother Jarles still regards emotionally, to serve in the Sanctuary. She, a well-known recalcitrant, with abnormal fear of the sanctuaries, refused. I then accused her of witchcraft, squeezing her shoulder to produce a witchmark. Brother Jarles struck me. We were both inviolable at the time. I was knocked down. Then I –"

" – your report ends, Brother Chulian," Goniface finished for him.

Across the ensuing silence Brother Frejeris' voice rang more musically than before. "If all we are to hear consists of such rash and mischievous madness as this – aimed directly against the stability of the Hierarchy – I will not need to ask for Brother Goniface's excommunication. Every archpriest will ask it for me."

"You will hear all," Goniface told him. "Hearing, you will understand."

But he could tell that his words fell flat. Even in the faces of his own Realists he could discern suspicion and distrust. Brother Jomald gave him a look as if to say, "The party disclaims all responsibility in this matter. You must handle it yourself – if you can."

The fat little priest seemed to want to say more. His cherubic mouth twitched anxiously. Goniface nodded to him.

"May I make an addition to my report, your reverence?"

"If it concerns your part in the action."

"It does, your resplendency. And it puzzles me. When I tore Sharlson Naurya's smock to expose the witchmark, there were three such marks where I am sure my thumb and forefinger alone had rested."

Goniface could have kissed the fat little priest. But his voice was faraway and musing as he replied. "And to think, Brother Chulian, that you might even now be a priest of the Third Circle, if you only had joined the virtue of deduction to the virtue of observation." He shook his head regretfully. "Well, I will give you a chance to redeem yourself. After all, it was a most peculiar coincidence. Take another priest, now that you no longer have your partner Jarles, and arrest – the witch!"

The fat little priest goggled at him. "What witch, your dread resplendency?"

"Sharlson Naurya. And you had best be quick about it if you hope to catch her."

Realization dawned in Brother Chulian's baby-blue eyes. He goggled for a moment longer. Then he spun around and scurried for the door.

But this time he had to stand aside for others. A meagre spindly man in the black robe of a deacon strode with brassy self-assurance into the Council Chamber, followed by several priests bearing oddly shaped rolls and canisters.

He planted himself before the Council Table with his entourage of priests. He was a paragon of sallow ugliness, with bulging forehead and jutting ears like three-quarter saucers. Nevertheless, the inscrutable mask he preserved was a painstaking copy of that which confined the coldly

31

handsome features of Goniface. He seemed to enjoy the animosity which greeted his appearance, as if he were well aware that, though his birth prevented him from ever entering the priesthood, he was nevertheless more feared than many an archpriest.

"And what has your servant Cousin Deth to tell us?" demanded one of the Moderates – not Frejeris.

The sallow man bowed low. "Your awful, august, exalted unimpeachabilities," he began with acid fawning. "I need make no verbal report. These unprejudiced witnesses will report for me." He indicated the rolls and canisters. "A moving solidograph of all that transpired in the Great Square. A transcription of each word spoken by Brother Jarles, and, synchronized with both, a visigraphic record of the major neuro-emotional waves emitted by the crowd during his harangue. A graphic analysis, made at Cathedral Control Centre, of the apparent physical nature of the shell which closed around Brother Jarles and carried him off. A transcription of the words and laughter that came at the end. With the usual supplements." And he bowed again, so low that his black sleeves swept the floor."

"We care not for your pretty pictures!" cried the same Moderate who had spoken before, face red with anger. "We want your story of what finally happened, Deacon!"

Goniface noted that Frejeris was unsuccessfully signing the man to keep quiet and not waste their advantage in petty outbursts. Cousin Deth, quite unabashed, looked inquiringly at Goniface, who nodded to him.

"All went as planned, as the records show," Deth began, the ghost of a cynical smile playing around his slitlike mouth. "At the end a mottled sphere, suggestive of hands, cupped around the priest. It sustained for an appreciable time the full power of the Great God's wrath. We were able to study it. Then it shot off, escaping us by a hairbreadth. For we had angels held in readiness to pursue, as you commanded." And he bowed towards Goniface, without mockery. "We know the quarter in which it vanished, and a search is now in progress."

Instantly Goniface rose, motioning Deth to approach the table and prepare the records for viewing.

Now was the proper moment, felt Goniface. Deth's words had angered all of them, but the Moderates most, while the Realists had been impressed in spite of themselves. He addressed the Council.

"Archpriests of Earth, it had been said: 'As Megatheopolis goes, so goes the planet.' But to turn that aphorism to practical use, we must know in what direction Megatheopolis is going before it goes!

"No government that calls itself realistic can neglect to answer that question.

"What archpriest here, saving perhaps you, Brother Sercival, believed that an enemy would openly strike at Megatheopolis itself?

"I did not so believe. But I wanted to find out. That was one of the reasons for the experiment in the Great Square.

"Brothers, you have the answer. Sathanas came.

"No longer can we deny that our fosterling, the Witchcraft, conceals an enemy – an enemy daring and dangerous.

"No longer can we deny that, within the debased Witchcraft which we tolerate, there is another Witchcraft, which seeks to use the weapon of fear, not only against commoners but against priests. There is reason to believe that the members of this Inner Witchcraft may be identified by certain marks on their bodies. They show themselves cunning and resourceful.

"No longer can we dismiss as some trifling case of mass hysteria, the Matter of the Frightened Priests. To give them courage, I told them it might be merely a test we had imposed upon them. But all of you know that three of our Fifth Circle scientists have admitted themselves baffled by those manifestations in the rural sanctuaries."

Goniface paused. The Moderates seemed angrier than ever. Plain talk of danger always angered them. But the Realists were listening. The look in Brother Jomald's face had become one of grudging admiration.

"To return to the question: 'How goes Megatheopolis?'

"Brothers, there is only one way to find out. Only one was to discover the true temper of the commoners. The closest observation of them in their normal round of life is insufficient. So are psychological tests. The one sure way, the only sure way, is to foment a sizable minor crisis and study it intensively."

The angriest Moderate started to get up. Frejeris forestalled him – with a certain unhappiness, as if he realized that they could no longer defeat Goniface by a straightforward attack.

"One does not fight fire by throwing oil on it," he began.

"One does!" Goniface countered. "Oil is more penetrating than water. There is a kind of hidden, smouldering fire which only oil can reach and which lacks sufficient oxygen to ignite the oil. Such a fire, Brothers, smoulders in the hearts of our commoners. And the force operating against us from under cover of the Witchcraft is another such fire, hidden but dangerous.

"To discover the secret temper of our commoners, to provide them with the instructive example of a priest blasted for blasphemy – or, in lieu of that, as actually happened, to lure the enemy into the open – I fomented a crisis.

"And now, archpriests of Megatheopolis, I give you a faithful recording of that crisis, for your contemplation and study, with a view to preventing the truly serious ones to come.

"After you have seen it, excommunicate me, if you still want to."

While Goniface spoke, Cousin Deth's assistants had worked a change in the seemingly fleckless surface of the Council table. A circular depression about six feet across had appeared in the centre. To one side were grouped smaller depressions, and certain slots had become apparent. The rolls and canisters had all disappeared – been inserted in the appropriate orifices.

Deth had touched a control and, while Goniface had been speaking, the pearly Council Chamber had slowly darkened, through an imperceptible series of greys. Now came utter blackness.

With the suddenness of creation a miniature scene sprang into being in the centre of the table. Only an occasional mistiness, and a slight blurring when many figures were grouped together, testified that it was only a projection –

a focusing of the patterns recorded on multiple tapes whirling noiselessly.

Pygmy figures in home-woven drab, scarlet-robed dolls of priests, tiny horses, carts, and wares, all complete – a sizable portion of the Great Square, without the surrounding architecture.

Only now, instead of the Great God, the archpriests of the Apex Council brooded over it.

Up from the smaller depressions rose stubby columns of light – yellow, green, blue, violet – fluctuating slightly but incessantly in height and saturation of colour – indicative of the massed changes in the major neuro-emotional responses of the crowd.

There rose the hum and babble of pygmy voices, the clatter of tiny hooves, the squeak of wooden wheels.

The scene in the Great Square was repeating itself.

Cousin Deth thrust his now-giant arm into the moving solidograph, momentarily intensifying, then shattering the illusion. His fingers negligently poked at and into two tiny red-robed figures.

"Jarles and Chulian," he explained. "In a few moments we'll give you their voices in full intensity."

Goniface leaned back with satisfaction. He was studying the expressions on the faces of the peering archpriests – eerily lit masks seeming to hang against the distanceless blackness beyond the table. But now and then he looked at the solidograph.

It was at the moment of the first accusation of witchcraft – the violet column concerned with fear, repulsion, and similar emotions had jumped abruptly and gone wan – that he chanced to note her face.

Almost, he jerked forward and grabbed at it.

But he caught himself in time and only leaned forward idly, as if it were his momentary fancy to take a closer look.

It couldn't be.

But there it was. That little coldly purposeful face, more perfect than any cameo, with its dark, fine-spun doll's hair. Not identically the same, of course, as the one printed in his memory. But if you allowed for the years and the maturing years would have brought –

Geryl. Knowles Geryl.

But Chulian had referred to her by another name – Sharlson Naurya.

A long-locked door in Goniface's mind groaned and reverberated, straining against the hinges with a formless pressure from the other side.

He looked across the table towards the yellowish caricature that was Deth's face in the darkness, caught the beady black eyes. Deth melted backward, was gone.

Goniface stood up quietly and walked behind the chairs, as though he were tired of sitting. Then he moved away from the table.

He sensed Deth's presence beside him, caught the thin, bony wrist in his hand, and whispered very faintly into Deth's ear:

"The woman I sent Chulian to arrest. Sharlson Naurya. Find her. Take her from Chulian if he has her. But find her. Make her my secret prisoner."

And then, like an afterthought. "Unharmed, mind you, at least until I have seen and spoken with her."

In the darkness Cousin Deth smiled crookedly.

## CHAPTER THREE

FOR a moment Brother Chulian thought a shadow was scuttling towards him in the deep grooves between the cobbles. He jerked away so that his halo reeled tipsily across the lightless street and his inviolability field bumped that of his companion.

"I slipped," he gasped unconvincingly. "Some nasty commoner must have thrown out greasy slops."

The other priests did not reply. Fervently Chulian hoped that he would not mind turning right at the next corner. It was a little longer that way, but you didn't have to pass the haunted house.

To his relief the fellow turned right without being asked.

Of course, the house wasn't really haunted, Chulian reminded himself quickly. That would be the sheerest nonsense. But it was such an ugly old relic of the Golden Age and the commoners told such unpleasantly grotesque stories about it at confession.

Why did the commoners have to have such narrow, twisty streets and why was there such a strict curfew, Chulian complained to himself, as if it were somehow the commoners' fault. Like a city of the dead. Not a person stirring, not a light showing, not a sound. Of course, all those rules were the laws of the Hierarchy, he remembered unwillingly. Still, there ought to be some provision for cases like this – say a law that the commoners ought to listen for priests coming at night and be ready to set out lighted torches. A halo hardly gave you enough light to keep from tripping over things!

Like twin will-o'-the-wisps the two circular violet glows bobbed through the crazily curving trenches in darkness that were the streets of Megatheopolis.

Behind rose the glow of the Sanctuary. To Chulian it seemed like a warm hearth from which he had been unfairly pushed out into the cold. Why did they have to pick on him for jobs like this? He was just an innocent clerk, bothering no one. All he asked from life was peace and comfort, a decent supply of his favourite goodies, a chance to lie in bed – at this moment he could almost feel its cushiony softness – and watch his favourite solidographic books read themselves, and now and again a bit of special fun with a Fallen Sister.

Who in the world could be so cruel as to object to that?

It all came from his miserable luck at having been paired off with Jarles, he told himself. That sullen fellow! If he hadn't been paired with Jarles, he wouldn't have been forced into this wild plot, which he didn't understand and which seemed to have been designed solely to bring trouble and danger into a world that would go smoothly if everyone were more like Brother Chulian!

Even then it would have been all right if he hadn't been so foolish as to mention those extra marks to Goniface. But if he hadn't told, they'd probably have found out and he'd have been punished.

Witchmarks! Chulian shivered. Almost he could see them burning in the white flesh of that nasty girl. Why did some commoner girls have to be brazen and sulky? Why couldn't they all be gentle and docile?

Witchmarks! He wished he could stop thinking about them. As part of his priestly education he had read a book about the Middle Ages of the Dawn Civilization and its primitive Witchcraft. A witchmark was supposed to be where a witch suckled her familiar. A familiar was supposed to be a little helper given her by Satan – Sathanas.

Of course, it had all been nonsense then and was nonsense now.

But why had Goniface called the girl a witch when he had heard of the extra marks, and sent Chulian to arrest her?

Chulian didn't really want to know the answer. He didn't want to be a Third Circle priest. He just wanted to be left in peace. If he could only make them understand that!

His companion nudged him into attentiveness, pointing at a rectangle of deeper blackness in the irregular rubble-and-plaster wall. They had arrived.

Chulian rapped loudly against the rough wooden door. When your fingers wore the Gloves of Inviolability you could hardly hurt them.

"Open in the name of the Great God and his Hierarchy!" he commanded, his reedy voice amplified by the silence.

"The door is not barred. Open it yourself," came the quiet, muffled, gently mocking answer.

Chulian bristled. Such insolence! But then they had come to arrest the girl, not to teach her manners. He jerked the latchstring and pushed.

The room was dimly and unevenly lit by the flickering of a thrifty fire. Faint coils of smoke, escaping from the fireplace, writhed about lazily, some of them eventually finding their way through the tiny square air hole in the low ceiling. Chulian's companion coughed.

Before the fireplace a shuttle was moving busily through the threads of a large loom, weaving some darkly figured fabric.

Its uninterrupted, snake's-head rhythm made Chulian uneasy. He hesitated and shot a quick glance at his companion. Side by side, close together, they moved forward

38

until they could see the other side of the loom and Sharlson Naurya.

She was wearing a close-fitting dress of grey homespun. Her rapt eyes seemed to be looking not so much at her work as through it, though her busy fingers never hesitated. Was it only cloth she was weaving, Chulian wondered, or something else – something bigger?

With almost a guilty start, he realized of whom she reminded him. Only a suggestion, of course – Still, there was in her face the same dark strength, the same sense of hidden yet limitless purpose, as he had just seen, and cringed before, in the archpriest Goniface.

After a moment she turned her head and looked at them. But there was no change in her expression – as if they were merely a part of that bigger, invisible fabric. Without haste she tucked the shuttle into the warp and stood facing them, folding her hands at the waist.

"Sharlson Naurya," Chulian intoned solemnly, but a trifle jerkily, "we come, inviolable emissaries of the Hierarchy, to do the bidding of the Great God."

Her green eyes smiled at that, if eyes can smile. But what Chulian wondered was what those eyes saw when they looked past him. Brazen girl! What right had she to take this so calmly!

He drew himself up.

"Sharlson Naurya, in the name of the Great God and his Hierarchy, I arrest you!"

She bent her head. And now there was something twisted and evil about the way her eyes smiled. She suddenly spread her hands outward from her waist.

"Run, Puss!" she cried with an almost mischievous urgency. "Tell the Black Man!"

A glittering talon ripped at the waist the grey homespun of her dress – from within. There was a rapid disturbance of the cloth. Then through the slit something wriggled and sprang.

Something furry, big as a cat, but more like a monkey, and incredibly lean.

Like a swift-scuttling spider it was up the wall and across the ceiling, clinging effortlessly.

Chulian's muscles froze. With a throaty gasp his companion lunged out an arm. From the pointing finger crackled a needle of violet light, scorching a zig-zag track in the crude plaster of wall and ceiling.

The thing paused for a moment in the air hole, looking back. Then it was gone, and the violet beam spat futilely through the air hole towards the black heavens, where one star glittered.

But Chulian continued to stare upward, his slack jaw trembling. He had got one look at the tiny face. Not when the thing had moved, for then it had been only a rippling blur, but when it had paused to glance back.

Not all the features of a face had been there. Some had been missing and others had seemed telescoped into each other. And the fine fur had encroached on them.

Nevertheless, where the features had showed through the fur, they had been white, and, in spite of all distortions, they had been a peering, chinless, noseless, hellish, but terribly convincing caricature of the features of Sharlson Naurya.

And the fur had been of exactly the same shade as her dark hair.

Finally, Chulian looked back at her. She had not moved. Still stood there smiling with her eyes.

"What was that thing?" he cried. It was much more a frightened appeal than a demand.

"Don't you know?" she asked gravely.

She reached for a shawl hanging from the end of the loom. "I am ready," she said. "Aren't you going to take me to the Sanctuary?"

And pulling her shawl around her, she walked towards the door.

It seemed darker than ever outside, and dead still. If any commoners had heard the disturbance, they had not come out to investigate. Of course, that was the law, but Chulian wished that some commoner would break it – just this once. Or if only they would meet up with a patrol of deacons!

Through the narrow, uneven streets hurriedly bobbed the two violet halos, straining towards the beacon-glow of the Sanctuary.

If only the girl wouldn't walk so slowly! Of course, they could hurry her up – each had an elbow in one of his puffed hands – but somehow Chulian didn't like the idea of hurting her, especially since she was otherwise so docile. After all, that thing of hers was somewhere on the roofs, perhaps following them. At any moment he might look up and see a tiny anthropoid muzzle poked over an edge, outlined against the stars.

When they got to the Sanctuary, things would be different!

Lightless doorways, lightless mouths of other streets, marched past them. At the next corner they must turn to the left to avoid the haunted house, Chulian reminded himself.

But when they got to the turn, the street to the left was walled – stuffed solid – with blackness.

Not the star-hazed blackness through which they had been passing, but blackness utter and complete, making the rest seem grey.

Nothing more.

Chulian looked sideways past the girl at Brother Arolj's face, sickly under the glowing halo, and caught an answering panicky glance.

In a rush so they wouldn't be able to flinch, they plunged into the blackness, the girl between them.

Their halos were extinguished. There was no light whatever.

As if out of a wall of ink, they scrambled back again, gasping. For one horrid moment Chulian feared they would be trapped in the blackness forever.

They turned to the right. Blackness filled that street mouth to brimming, too.

Yet Sharlson Naurya still stood obediently between them. She could have escaped merely by staying in the blackness – they had both let go of her. Of course, she might be afraid of the blackness, too. But Chulian did not think so.

From the corner of his eye he darted a backward glance. It was as he feared. The blackness had followed them down the street by which they had come.

The only way open was directly ahead, past the haunted house. Something wanted them to pass the haunted house. But it was that or nothing – before the blackness should decide to encroach still farther and swallow them up.

That last fear must have occurred simultaneously to Brother Arolj, for they started forward at a panicky trot, fairly dragging their prisoner between them.

Behind them steadily flowed the wall of blackness, lapping round their heels when they faltered. By the time they reached the little neglected square and the haunted house, they were running.

Much taller than the other houses it stood, a landmark of desolation. But Chulian only caught a glimpse of its entirety of crazily sagging, strangely slack walls and drooping circular windows, like pouched and leering eyes. For the blackness suddenly closed in from several directions, like a huge sack, cutting off the way ahead, blacking out the stars, driving them across the rubbly ground towards the mouth of the sack and the wrinkled, oval doorway of the house itself.

There Chulian had his one burst of desperate, fear-inspired courage. He pointed his finger at Naurya.

"In the name of the Great God, if you don't make it go away, I'll blast you!" he threatened through trembling lips.

Instantly the blackness swooped inward, closing about them like an envelope, bare inches away, half blotting out their view of each other.

"I won't! I won't!" Chulian cried, dropping his hand. The blackness retreated somewhat.

And now Sharlson Naurya finally smiled at him with her lips. She reached out, and before he realized what she was going to do, slapped his chest smartly at a certain spot.

His inviolability field went limp. His halo winked out. His scarlet robe hung loosely.

She patted his cheek, as one pats the cheek of a child. His flesh crawled at the gentle touch.

"Good-bye, Little Brother Chulian," she said, and slipped through the sagging doorway into the haunted house.

The blackness shot back, was not.

And up from the street Cousin Deth came running.

"Your prisoner! Where is she?" he demanded curtly of Chulian.

"Didn't you see it? That awful blackness?" Chulian countered unsteadily.

Cousin Deth drew back from him. "I wasn't aware you priests were afraid of the dark."

For a moment Chulian was conscious only that he had been insulted by a mere deacon.

"She went in there!" he retorted angrily. "And if you're so eager to get her, why don't you go in after her yourself?"

Cousin Deth turned towards the street.

"Rouse commoners!" he shouted to someone. "Set a cordon round the house!"

Then he turned back to Chulian.

"I shall probably be asked to enter this place tomorrow to cleanse it of evil," he said. "Since you are so desirous of seeing me enter it, your reverence, I will petition that you be made my priestly director, to guide me."


## CHAPTER FOUR

THE hands left Jarles' elbows after a slight, momentary tightening of their grip, which seemed to mean, "Stay there!" He felt the edge of a box or bench against the calves of his legs, but he did not sit down.

Gradually the faintest suggestion of his surroundings was revealed, like a midnight picture deftly painted by a master artist in brief phosphorescent strokes against a black surface tinged with violet.

He was in an extensive, very low-ceilinged room. Air currents and the way his footsteps sounded told him that.

At what seemed the far end of the room, on a low dais, was a kind of chair or throne, faintly glowing, with a squat table in front of it, and on the table something that might have been a huge, old-fashioned book, open. Little creatures of some sort seemed to be playing around the throne, for he could discern a scampering movement close to the floor and

43

hear an indistinct scratching and scuffing – and once or twice a faint *plop,* as if something suctorial had been pulled away from a flat surface.

Then one of the creatures sprang up on the throne, squatting there impishly – a tiny, very lean, vaguely monkeylike silhouette.

What came next sent a dry shiver up Jarles' back and started his scalp pricking. For the creature spoke. Or at least whispers came from the direction of the throne in voices too threadlike and shrill and oddly mumbling to be human – and yet human nevertheless. He could only make out a little here and there.

" . . . been tonight, Mysie?"

" . . . inside his robe . . . a Fourth Circle priest . . . scared . . . wits."

"Jill?"

" . . . on a visit far away, to tell . . . "

"Meg?"

" . . . on his chest, as he slept . . . "

"And Puss? But I know . . . "

"Yes, Dickon."

The one perched on the throne seemed to be asking, the others to be answering the questions, as if in parody of human beings making reports to a leader or chairman. The last voice had a disturbing familiarity which set Jarles quivering.

"Who are you?" he called loudly – and with more confidence than he felt. "What do you want of me? Why this mystery?"

The echoes died hollowly. There was no reply – only a sudden scurrying. In a moment the dais was empty.

Jarles sat down. If they chose to play this sort of game with him, there was nothing he could do about it – save refuse to be impressed, or at least refuse to show it.

But what could be the purpose of their game? In an effort to find some clue to his rescuers – and captors – he rehearsed in his mind what had happened since he had stood awaiting death in the Great Square.

The first section of his memories was clouded by shock. The impression of something solid, semi-transparent, and

44

blackly streaked closing around him. Blinding blue light and a crackling, howling, laughing pandemonium of sound. A nauseating swoop upward and then down again into a black hole that suddenly yawned.

After that, a brief period of waiting in absolute darkness. Then hands. Hands which eluded him when he sought to catch hold of them. Hands which guided him for an indeterminate distance and then left him in what cautious exploration showed to be a small cell. A long period of waiting. Again hands, bringing him here.

For a long time he peered towards the ghostly dais and throne, until he began to think he could make out other silhouettes, much fainter even than those of the small scampering creatures, so faint that they vanished when he looked at them directly. Larger silhouettes of figures seated midway between him and the violet-tinted blackness of the far wall, though none directly between him and the throne.

Suddenly his eye was caught by a fleeting smudge of phosphorescence on one of the silhouettes – where the teeth should be. Then brief yellowish tracks in the air, as if made by the waving of fingertips dipped in phosphorescence.

He looked at his own hand. Each fingernail glowed yellow. The room must be bathed in ultraviolet light. Perhaps the others were wearing some sort of transformer goggles.

"The Black Man is delayed, Sisters."

He started violently. Not because the voice – a woman's – was the first undeniably human one he had heard. Not because the words were mysterious and darkly suggestive. But because it was so devilishly akin to one of the shrill, sub-human voices he had heard mumbling earlier. As if this were the voice which the weaker one had been mimicking.

"Dickon is here. The Black Man cannot be far away."

Another woman's voice. Another impression of shuddering similarity.

The first woman: "What work did you do tonight, Sister?"

The second woman. "I sent Mysie to trouble a Fourth Circle priest – may Sathanas torment him eternally! She

45

crept in his robe and scared him into white fits – if I can believe her. She's such a sweet little liar when her mind is away from mine. Whatever happened, Mysie was famished when she came back. She'd drain me green if I let her. The little glutton!"

Abruptly his mind grasped the thread linking together all this shivery confusion.

The Witchcraft of the Dawn Civilization.

This would be a meeting of witches to report their exploits – a coven meeting. The Black Man – that would be the chief of this group or coven. And those little servant-creatures supposedly suckled on witch's blood, drawn through the witchmark. What were they called? Familiars!

But he had told the commoners, and he believed it, that there was no Witchcraft, save the debased and harmless remnant which the Hierarchy preserved for its own purposes.

This seemed debased enough, in a sense, with those bestial little manikins – phantasms of retrograde evolution. But harmless? He did not get that impression.

He turned again towards the dais, intending to address further demands to the darkness and seek to force an answer.

But the throne was no longer empty. A dead-black, man-like shape was sitting in it.

And then a voice from the shape – a silky, steely voice, bubbling with malefic mirth.

"Your pardon for my delay, Sisters. But tonight I was as busy as a priest. First must I guide the Hands of Sathanas to snatch a renegade priestling from under the very nose of the Great God. He almost sneezed in surprise, Sisters! Next Puss came scampering to tell me that the Hierarchy had seized our Sister Persephone and was conveying her to the Sanctuary. So Dickon and I must float over the roofs and drop down the Black Veil to fuddle her captors and persuade them to escort her to a safe place of refuge."

The voice was at once attractive and repellent to Jarles. He felt that he would like the man – and hate him!

"It tickles me, Sisters, now and then to use the priests' science against them. And no doubt our master is grateful to be relieved of a bit of extra work. Do you know the Black Veil, Sisters? One of the little tricks we have developed from the Hierarchy's solidograph. Two lights can make a darkness, Sisters, if they're of the same frequency – interference, it's called. The projector of the Black Veil sends out multiple frequencies which automatically adjust to neutralize all light in the focal region. That's the old real darkness, for you, Sisters – one that is born of two conflicting lights!

"But I monopolize the conversation, while all of you have doubtless as amusing tales to tell. First, though, our reverences to our masters!"

The Black Man rose, stretching his arms outward and upward in invocation – a batlike shadow against cloudy phosphorescence.

"To Black Sathanas, Lord of Evil, our eternal allegiance!"

To Sathanas, our allegiance," echoed the shadowy ring of witches – a dozen voices at least.

And with those voices, like a parody of a boys' choir, the shrill falsetto parrotings of the familiars.

"To Asmodeus, King of the Demons, on earth our master, our lifelong obedience!"

"To Asmodeus, our obedience." Again that half-chanted response with its piping overtones.

"To the covens and the Witchcraft, to our sister witches and brother warlocks, both here on Earth and secretly dwelling in heaven, to the little ones, and to the commoners sweating under the Hierarchy's yoke, our loyalty and love!"

"To the covens, our love."

"For the Great God, self-styled ruler of the universe, fat and impotent phantom, our laughter and hate!"

"For the Great God, our hate."

"For the Hierarchy, his underlings, puffed red parasites, our devices and doom!"

"For the Hierarchy, our doom! "

Then the Black Man's voice went low and ominous – a far-carrying , shivery half-whisper.

"Creep night, and enshroud the earth! Come, fear, and shake the world!"

47

"Gather, darkness!"

The next moment the Black Man was again reclining in the throne. And now his sardonic voice was more leisurely.

"Before we proceed to our regular business, there is the matter of new members. Persephone?"

From just behind him in the darkness, Jarles heard Sharlson Naurya answer.

He was triply confounded – by her unsuspected close presence, by a realization of what had made the voice of the creature called Puss disturbingly familiar, and by what she went on to say.

"I propose for membership the former First Circle priest, Armon Jarles! He has proved himself by publicly blaspheming the Great God and daring the Great God's wrath. He should make a cunning and potent warlock."

"Bring him forward," commanded the Black Man, "first taking from him that which must be taken!"

A pair of hands gripped each of Jarles' arms. He felt something needle-sharp prick his back deeply. He gasped and floundered forward, struggling.

"Be not alarmed," called the Black Man, mockingly. "We have what we want – the seed for that which must be grown. Bring him to the altar, Sisters, that he may bow his head to the Book and be baptized by me with his new name – his witch-name – Dis!"

At that Jarles found his voice.

"Why should I join with you?"

A startled silence. Then, close to his ear, Sharlson Naurya's whisper, "Be quiet!" And a sharp pressure from the fingers on that side.

The warning only stung him on. "What makes you so sure I'll enter your Witchcraft?"

Again Naurya's whisper, "Where else do you think you can find refuge, you fool!"

There was a flurry of murmurings, human and subhuman.

But the Black Man had risen. "Softly, Persephone," he called. "Remember, no one may become witch or warlock save of his own uninfluenced free will. It seems that your recruit has certain reluctances. Let him tell us about them."

"First tell me what you would expect of me," Jarles replied.

The Black Man's voice was faintly edged with derision. "I thought you had guessed. To abjure the Great God. To give yourself, body and soul, into the service of Sathanas. To sign your name in his book by touching your forehead to it, so that it will receive the individual and unique pattern of your thought waves, which cannot be counterfeited. To submit to certain other formalities."

"Not enough!" retorted Jarles. "I might be entering the Hierarchy, in view of all this supernatural mummery! What are the aims of this organization, whose slave you ask me to become?"

"Not *ask*, Armon Jarles," said the Black Man. "And not a slave – only a free man who has contracted certain obligations. As for our aims – you heard our ritual. Overthrow of the Great God and his Hierarchy!"

Jarles' bitter reply started another flurry of murmurs.

"In order that you may raise up your own degraded superstitions to be the decalogue of a new Hierarchy, and tyrannize over the world in your turn? The scientists of the Golden Age had good aims, too, but they forgot them as soon as they tasted power. For that matter, how do you know that you yourselves are not the dupes of the Hierarchy? True, you rescued me. But the methods of the Hierarchy are devious. They let me speak to the commoners when they could easily have silenced me. Perhaps they also let me be rescued, for some indecipherable purpose."

"I do not quite know how to satisfy you, Armon Jarles – if you can be satisfied," replied the Black Man with amused perplexity. "Regarding the ultimate intentions of the Witchcraft, when and if the Hierarchy is overthrown – that involves matters of high policy which I may not discuss.

"But, Armon Jarles, if there is anything within reason which I can do to satisfy you of our purposes, name it!"

"There is!" Jarles declared hotly, disregarding the imperative pressure of Naurya's fingers. "If you are sincere in your opposition to the Hierarchy and your love of the commoners, drop all this mummery and deception! Don't add to the commoners' superstitions. Can't you see that

49

their ignorance is at the root of everything? Tell them the truth! Rouse them against the Hierarchy!"

"And suffer the consequences?" the Black Man mocked. "Have you forgotten what almost happened to you in the Great Square – and how the commoners took your words?"

"I ask a favour," interjected Sharlson Naurya hurriedly. "This man is a thick-headed idealist. He is suspicious and fault-finding by nature. Make him a warlock by force! He'll come around to our way of seeing as soon as he's had time to think things over."

"No, Persephone. I am afraid we cannot make an exception – even for a thick-headed idealist."

"Lock him up safely, then, until he sees the light!"

"Nor, Persephone, may we use force – whether compulsion or restraint. Though I confess there are times when I itch to!" And he laughed.

His voice immediately became serious then – in so far as such a bubblingly mirthful voice ever could.

"I'm afraid it's now or never, Armon Jarles. What do you say to joining the Witchcraft? Yes or no?"

Jarles hesitated, looking around at the circle of black, phosphorus-touched forms that were now very close. They would probably kill him if he refused. He knew too much.

And then there was Naurya, whom he had thought lost to him forever. If he went through with this, he would be near her. And she seemed to want him. Weren't Dis and Persephone king and queen of Hell?

And then all these people – the Black Man and the rest of them. His feelings towards them were mixed. He might dislike what they did, but he couldn't hate them personally. They had saved his life.

He was terribly tired, he realized suddenly. He couldn't be expected to dare death, of his own free will, twice in one day.

And Naurya's fingers were conveying an insistent, anxious message. "Say yes! Say yes!"

When he opened his lips, it was to say "Yes."

But – just as had happened in the Great Square – his idealist's white-hot anger at all shams and supernatural mummery, like some possessing demon, seized control of him.

"No! What I said I meant! I will not compromise with hypocrisy! I will have no part in your Black Hierarchy!"

"Very well, Armon Jarles! You have made your choice!" rang the Black Man's answer.

The hands let go his arms. The Black Man seemed to spring at him. He flailed out wildly. The picture that had been painted indistinctly in blackness and phosphorescence now whirled with movement, became a formless chaos.

He was seized by other hands – smooth, rubbery-hided, and very strong. He sensed in them the pressure of some kind of field, though different in texture from the inviolability fields of the scarlet robes. He struggled futilely.

Something small and furry, but with claws, grabbed his bare leg. He kicked out convulsively. He heard the Black Man order, "Back, Dickon! Back!" His leg was free.

He had time to cry out, "It's all shams and lies, Naurya! All shams and lies!" And to hear from the darkness her angry laughter and her scathing cry, "Idiot! Idealist!"

Then he was being rushed along by a power he could not resist. Out of the room, down some narrow corridor that turned and turned again, and then reversed, like a maze. Staggering, stumbling, his shoulders buffeted by unseen walls. Then upstairs. A blindfold quickly whipped over his eyes. Another corridor. More stairs. His thoughts whirling as dizzily as he.

Finally, cold night air thrusting up his nostrils and chilling his sweaty skin. The feel of cobbles under his feet.

And, in his ear, the mocking voice of the Black Man.

"I know idealists never change their minds, Brother Jarles. But if you should prove the exception to the rule, come back to the spot at which I shall release you, and wait. We might contact you. We might give you a second chance."

A few more steps and they halted.

"And now, Brother Jarles," said the Black Man, "go practise what you preach!"

A shrewd push sent Jarles spinning, so that he stumbled and fell painfully on the cobbles. He jerked himself up, whipping off the blindfold.

But the Black Man was nowhere in sight.

He was in the mouth of one of the streets that opened on the Great Square.

In the sky was the first suggestion of dawn, magnifying the empty immensity of the square, touching with lovely shades of opalescence the towering domes and spires of the Sanctuary, paling a little the blue nimbus of the Great God.

And from the hillside farmlands, gathering power in its sweep across the Great Square, came a bitter wind that cut his naked flesh to the bone.


## CHAPTER FIVE

THE silver clashing of unseen cymbals and a mighty choir of invisible voices, stirring yet heavenly sweet, heralded the approach of the exorcisers to the haunted house. The commoners blocking their way drew back to let them pass. But since the streets enclosing the square were wedged tight with commoners, and since other commoners crowded in to get a closer view of the procession, and since none of the commoners were willing to encroach on the unkempt and accursed grounds surrounding the haunted house, and frantically resisted being shoved in that direction, there were several of them gently cuffed aside by inviolable, red-gloved priestly hands, and one or two children knocked down, before the exorcisers issued into the square.

An excited murmur greeted them. Megatheopolis was astir with rumour of mighty doings in the supernatural world and the close presence of dread Sathanas, who had once again risen from Hell to challenge the omnipotence of his master.

Early this morning had come word that the Hierarchy would cleanse the haunted house of evil. This seemed an exceedingly wise and logical procedure, since the haunted house was a relic of the Golden Age and therefore a likely lair of Sathanas and his friends, who dearly loved those ancient, overweening, star-storming sinners. No matter how hard and wearisome an age this might be, it was certainly a very exciting one with regard to manifestations of the supernatural. That couldn't be denied.

The music and the pomp of the procession of exorcisers were well designed to whip up the mob's anticipations to a high pitch.

First came the four young priests, handsome and tall as angels, each bearing before him, like a truncheon, a gleaming rod of wrath.

Then two deacons bearing censers from which a sweet incense dispersed.

Next a priest who walked alone, apparently the one in charge. Rather short and dumpy he seemed, but well puffed out and carrying his head high. The Fifth Ward goggled to see their ghostly counsellor, Brother Chulian, in such a position of authority.

After him, almost a score of priests, some with the lightning-and-coil insignia of the Fourth Circle emblazoned on their chests, bearing all manner of awe-inspiring implements – globes that glowed even in the bright sunlight, tubes, canisters, and oddly shaped metal boxes – all of them ornately decorated and bejewelled, and decked with religious emblems.

Last of this group, four grim-faced priests, easing along something that resembled a gigantic metallic snailshell. It floated unwieldly at shoulder height. They guided it to the top of a tiny knoll on the desolate grounds and stepped away. Then, while the crowd gaped, one of them made mystic passes in the air, whereupon it slowly sank, crushing the weeds and bushes beneath, until it came to rest with its flaring muzzle pointing towards the haunted house.

But the rear guard of the procession rather distracted from this exhibition. The excited babbling of the crowd dropped momentarily into a whispering, as those in front told those behind about the presence of the little man in black. Cousin Deth had quite a reputation.

And at the sight of the object borne behind him, several children set up a wail. It looked like a large, deep bowl, tightly covered. From it trailed downward a white mist, and it was dripping slowly, leaving a trail of little white pellets, which melted into nothingness but were bad to step on with bare feet, because they stuck and burned. The commoners in the front ranks felt an icy wave pass.

Such containers of holy water normally flanked the doorway of the Cathedral, chilling the entry. More than one child had had skin torn from his fingers, when he had inquisitively touched one of them and then been jerked away by a screeching mother. No wonder the priests carrying it exerted their inviolability to the fullest!

The invisible music rose to an exalting climax, then broke off. The murmuring of the crowd was hushed. For a moment there was silence. Then one of the young priests strode with great dignity towards the house, bearing his rod of wrath above his head like a gleaming sword. Heads turned as, breathlessly, every commoner watched his approach.

"This place is evil!" he cried suddenly in a great voice. "It is offensive to the nostrils of the Great God. Tremble, Sathanas! Cower, ye fiends! For, lo, I inscribe here the brand of the Hierarchy!"

He stopped directly in front of the oddly wrinkled doorway. There gushed from the extended rod a violet brilliance of the same hue as his halo, which was almost invisible in the sunlight. Slowly he traced a burning circle above the doorway.

What happened next did not seem to be part of the programme. He leaned forward suddenly to peer through the irregular orifice of the doorway, leaving the fiery circle unclosed. He must have seen something of exceptional interest, for he thrust in his head. Instantly the doorway puckered and snapped tight around his neck, leaving him frantically kicking and plunging, while his rod, still gushing violet light, set the green weeds smoking.

There were gasps and scattered screams and a few shrieks of hysterical laughter from the crowd. The three other young priests dashed forward to help their companion, one of them snatching up the fallen rod, which instantly ceased to flame. They tugged and pushed at him violently and pried at the doorway. The wall gave a little, as if semi-elastic. That was all.

Then the door opened wide of its own accord and they all sprawled backward in the smoking weeds. The young priest who had been trapped sprang up and darted into the house before the others could stop him. The door clenched shut behind him.

The house began to shake.

Its slack walls tightened, bulged, were crossed by ripples and waves of movement. Its windows all squeezed shut. One wall stretched perceptibly, another contracted. There were other distortions.

An upper window dilated and through it the young priest was ejected, as if the house had tasted him and then spat him out. Halfway down he exerted his inviolability, so that his fall was slowed and cushioned. He bounced gently.

This time the laughter of the crowd did not sound entirely hysterical.

The house became quiescent.

There was a flurry of activity among the priests tending the instruments. Hurried consultations. Two of them darted over towards Cousin Deth. Those tending the great coiled tube atop the knoll looked inquiringly towards him.

But of all the exorcisers, none felt so futile and confused as Brother Chulian. Why must things like this happen to him? Thrust into a position of seeming importance by Deth's malicious whim, he knew less of what was going on than any of the others. If only he hadn't forgotten himself last night and insulted the cruel little deacon!

The four young priests, retreating at last from the haunted house, stopped near him. Made careless of dignity by excitement, they argued together. The one who had been tossed from the upper window was being questioned by the others.

"Who wouldn't have looked inside?" he asserted, heatedly. "Two bare feet scampering, that's what I saw, I tell you! Just those two little bare feet, with nothing on top of them. When they danced off, I just had to see where they were going! Then, when I was caught in the door, a lot of ratty little commoners came in from somewhere and began making the most insulting remarks about my head. As if it were something stuffed and hanging on the wall! You'd have lost your temper, too! I wanted to chastise them. That's why I ran inside."

"But what made you jump out the window?"

"The house, I tell you! I didn't see the commoners anywhere. But it all began to heave and shake. The floor lifted under my feet and knocked me against a wall. The wall bounced me to another. Then the floor got me again. Before I knew it I was upstairs, I got a last bang, and a window opened in the wall just before I hit it. I couldn't help myself!"

Chulian did not want to listen. It was all too disturbing and confusing. Why did the Hierarchy want to do things like this? Why, the commoners had laughed! The deacons in the crowd had shut them up pretty quickly. But they had laughed.

Cousin Deth strolled up, followed by priests.

"And now that your reverences have edified the mob with this little display," he was saying, "perhaps we can carry through the original instructions given us by the archpriest Goniface."

"Given you, you mean!" one of the young priests retorted hotly. "We all had our orders from Sanctuary Control Centre and the Apex Council. We were told to proceed in the usual manner."

Deth surveyed him coolly. "But you see, your reverence, this is not the usual haunted house, set up for you to knock down. This, I fear, is a kind of war, your reverences. And perhaps war is something that only a contemptible and misbegotten deacon knows how to dirty his hands with. Unlimber the zero-entropy spray, Brother Sawl!"

A long, light, slim projector was attached to the container which had originally been carried behind Deth. Brother Chulian felt the chill strike through his inviolability field, and he edged away, shivering.

"A brief medium spray over the whole building," Deth was directing. "Enough to stiffen the outer walls. Then full intensity straight ahead. We'll make our own doorway. Ready? Very well. Brother Jafid, speak your piece!"

Brother Jafid's voice, mightily amplified, was unpleasantly sweet.

"Let the Waters of Perfect Peace infold this place. Let them lull its unrest. Let them draw from it all motion and all evil."

With a faint screaming sound of almost inaudibly high pitch, suggestive of ice scraping ice, the zero-entropy projector opened up. Snowflakes and flakes of frozen air traced the widening path of its spray. The haunted house was engulfed in a swirling miniature snowstorm. Back from it rebounded a blast of arctic cold. The crowd, tight-packed as it was, seemed to draw back still farther, huddling.

The path of the spray narrowed, concentrated around the doorway, crusted it frostily. Then the faint screaming ceased.

A priest walked up to that gleaming, icily opalescent patch and rapped it smartly with his rod of wrath. The hyperfrozen materials shattered, leaving a large, jagged-edged hole. The priest ran his rod around the edge, knocking down splinters, which tinkled like icicles as they fell.

"Now we can proceed," said Deth sharply. "Projector and rods first. Keep together. Watch for traps. Wary of doors. Listen for my orders. If the young witch is found, inform me at once."

Then, just as they were starting, he noticed Brother Chulian standing to one side.

"Oh, your reverence, I had almost forgotten! This was the very thing you wanted so much to see. You shall have the place of honour. Lead the way, Brother Chulian!"

"But – "

"We are waiting for you, Brother Chulian. All Megatheopolis is waiting."

Reluctantly Chulian picked his way through the frost-bitten weeds. Cold pushed upward around his ankles through the lower orifice in his inviolability field, urging his knees to tremble.

Unwillingly he studied the house, whose frosted walls were already beginning to steam in the hot sunlight. Even in its present dilapidated state, the haunted house had a certain beauty of proportion. But its potential fluidity was very repugnant to one used to the ponderous, rigid plastics of Hierarchic architecture.

Somewhere he had read of the adjustable houses of the Golden Age, with elastic walls made tense by force fields, akin in structure and motivation to the mobile figure of the Great God on the cathedral.

But the idea did not appeal to Brother Chulian. To a considerable degree he shared the commoners' fear and awe of the Golden Age and its proud inhabitants. They must have been as unpredictable and self-willed as their houses – rebellious and critical like Brother Jarles, brazen and mocking like that witch woman.

Chulian believed that it would have been extremely unpleasant to have lived in the Golden Age, with your own free individuality continually threatened by that of everyone else and with no Hierarchy to plan your life and guarantee your security.

He was very close to the ice-rimmed opening. What if the ancient dwellers had come alive with the house? Silly thought. And yet –

"If the interior shows signs of movement, we'll be giving it a light entropy spray to freeze it, your reverence," he heard Deth call to him. "You'd better step lively if you don't want your inviolability field to go into stasis, your reverence."

Hurriedly Chulian entered the haunted house and ducked through the first interior doorway he caught sight of. It would be just like the mean little deacon to carry out his threat and the thought of being held helpless in a rigid field in this place, even temporarily, was distinctly disturbing.

The feeble glow of his halo partly revealed a domed chamber of moderate size, with furnishings whose colours had faded with the centuries, but whose general lines still conveyed an impression of graciousness and comfort. Chulian coughed. Dust, churned up by the recent commotions, was everywhere resettling thickly. The floor gave slightly under his feet.

Despite his general revulsion, the room exercised an odd fascination on Brother Chulian. Some features seemed almost attractive. Particularly a certain couch, which looked rather like the bed in his luxurious little cell in the Sanctuary.

A chilling sound, as if someone had grated his teeth just behind him, made him whirl around. There was no one there.

58

But the door had vanished. He was cut off from the others.

His first thought was, "What if the walls should close in, and in, and in."

The couch which had first attracted his attention began to creep towards him, oozing across the dusty floor like a gigantic snail.

With a little gasp of choking, panic-inspired laughter Chulian dodged past it. It changed its course to follow him. Faster.

There were no doors. He tried to get solider pieces of furniture between him and the thing. It shoved them aside. He darted past it again. It swerved towards him quickly, as if it were a very intelligent, evil slug. He tripped, fell awkwardly, managed to scramble up, dart blindly forward.

It had him trapped in a corner. Very slowly now, as if gloating over his terror, the couch writhed closer, suddenly reared up, quaking obscenely, and thrust out stubby arms towards him – a vile personification of the fleshly comforts so dear to Chulian. Then it embraced him.

Its pressure against his chest activated the controls of his inviolability field, switching it off. His halo, carried by the funnellike extension of the field above his head, was automatically extinguished.

Darkness, then, and the suffocating, obscene endearments of the thing. Desperately he fought against it, straining his head backward, pushing out wildly.

If it touched his face he would go mad. He knew it.

But it did touch his face. Gently at first, recalling the feel of Sharlson Naurya's fingers. "Good-bye, Little Brother Chulian."

Then tighter and tighter, stranglingly, crawling over his mouth. And Brother Chulian wished he would go mad.

One useless thought insisted on staying in his mind. If he ever escaped, he would never again be able to sleep easily on his little bed in the Sanctuary.

Abruptly the pressure receded. A door appeared in the wall ahead, letting in wan light. He stared at it stupidly, swaying, feeling as weak as water. Then the realization that escape was possible penetrated his fear-numbed mind. He staggered forward.

Just outside the door he was bowled over by a scarlet tide of fleeing priests. Cousin Deth was in their midst. From the floor Chulian caught one glimpse of Deth's distorted, sallow face, white showing all around the irises of the eyes.

Cousin Deth was screaming, "The thing! The thing in the hole!"

Painfully Chulian half-scrambled, half-crawled after them, out through the chilly, ragged doorway.

In his ears thundered the uncontrollable, crazy laughter of the crowd.

Nimbly, the fingers of the Black Man rippled over the banks of close-set controls. His glistening eyes scanned the tenuous solidographic miniature of the haunted house set in front of him. Through the faintly projected walls he watched the tiny scarlet-robed manikins flee from the place, disappearing abruptly as they got outside the visual field of the mechanism. Watched Brother Chulian hobble after.

His intense concentration took the form of a very gleeful, but rather taut smile. Snub nose and short, bristling, red hair emphasized the impression of impishness.

He murmured a swift aside to his companion: "I am becoming very fond of that tubby little man. He scares so beautifully." He jerked backward. The little scene had erupted with blinding light.

"At last they blast the place," he cried. "But Sathanas always laughs last!"

And lifting a microphone to his lips, he howled manically.

It was as if a volcano had erupted. The haunted house glowed, flared, writhed, melted. The four priests on the knoll had finally received orders to get their warblast into action. But its smoky red flare was more suggestive of hell than heaven, and from the crowd beyond came screams of agony, where a momentary puff of its carelessly handled heat had inflicted serious burns. Each narrow street was jammed by fear-crazy, fleeing commoners. Others were seeking to scramble onto the roofs of surrounding houses.

The haunted house collapsed, ceased to be.

But from the flaming, heat-blasted ruins rose a shuddering triumphant laughter.

The Black Man switched off the master controls and stood up, eyeing the great keyboard with regret.

"Too bad its usefulness is over. It was a lot of fun to operate. I shall miss it, Naurya."

"But it was certainly worth it." She was looking at him seriously.

"By Sathanas, yes! Commoners laughing at priests – that's a major achievement. Though the poor devils will be sorry they laughed, when the Hierarchy doubles the tithes. But it was a very neat little instrument, just the same, and I have a right to mourn its passing. See, that top bank controlled the walls; the next one below it, floors and ceilings. You mightn't believe me if I told you how many hours of practice I put in before I developed the technique required for such stunts as bouncing that first chap upstairs and out again. Quite a problem in timing.

"Third bank – windows and doors. Fourth – ventilators, and such furniture as we decided to animate. Including Brother Chulian's overaffectionate couch." He patted a half dozen keys tenderly.

"Tell me," asked Sharlson Naurya, leaning forward curiously, "did the people of the Golden Age usually have houses that played such tricks?"

"Asmodeus, no! They were just a fad, I imagine, and a very expensive one. The idea was to have a house whose shape you could change to suit your fancy. Say you had a big crowd in for a party and needed a larger ballroom. You just activated the proper controls and – presto! – the walls would recede. And why not make it an oval or octagonal room while you were at it? Just as easy!"

He laughed happily.

"Of course, it all worked in slow motion. But when our investigations showed that the old equipment was still pretty much in order, it was very simple to shove in more power and speed up the tempo, so that the old place could dance a jig if we wanted it to. Then we hitched up our remote controls, and there we were!"

Sharlson Naurya shook her head. "I can't get over thinking that there's something disgusting about the luxury of a house like that. Imagine summoning a chair across the room because you were too lazy to walk! Or changing the shape of a couch to ease a crick in your back! Sounds too voluptuous." She wrinkled her nose in disgust.

Looking like some ancient jester, in his black tunic which left arms and legs bare, the Black Man spun around and pointed a mocking finger at her.

"You've been bitten by the toil-for-its-own-sake morality that the Hierarchy dredged out of the dirty past!" he accused laughingly. "But for that matter, none of us can escape it. I'm glad that in my case it took the form of an urge to play exceedingly laborious and complicated practical jokes."

Naurya studied him intently, leaning her arm lightly on the edge of the control panel that occupied much of the tiny, bare-walled, windowless room. He lolled back across the padded seat in front of the controls –the only piece of furniture in the room – eyeing her humorously. She seemed much wiser and more experienced than he, with her coldly purposeful features and enigmatic eyes.

"Are practical jokes your life's goal?" she asked finally. "I watched you all the time you were operating this thing. As you peered down at those scuttling little images, you kept smiling as if your sole ambition in life were to play at being a malefic demigod."

"You've touched my weakness there! But the telesolidograph always gives you that godlike feeling. You must have felt it yourself. Confess!"

She nodded soberly. "I did. How does it operate? That was the first time I ever saw one."

"So? I would have thought otherwise, since you are so close to Asmodeus."

She shook her head. "I know nothing of Asmodeus."

He looked at her sharply. "He takes a very special interest in you, as if you were one of the most important of us."

She did not answer. "But you know the job he's saving for you, Naurya. Do you mean to say that Asmodeus informed you of that job in the same manner that he informed me – by indirect communications?" He watched her for a moment longer, then shrugged his shoulders carelessly. "I can believe you don't know him. I've never met witch or warlock who did, myself included – and in one sense I'm his second in command. Just orders from above, that's all he is to any of us. An invisible fountainhead of instructions. The great mystery." His voice had a jealous tinge. He changed position, snapping his fingers restlessly. "But if Asmodeus gives you the run of our headquarters here and asks me to look out for you, I suppose it's quite proper for me to tell you about the telesolidograph. It's simple, really. The Hierarchy's solidograph is a three-dimensional motion picture. The telesolidograph is the same sort of thing, except that the primary multiple-beam is invisible, long-range, and highly penetrating, only erupting into a visible, three-dimensional image when it reaches the focus. Slightly analogous to a needle-point spray. So, for instance, if we want bare feet scampering around, or what not, we just fake a solidograph of them and feed the tapes into the projector. Phantoms to order! Vocal manifestations work in about the same way.

"The instrument I used is a bit more complicated, of course. Two-way. Viewer and projector. So I'd have a miniature image of the general focal region to guide me in operating my life-sized phantoms and manipulating the remote controls of the house.

"All our tricks are like that, Naurya. Relatively slight improvements on Hierarchic science. As soon as the priests get on the right track, it'll only be a matter of time before they find the answers. They've started already. Zero-entropy to put the walls in stasis wasn't a bad dodge.

"That's why, in handling the haunted house, I went light on telesolidograph – one of our real triumphs, worth holding up – and heavy on house controls, which we couldn't have hoped to keep a mystery. Only used telesolidograph on the first chap – and on Deth." He smiled reminiscently. "Odd that such a trivial thing should scare our dear deacon. But when Asmodeus sends you a detailed fear-biography of a man, it isn't difficult to put your finger on the weak spot — even of such a cruel crook as the deacon. What's the matter, Naurya? He one of your pet hates?"

She shook her head, but her eyes stayed as stonily hating.

"The man behind him," she said softly.

"Goniface? Why? I know, of course, that the special job for which you're being saved involves Goniface. Something personal about it? Maybe revenge?"

She did not answer. He stood up.

"A little while ago you asked me about my aims. What are yours, Sharlson Naurya? Why are you a witch, Persephone?"

She took no notice of the questions. A few moments, and her expression changed.

"I wonder what is happening to Armon Jarles."

He looked at her quickly. "Does he figure in your aims? You were hurt when he balked last night. Are you in love with him?"

"Perhaps. At least, he has a deeper motivation than the urge to play practical jokes. There's something firm-rooted about him, solid as a rock!"

The Black Man chuckled. "Too solid. Though I was sorry we lost him. Sathanas, but we need men! Men of ability. And it's just those that the Hierarchy grabs."

"I wonder what is happening to him," she persisted.

"Unpleasant things, I fear."


CHAPTER SIX

ARMON JARLES crouched where the shadows were darkest, trying to force himself to make a plan. But the deep wrath-ray burn on his shoulder had already started a fever, so that the throbbing dance music and squealing laughter from the house behind him became an evil thing, weaving nightmarish visions in his pain-racked mind.

This was the only part of Megatheopolis where curfew violations were tolerated. This district sacred to the ministrations of the Fallen Sisters. This place of slinking forms, priests without halos, cracks of light, doors that swiftly opened and closed, whistles, whisperings, throaty greetings, and invisible merriment with overtones of a desperate melancholy. A wanly beautiful, flimsily clad girl, standing in a lighted doorway, had seen him pass. There must have been something hunted about his manner, for her eyes had gone wide with terror and she had screamed, once again bringing pursuit down upon him.

For a moment they were off on a false scent, beating up another street. But they would be back. They would be back.

He must think of a plan.

Fever dulled hunger, but his throat was dry. Ill-made sandals cut his swollen feet. He had not realized how two years in the Sanctuary had softened him.

But other pains were nothing to the rasping of the coarse, stolen tunic against his unbandaged shoulder.

He must make a plan.

He had thought of leaving Megatheopolis. But neatly cultivated fields offered poor concealment, and if the farmers proved themselves half as hostile to him as the commoners of Megatheopolis had –

He must –

But an agonized swell in the sultry music conjured up an evil vision of his mother's work-worn face. Even now it was hard for him to realize that she had betrayed him. That his father and brother had done the same. Home. The one place where he had been sure he could find refuge. Even their obviously cold, unfriendly, panicky reaction to his sudden appearance had not put him on guard. But sideways glances – and that matter of sending his brother off on an unexplained errand – had finally forced him to recognize the truth. Almost too late. He had barely outsped the deacons his brother had brought. That was when he had got the wrath-ray burn. It was then, too, that he had learned there was a price on his head, a price which every commoner lusted to earn.

He had had to grapple with his father and knock him down, when the old man had tried to hold him.

His mother's shadowy face, like something seen through

heat waves, seemed to leer at him in the darkness. He reached out his hand to brush it away.

Perhaps, he told himself, feeling all the while that the universe was crazily tipping, he ought to be glad they had acted as they did. It showed that deep in their beings the commoners nursed for the Hierarchy a hate almost beyond belief. A priest backed by the Hierarchy was something to fear, to fawn upon, almost to worship. But a priest whom the Hierarchy cast out – their one chance to give expression to their hatred! It was commoners who were pursuing him now. Commoners led by deacons. But commoners.

Two years ago he had passed his examinations and set out, his head crammed with determinations to improve the morality and living conditions of the commoners and to do his part in hastening the New Golden Age. He had thought of himself as helping his family.

But on that same day his family had looked upon him as someone lost to them forever, as having become something more and less than a man – a priest – inhuman.

"Look! There he is!"

He shrank, blinking, from the searchbeam. Pain lashed through his stiff muscles as he lunged into a run and darted up the alley across the street. A wrath ray sizzled against the far wall.

Cobbles. Bite of the sandal thongs. Rasp of the tunic. His hurt arm dangling. Darkness. Rectangle of light. A woman's painted face. Screams.

Running. Running. Running.

Sudden swell in the shouts behind him, as they reached the mouth of the alley. Violet needle of a wrath ray over his head.

But before it chopped down into him, he had swerved into the next street, crossed it, and plunged into the ruined area towards which he unconsciously had been heading.

Rubble. Matted weeds. Feeling his way. Great blocks of stone and fractured plastic. Ragged wall that might have been erected before the Golden Age. Narrow, twisting spaces. Blind alleys. A maze built by the dilapidation of mighty structures.

Shouts from behind. Circle of light just above his head,

against a vast, jagged block. Ducking. Wriggling. Crawling.

More shouts, very close. Panicky rush for cover. Flood of pain, like blinding light, as his burnt shoulder rammed rock. Biting his cheek to hold back the scream. Salt taste of blood.

From that point onward he had no object but to burrow deeper and deeper into the ruins. Always to take the darkest and narrowest turning available. Sometimes the shouts moved away. Sometimes they drew close. That in the course of his aimless progress he would eventually crawl into the hands of his pursuers, was a fact depending on a kind of reasoning that no longer held significance for him.

It seemed to him he could still hear the dance music, throbbing in rhythm with his shoulder, screeching obscenely, wailing raucous despair. And the whole universe was dizzily swaying to the tune. He wanted to dance, too, but it hurt too much. He was someone else. He was Armon Jarles, but Armon Jarles was someone else. His father – his father was an archpriest. Those grim old arms were hugging him and would not let him go. His brother was a chubby, cooing little baby, named Brother Chulian. His mother –

A beautiful girl stood in a doorway, smiling at him, beckoning. Closer and closer he edged, his suspicion melting. Then she reached suddenly forward, and caught his hurt shoulder, and wrenched it, and from behind her poured a tide of scarlet robes. And her features grew old and work-worn, and his mother, dressed in a tawdry tunic, leered at him.

But her features were getting old, much too old even for his mother. Cheeks were sinking, lips puckering, nose growing to a thin beak, chin becoming a brown knob.

"Wake up, Brother Jarles!" A cracked whisper.

Something was wrong with the face. It was real, and he did not want to look at reality now. But the hand kept hurting him. He tried to push it away, looked up, saw, in the glow of a searchbeam striking above the narrow passageway, the same crone-face, recognized it.

"Come with me, Brother Jarles! Come with Mother Jujy!"

Almost, he smiled.

"I'd sooner you had the reward than my father," he murmured.

A bony palm was clapped over his mouth.

"You'll bring them down on us! Get up, Brother Jarles! It's not far, but we must hurry, hurry!"

It was less painful to get up than to lie there and be tugged at. After a little while he managed it, though the effort made the darkness real dizzily and brought back the visions. As he staggered along beside her, leaning on the skinny shoulder, it seemed to him that she kept changing. First his mother. Then Sharlson Naurya. Then Mother Jujy. Then the girl in the doorway. Then his mother –

"Let me call them," he said, smirking foolishly. "No need to look for them. Just let me call them and they'll come. Then – just think – you'll have the reward all to yourself. Or are you afraid they'll cheat you out of it?"

For answer, he was rapped across the mouth with a cane.

"There he goes! There he goes! Someone with him!"

Sudden turn into a side passageway. Eager voices baying from all directions. Another sharp turn. Then he saw Mother Jujy tugging at the weeds, tilting up a whole section of them.

"In! In!"

The blow had given him a little sense. He let himself down into the black hole she had uncovered. He half-climbed, half-slipped down a short ladder, rolled away from the bottom of it, lay there.

The shouting was cut off. Pitch darkness. Silence.

After a while a light was struck, and he saw the ancient face grinning toothlessly at him over a candle flame.

"So you see how Mother Jujy claims her reward, Brother Jarles!" she crackled.

She hobbled over to him and poked at his shoulder, lifting the cloth. He gritted his teeth.

"I must fix that," she mumbled. "Fever, too. But we must go aways first. Drink this."

She put a little bottle to his lips. The fiery liquid made him gag and gasp.

"Burns, doesn't it?" she observed gleefully. "Not like the

wines of the Hierarchy, is it? Mother Jujy makes her own nectar. Mother Jujy has a still."

He looked around.

"Where are we?"

"In one of the tunnels of the Golden Age," she replied. "Don't ask me what they were for. I don't know. But I know what they're for now." She giggled slyly, bobbing her head. "Just ignorant old witches! The priests know all about us! Oh, yes!"

He stared at her, puzzledly.

"Ah, don't bother your addled wits, Brother Jarles. Just come with Mother Jujy."

He followed her. In places the tunnel was almost whole – a circular tube of dull metal, big enough to stand in. More often it was cracked, and floored with dirt. Once or twice they passed crude shorings, obviously recent.

The trip seemed endless. Before it was over, he was very sick. His fever had gone up, fanned by exertion and perhaps by Mother Jujy's flaming nectar.

He began to stumble. The visions came back. Only now Sharlson Naurya walked at his side, nibbling a pomegranate. They were King and Queen of Hell, making a tour of the Underworld, conducted by their prime minister, Mother Jujy, whose cane had become a staff coiled with living serpents. Behind them walked a man who was all blackness. And around their feet gambolled half-human little apes.

Another ladder. Mother Jujy driving him up it. A narrow bed like a box with one side open. Short for him, but wonderfully soft. Against his tortured shoulder the blissful coolness of a bandage soaked with a dark, aromatic liquid. Momentary twitch of fear because he had never been doctored by anyone but a priest. The priests doctored everyone. Something warm trickling down his throat. Softness. Sleep.

His next conscious moment, omitting feverish visions with perhaps bits of reality jumbled in, began when he saw a black, blurred something squatting on the bedclothes over his feet. He concentrated on it patiently until it came into focus.

It was a large black cat, washing her paws and regarding him with a stony judiciousness.

That didn't seem right. It oughtn't to be a cat. Mother Jujy ought to have something small and furry and alive – but not a cat.

For an interminable period, he vaguely pondered the problem. All the while he watched the cat, half expecting it would speak to him. But it only went on washing its paws and judging him dispassionately.

Gradually he became aware of his surroundings. His bed was a box, after all. A box built into the wall of a room. His view of the lower part of the room was cut off by a solid side which held in the bedclothes.

The ceiling of the room was low, with all sorts of things hanging from the rafters. He could hear a little fire singing and something bubbling in a pot. It smelled good.

He tried to look over the side. That brought twinges of pain, not very bad but enough to make him catch his breath.

The old crone hobbled into sight.

"So you're back with us again, eh? For a while Mother Jujy thought she was going to lose her little boy."

He was still obsessed by his problem.

"Is that just a cat?" he asked weakly.

The witch's eyes, bright in their leathery sockets, regarding him narrowly. "Course! Though she gives herself awful airs!"

"She doesn't suck your blood?"

Mother Jujy made a contemptuous sound with her gums and tongue. "Maybe she'd like to. But just let her try!"

"But . . . then . . . are you a witch, Mother Jujy?"

"Do you think I make myself unpopular for fun?"

"But . . . I thought . . . I mean, the other witches I met –"

"Oh, *them!* So you've met some of *them*, eh?"

He nodded feebly. "Who are they?"

She glared at him. "You've asked too many questions already. Besides, it's time for soup!"

While she was spooning hot broth into him, with the cat come up to sniff the bowl and follow the movements of the spoon, there was a knock at the door. Mother Jujy hissed, "Not a peep out of you, now!" She slid a section of the wall across the front of his box, leaving him completely in the dark. He heard a muffled flop, as if a hanging of some sort had been dropped down.

The cat stood up on his chest. He could feel the pressure of the four paws, like a little table.

From the room came the sounds of talk, but he could not make out what was being said.

Presently the cat lay down on his good shoulder and began to purr. Jarles fell asleep.

During the next few days, the section of boarding was slid in front of Jarles' bed many times. After a while Mother Jujy omitted to drop the hanging, so he could hear fairly well what went on. He listened to the old witch dispense dubious-sounding magic and hard-headed advice to all sorts of commoners, especially girls of the Fallen Sisterhood, who couldn't have their fortunes told often enough. He made the acquaintance, in this indirect way of Megatheopolis' scanty and indigent criminal class, with whom Mother Jujy seemed on suspiciously good terms. Apparently she acted as a fence.

But those were not all her visitors. Twice, deacons came. The first time, Jarles was tight with apprehension. But, strangely enough, the fellow turned out to be genuinely desirous of obtaining Mother's Jujy's sorcerous aid in winning back a girl who had been stolen from him by a priest. The second time was worse. The deacon sniffed around suspiciously, spoke meaningfully of the penalties for illicit distilling and other illegal activities, and rapped the wall in one or two places. But apparently that was merely an attempt to get services for nothing, for he finally got around to telling a story somewhat similar to that of the first deacon. Jarles was vaguely glad when he heard Mother Jujy sell him a piece of magic the performance of which would involve several toilsome and degrading actions.

And he sometimes thought of the Black Man and Sharlson Naurya, though the coven meeting now seemed almost a part of the hallucinations of his fever. But he thought about it a great deal. And he plagued Mother Jujy with questions about *them*, until he had wormed considerable information out of her, although he had the impression that she knew a little more about them than she would admit.

According to Mother Jujy, it was only a very few years ago that the "new witches" had first cropped up. At first she had thought that they were directly inspired by the Hierarchy, and that the priests had decided to "run us old women out of business."

After a while she had changed her opinion of the new witches, until now she seemed to regard them as not altogether unfriendly business rivals. She admitted to certain sketchy dealings with them, though of what sort she would never tell Jarles.

As his burned shoulder healed, with a white-ridged pit in it, and his fever abated – slowly, since the marvellous restoratives of the Hierarchic physicians were lacking – Jarles mulled this information and one day he asked Mother Jujy straight out, "Why did you rescue me?"

She seemed perplexed. Then she leered at him and said, "Maybe I'm in love with you! There's many a pretty boy Jujy helped out of scrapes and hid away when she was the sweetest little dickens in the whole sisterhood."

After a moment she added gruffly, "Besides, you were half-way decent to me when you wore the robe."

"But how did you ever find me? How did you happen to be there in the ruins, when they were tracking me down?"

It was merely chance, Mother Jujy told him. She had just happened to be coming out of the tunnel. Later she amended this by claiming to have had a "vision" of his predicament. He knew she was not telling the whole truth.

Late one evening he felt restless and insisted on getting out of bed and walking up and down the room, ducking and weaving around the stuff hanging from the rafters, impatient to grapple with reality. There came a knocking at the door, quite different from any of those he had learned to recognize. A lilting tattoo of rippling fingers. Grimalkin, the cat, snarled menacingly. Mother Jujy drove Jarles back into the wallbed. Then she went to the door, unbarred it, slipped outside, and closed it behind her.

It was very dark, but confronting her was a deeper darkness, man-shaped.

"I see you," she said tartly, though a little nervously, pulling her ragged shawl a little tighter against the cold.

"And you needn't go pulling tricks to show off. You can't faze me."

"Grimalkin knew my knock," answered a laughing voice. "Shall I send Dickon in to play with her?"

"She'd scratch her eyes out! Creepy, crawly snuggly, dirty-minded little brute! What do you want?"

"How is our patient?"

"Wants to get up and set the world on fire! I have to tie him down."

"And his – education?"

"Oh, I think he's getting a little sense. Hard knocks have a way with them. He's tough, though. Got a slam-bang, drag-out mind, for all he's a gentle boy. Still, I think he's softening towards you people – worse luck for him!"

"Good! You are too modest, though. You underestimate the influence of your companionship on him. We are much beholden to you, Mother Jujy."

"Beholden pudding!" The old crone drew herself up, and stuck out her shrivelled chin. "Listen, I'm willing to help you people now and then, because I know you're out to get the priests. But there's one thing I always want you to understand: I saw through you from the first. In spite of all your tricks and stunts and gibbering little monkeys, you're not real witches!"

There was a half-pleased chuckle from the darkness. "Let us pray that the Hierarchy never achieves your penetration, Mother Jujy."

She ignored the compliment. "You're just fakes," she persisted. "I'm the real witch!"

The darkness bowed. "We will not dispute the honour with you."

"That's right!" said Mother Jujy.


## CHAPTER SEVEN

"ASMODEUS says we're stepping up the pressure, Drick. Tonight the wolves come to Megatheopolis. Just sniff around the outskirts at first, but they'll get bolder afterward. Beginning at midnight, telesolidographs in all key cities will be working twenty-four hours a day. We should have our second one set up here by then. You boys can operate it in shifts. Fun. But watch out for eyestrain. Meanwhile, all covens are to put everyone they've got on second-stage persecutions of priests of the top four circles. Here are the tapes listing the basic individual fears of susceptible priests holding key positions. You can attend to distribution."

The Black Man shoved across the desk a box packed with tiny wheel-shaped containers. The other young man – short, burly, shrewd-faced, and wearing a similar black tunic – glanced at the identifications on them and snapped the box shut.

"I'd like to know where Asmodeus gets such detailed information," added the Black Man, rubbing his dark-circled eyes. "If I were religious, I'd say he was the Great God – he knows so much about the Hierarchy."

Drick leaned forward. "Maybe he's in the Hierarchy."

The Black Man nodded, frowning thoughtfully. "Maybe. Maybe."

Drick looked at him queerly.

"I'm not Asmodeus, Drick. I'm not even sure that I'm top man in Megatheopolis, though I do seem to be the first to get instructions."

"From where?" Drick put his hand on the box. "A thing like this. It's a physical link. You had to get it from someone."

"Surely." The Black Man smiled, a little wearily. "It's logical to assume, if I walk into this room and find a box on my desk, that I got it from someone. But whom?"

"That's how it came?"

The Black Man nodded.

Drick shook his head, dubiously. "We sure do a lot on trust."

The Black Man chuckled. "Still, there are advantages to the arrangement. If any one of us is caught, he won't be able to give the whole show away, even if he's – persuaded to."

"They haven't caught any of us yet." Drick sounded a trifle cocky.

The Black Man looked up at him slowly, his impish face

suddenly dead serious. "You're not, by any chance, thinking that's because they can't? You're not doubting that they haven't spotted some of us, and are just waiting to get an angle on the higher-ups before they pull in the net?"

Drick looked a trifle taken aback. He frowned. "No, I'm not." He picked up the box and stood up. Then he remembered something. "I've been with Sharlson Naurya. She's getting restive. Doesn't like being cooped up here."

"Asmodeus' orders again. He's got something up his sleeve – a special job for her when the right moment comes. Spend some time with her, Drick, if you get the chance. Entertain her."

"Now those," said Drick, "are pleasant instructions."

"Better not set your hopes too high, though. I fancy we'll have a certain renegade priest back with us shortly."

"Mother Jujy's patient? He's changed his mind?"

"Changing, I think."

Drick nodded. "Not a bad fellow. And I guess Naurya does favour him." In the doorway he looked back suddenly. The Black Man had slumped a little and was rubbing his eyes. "Oh, say," Drick suggested casually, "If things are going to be much tougher from tonight on, why not take yourself a six hour vacation while you've got the chance?"

The Black Man nodded. "Not a bad idea."

After Drick was gone, he sat looking at the wall.

"Not a bad idea," he repeated.

Somewhere far off a mighty bell began to toll. A mischievous smile slowly crept into his lips. He frowned and shook his head, as if putting away a temptation. The bell continued to toll. The smile forced its way back. He shrugged his shoulders and jumped up.

He seemed all energy now.

From a closet in the wall he took a rather thick, black sheath, that suggested in part a coil or network of wires, and bound it to his right forearm. On a cabinet across the room was a shallow brass bowl, with some flowers floating in it. He pointed his right hand at it, experimentally, seeming to feel for some kind of contact. The bowl rocked slightly, rose an inch or two off the table, and suddenly upset, spilling water and flowers. He smiled satisfiedly.

To his left arm he bound a different sort of sheath, one with keys which he could touch by bending his fingers across his palm. He fiddled with the cabinet, setting some music going – a solemn melody. Then he backed away, moved his left arm as if again feeling for some sort of contact, and began to finger the keys. The solemn music squawked, became discordant, changed into something raucous.

From a rack in the closet he took down the costume of a commoner – coarse, long-sleeved smock, leggings, boots, hood.

A thin, muffled, piping voice without apparent source, commented, "Up to tricks again! I suppose I'll have to do all the hard work!"

"For that, Dickon, my little familiar, I think I'll leave you at home," said the Black Man.

The great bell had ceased to toll, but its reverberations seemed to linger on unchanging, like some mysterious message from eternity. Hushed and reverent commoners almost filled the Cathedral – a place of vast and pleasant gloom, aglow with soft rosy lights and the glitter of gold and jewels, the air swimming with sweet incense. Priests hurried softly up and down the aisles, slack robes swishing silkily, bound on mystic errands.

The Black Man made the customary ritualistic obeisances and hunched himself into an aisle seat on one of the rear benches, just opposite the gleaming wonder of the organ, from whose golden throats soft music had begun to breathe, blending itself with the fancied reverberations of the bell. He seemed half stupefied, sunk in an ignorantly groping meditation, chewing his tongue as if it were an animal's cud, piously brooding on his sins.

There descended upon him a feeling of peace and well-being, greater than could be accounted for by the warm gloom, the misty lights, the soothing music and incense. But since he knew it was due to radiations which depressed his sympathetic, and stimulated his parasympathetic nervous system, he could disregard the influence – indeed, enjoy it. If he had any lingerings of nervousness, the radiations nullified them. Covertly he noted their effect on the others

– the loosening of work-taut muscles, the smoothing of worried frowns, the stupid dropping of jaws.

"Great God, master of Heaven and Earth, priest of priests, whose servant is the Hierarchy – "

A devout, half-chanting voice pulsed through the lustrous dimness. From behind the altar, lights blared upwards like muted trumpets, revealing the image of the Great God, which seemed a diminished reflection of the vaster image atop the Cathedral. The commoners bowed their heads. From them rose, like a tired sigh, a mumbled response. The service had begun.

The pious atmosphere deepened, as response followed droning response. There was only one suggestion of a hitch – when a number of older commoners automatically responded to the "Hasten your New Golden Age" line, which had been recently cut from the service.

The priest on the rostrum was replaced by an older one, who began to preach. His voice was marvellously flexible, one moment stern as wrath itself, as sweetly soporific as dugged honey the next. His words were admirably suited to the mentality of his audience. Not one could fail to hit its mark.

He spoke, as usual, of the hard lot of commoners and of the never-ceasing endeavours of the priesthood to alleviate their sin-begotten misery. He painted a simple, compelling picture of a universe in which only endless toil could expiate the evil taint inherited from the Golden Age and so keep damnation at bay.

Then all the honey went out of his voice, as he began to speak of a matter more pressing and closer at hand – the increasing boldness of Sathanas and his imps. There was a subdued scraping of feet and friction of homespun on benches, as the commoners shifted around to listen more intently. He told them that the boldness of Sathanas was entirely due to their own increasing sinfulness, warned them of the dire fate in store for those who did not repent and improve, and commanded each man to keep close watch upon his neighbour.

" . . . for none may say from where sinfulness will next spring. Its seeds are everywhere, and Sathanas waters and manures them daily. Beyond all else he loves that crop. The Hierarchy can smite down Sathanas when it wills. But there is no merit for you in such a victory, unless each of you tears Sathanas from his heart and keeps the seeds of sin dry and sterile."

On this note of stern and ominous warning, the sermon ended. First Circle priests appeared at the head of the aisles, bearing gleaming plates, and yet another priest entered the rostrum to exhort the people to contribute as much as they felt able to the coffers of the Hierarchy. Such free gifts had a special virtue.

Hands fumbled in pouches. The plates passed up and down. Metal clinked in.

The priest on the centre aisle had worked back almost to the end. As he reached once again for the plate, now grown heavy, the commoners holding it seemed to pull it away from him a little. The priest reached out farther, grasped it, and – because he was glaring suspiciously at the commoner who had been so awkward – handed it without looking towards the row across the aisle. He felt it taken from him and dropped his hand. Then he noted something queer in the expression of those around him – perhaps he heard the faint initial gasp of surprise – and he turned around.

The first commoner across the aisle had indeed reached out to take the plate, but before he could quite get his hand on it, another force had taken it from the priest. The commoner shrank back, goggling.

The plate hung unsupported in the air.

The priest quickly grabbed for it. It eluded his fingers, moving higher.

He grabbed again, standing on tiptoes. The plate kept just out of reach.

Suddenly conscious of dignity, he stopped grabbing and stared around at the gawking faces, including a red-headed fellow four rows back, who seemed if anything more oafishly dumfounded than the rest.

His attention instantly returned to the hanging plate, when it jogged up and down sharply, so that the coins jangled and one or two dropped out.

More and more commoners were staring at it.

Abruptly it shot off and upward, describing a gleaming curve in the gloom, and overturned, spilling a shower of coins on the commoners below. It fell a distance with the coins, then righted itself, and again hung quietly.

With admirably quick wit, perhaps thinking this a demonstration of which his superiors had neglected to inform him, the priest cried, "Lo! A miracle! The Great God gives of his infinite bounty! To each he gives as each deserves!"

Instantly, in response to his last words, the plate swooped towards him, intent on braining him. He ducked, then quickly looked up. The plate reversed its course and made another swoop. Again he ducked, and this time he did not look up. The plate came to a sudden stop over his bowed head, like a halo of brass, and then dropped downward, thumping his shaven pate twice with audible clanks.

The priest bellowed with pain and surprise, and remembered at last to switch on his inviolability.

The plate retreated upward and hung.

There were already the beginnings of a panic – or riot. One whole section of commoners was grubbing around under the benches for fallen coins. Others were crowding in fear towards the entrance. While the majority were staring upward, excitedly nudging each other.

In response to a hurried order, the organist started a loud, solemnly blooming melody. That would have been a good idea, except that it did not stay solemn. With a discordant bray, its rhythm changed and quickened, until – as the organist stared horrifiedly at the score and continued to press the keys in frantic bafflement – there squawked from the golden throats the seductive swing of something that all of the priests and many of the commoners recognized as the latest ditty to find popularity in the houses of the sisterhood.

Radiations stimulating the parasympathetic nervous system are tricky things, encouraging instinctive, animal responses. Only a few at first, but swiftly more – the commoners began to sway, to writhe, to whirl and dance in quasi-religious ecstasy, yelping, screaming, panting, grunting like animals, as if this were one of the mammoth revivals and not an ordinary religious service.

In a side aisle, a group of them careened into a priest, upsetting the collection plate he was still holding, sending coins spinning in all directions. There was more scrambling and crawling under benches. Many of those on the floor forgot to look for coins and began to roll, groaning and howling with devout fervour. Some embraced.

Then the organ began to laugh insanely, mechanically, and the hanging collection plate began to swoop about, skimming heads, like a brass bat, finally darting towards the altar and dashing itself with a clang against the image of the Great God. At that, a sizeable portion of the crowd broke in panic and rushed towards the door.

There was an ear-splitting roar – not from the organ. Those in flight came to a dead stop. The less intoxicated dancers looked around frightenedly. Everywhere people cringed from the sound.

Then a stern voice filled the Cathedral:

"Move not a step! There is an imp of Satan in this place. Each commoner must be examined to see if he be the sinful one – the one possessed. Return to the benches. He who moves towards the door will feel the Great God's wrath!"

Substantiating this statement, a dozen black-robed deacons filed in to block the wide, high-arched doorway, each bearing a rod of wrath.

The Black Man, in the van of the fleeing crowd, felt a sudden change in his emotions, indicating that the parasympathetic radiations had been replaced by the sympathetics. That was not altogether a wise move. Although the remaining dancers and rollers stopped almost instantly, the sympathetics were favourable to fear. The crowd surged forward unevenly, like animals about to stampede. The rods were lifted. The crowd came to a nervous halt.

The Black Man's right arm, bent at his side, moved a little, feeling for contact. He leaned a little to the left to balance the weight of the force pencil.

A deacon towards the centre of the line turned suddenly on the man beside him, rubbing his elbow. His whisper was audible: "Watch out, you clumsy fool!" The other deacon turned on him as suddenly. "You bumped *me!*"

A similar altercation started towards the end of the line.

There were more angry words. Others joined in. Then actual pushes, shoves, raised fists, threats – for deacons were not trained to be as gentlemanly as priests.

And still the imp of discord moved among them, setting them against each other. The sympathetics, as favourable to anger as to fear, played their part. Fists struck out. The line of deacons tied itself into a struggling knot of men, each enraged against the rest. Some dropped their rods. Others used them as clubs.

This mysterious brawl, and the fact that a way of escape now lay open, was enough for the fear-skittish crowd. In a great ragged wave it poured out of the Cathedral.


## CHAPTER EIGHT

Up from the black infinite abyss of sleep shot the arch-priest Goniface.

First a dream. A dream so deep, so primal, that it lacked vision and sound. Horror. A writhing in darkness that was himself. Restraint. Himself struggling futilely against it. Deep, pricking pain. Something essential being cut from him, to be used against him. It was his secret, his one and only weakness. It could destroy him. A spasm of convulsive, futile and horror-stricken writhing.

Then a more definite dream. He wandered among the corpses of those he had killed because they knew his secret. Very white and stiff and still they seemed, each laid out on its table under a glaring light, and he felt very safe. Then, three tables away, one sat up suddenly. An immature girl with dark hair streaming over her marble shoulders. She pointed at him and her mouth opened and she said, "Your name is Knowles Satrick. You are the son of a priest. Your mother was a Fallen Sister. You have transgressed the most jealously enforced law of the Hierarchy. You are an impostor." He ran towards her, to force her down again and shut her mouth. But just as his fingers touched her, she slipped away from him. Around and between the tables he pursued her. Some were overturned. He stumbled over his mother's corpse. Around and around. Staggering. Gasping.

And still she eluded him, crying all the while in a loud voice, "Drag down the archpriest Goniface! His name is Knowles Satrick! His father was a priest!" And the mouths of all the corpses opened and they began to cry loudly, "Knowles Satrick! Priest's son!" until the whole world was screaming it at him and there were a thousand hands upon him. And suddenly he was a boy again, and his mother was bitterly muttering, "Priest's son!" to shame him.

Then memories, close to the surface of awakening. The white, upturned face of his half sister, Geryl, with the dark hair streaming upward around it, as she fell from the bridge into the dark distant torrent below. His secret wholly safe at last. Then the Apex Council Chamber and the solidographic miniature of a mature woman, whose face wore that same expression of hate and implacable purpose as he had glimpsed on the face of that immature girl, as she fell towards the torrent. The same face. Geryl. Sharlson Naurya. His secret come alive.

Then illusion. He was where he should be, in his chamber at the Sanctuary. Grey darkness let him see the outlines of the room and silhouetted, at the foot of his bed, a grotesque anthropoid shape, skinnier than any monkey, but furry-seeming. Only for a moment was it visible. It dropped out of sight, and there came the faintest pattering of tiny paws.

Then complete wakefulness. He sat up, breathing a little heavily, his eyes refamiliarizing themselves with the shape of his room, putting every object in its right place in the semi-darkness. Odd, how that last brief dream had reproduced the outlines of his room almost as they were in reality. But there were dreams like that. Perhaps the rural priests, with their talk of furry things which squatted on their chests, had been responsible for that last dream-imagining.

He fancied a slight pain in his back – another dream echo.

Unpleasant, that memories of his past deeds should sometimes pry their way into his dreams. But that was the way the human mind was constituted. Nothing could ever be wholly forgotten.

And what difference did it make? The secret of his birth

was no longer of great importance. It had been, when he was a First Circle priest. But now he was too powerful to be dragged down, or even seriously endangered, by any such accusation.

Still, if Geryl had actually escaped, and if Geryl were Sharlson Naurya, and if the Moderates got their hands on her, they could make it embarrassing for him. Best that Deth should find her and put her out of the way.

It seemed she was in the Witchcraft. Did the Witchcraft, then, know of her relationship to him and plan to use her against him? If that were true, why had she been spirited away? What good was she except to accuse him openly of being a priest's son and having entered the Hierarchy illegitimately?

As Goniface pondered, the range of his thinking widened, until, almost before he was aware of it, he was surveying in imagination the vast empire of the Hierarchy.

Out there in the darkness – and on the day-side of Earth, too – something was gnawing at that empire, as mice might gnaw at the strands of some vast net. The New Witchcraft, every day growing bolder. Creeping from farmland to town and from town to city. Only yesterday striking in the Cathedral itself.

Most of all, his thoughts were concerned with the problem of the Witchcraft's leadership. Out there, somewhere, was a mind daring enough to challenge the Hierarchy. Beyond all else, the identity of that mind fascinated Goniface. Did it come from beyond Earth? That was barely conceivable. Or should he look for it closer at home?

One of the televisor panels beside his bed flashed on and there appeared the face of one of the Fourth Circle priests on duty at Web Centre.

"I am sorry to disturb your archpriestship – " the priest began.

"What is it?"

"It began approximately an hour ago. A sudden, sharp increase in all manifestations of the Witchcraft. Communications have been coming in from all over the planet. There have been panics in several rural sanctuaries and at least two have been deserted by their occupant priests. There is a confused and ambiguous message from Neodelos. Beasts of some sort, or phantasms of beasts, have been reported in and about our own city. Many local priests report hallucinations – or persecutions of some sort – and clamour for treatment. There has been a riot or panic in the dormitory of the novices."

"Can you inform me," inquired Goniface, "if the counter-measures covering this type of emergency have been put into action?"

The face in the televisor nodded. "To the best of my knowledge, they have. But the Chief of Communications desires to consult with you. Shall I flash him on?"

"No," said Goniface. "I'll come down."

The televisor flicked off. Goniface touched a switch and soft light flooded his spacious cell, with its Spartan luxury.

He rose quickly from the couch, then – moved by a sudden impulse – looked back.

He immediately remembered the stinging pain he had felt momentarily in his dream.

For near the centre of the couch, on which he had lain, was another echo from his dream – an echo of a very different sort.

A small spot of blood.


## CHAPTER NINE

THE second night of fear had settled on Megatheopolis, imparting a shuddering menace to the curfew-darkness and the curfew-silence. That day special prayers had been addressed to the Great God, both in the Cathedral and the chapels, for protection against the forces of evil. Tales of strange phantasms, which last night had defied even priests, were whispered everywhere. More commoners had clamoured to confess their sins than the priests could take care of. Before being dispersed, an hysterical mob had torn to pieces two old crones, known to be witches. Each man looked with suspicion on his neighbour, wondering if he might not be in league with Sathanas. An hour before curfew, the streets were almost deserted.

Along those mazy streets, staying close to the squat rooftops, the Black Man floated, relishing the atmosphere of terror and suspense, just as an actor enjoys knowing that the play in which he has a part is going well. Over the Cathedral, the halo of the Great God glowed with a double brilliance, and the whole Sanctuary was ablaze with lights. A few streets away the search beam of a patrol of deacons moved about restlessly. But in between all was darkness.

As a swimmer in darkness, the Black Man moved, poling himself along by varying the direction and intensity of the pencils of force emanating from his forearms. The repulsor field generated by the garment he wore, skintight over his whole body, was sufficient to counteract gravity at this slight elevation. The field also had the property – save at points over sense organs – of absorbing all radiant energy that impinged upon it. This radiant energy in turn helped power the field.

Technically he was off duty. An hour ago he had finally been relieved at the telesolidograph by another operator – there was a shortage of operators now that they had two projectors working – and had satisfied himself that as much of the general plan as he knew was progressing satisfactorily. But after that, like an actor who is off stage for a time, he had been unable to resist the temptation to sneak out in front and see how the play was going.

He had an excuse of sorts. Word had come from Mother Jujy that Armon Jarles intended this night to attempt to recontact the New Witchcraft. Meanwhile, Mother Jujy was retiring into her tunnels "until the mob gets a little less frisky."

Of course, he could have sent someone to pick up Armon Jarles at Mother Jujy's. But with a man as peculiarly stubborn as Armon Jarles, it was well to let him take the initiative. And it was dramatically more pleasing that Armon Jarles should go to the appointed rendezvous on the edge of the Great Square, the spot where he had been cast out by the Witchcraft.

Meanwhile, he trailed him, to make sure he didn't get into trouble, hovering noiselessly above while Armon Jarles, clad as a lowly commoner, stole furtively through the narrowest streets and alleys, seeking the deepest shadows, stepping carefully to avoid the mouths of drains, stopping at intervals to spy warily for patrols, frequently glancing over his shoulder, but quite unaware of his guardian demon overhead.

They were nearing the Great Square. The Black Man was tempted to put an end to this rather purposeless pilgrimage, but was held back by his love of dramatic denouements. The fun would be over soon enough.

Bobbing violet rings warned of the approach of two priests bound on some nocturnal mission. Jarles hesitated, then shrank back into a narrow passageway between two buildings. The Black Man sank gently to the edge of the roof above, alert for emergencies.

But the two priests hurried unconcernedly on. As they neared the passageway, the Black Man felt a start of pleasure. He had recognized the smaller, dumpier priest as the little fellow whom he had so thoroughly scared, in front of the haunted house, with the Black Veil, and later, inside the place, with a nastily animated couch. His feeling towards Brother Chulian was one almost of affection. It would be too bad to miss this opportunity. Naurya said the little priest had been inordinately frightened by Puss, her familiar. It would only take a moment to switch off his repulsor field, set Dickon riding on the end of his force pencil – Dickon would like that – and dangle him in front of Chulian's face.

Almost before he had decided to, it was done. A tiny anthropoid shape was slanting down through the darkness towards the bobbing halos. The Black Man's mind was all mischief.

Then – ominous windy rushing in the darkness overhead and the emptiness of dismay at the pit of his stomach before he had time to reason why.

Wrench of his neck, as he slewed around to look behind and above, from where he rested on the edge of the roof.

Then – one frozen instant.

One frozen instant to damn himself as an adolescent prankster who would walk into any trap so long as it was baited with an opportunity for a practical joke, to think, with poignant intensity, of what a swift blotting out was in store for the Witchcraft, if it were all manned by as reckless and negligent fools as himself.

One frozen instant to comprehend the thing swooping towards him. Its rigid, manlike form – but twice as long as a man. Legs stiffly extended, like a diver's. Arms threateningly outstretched, fingers spread like talons. Huge sculpturesque face, framed by great golden curls, handsome with the super-human, unearthly beauty of some heroic painting, visible in a faint glow from the stern, staring eyes, which could flash forth death if they willed.

An angel.

Then – one whirling instant.

One whirling instant to repower his repulsor field, launching himself simultaneously down into the street – the angel was too close to permit a try over the roofs.

One whirling instant to swerve frantically from side to side of the street, like a low-lurking hawk pounced upon in turn by an eagle; to see the two priests ahead stop, but not time enough to see them turn around; to see slim Dickon, hurled from the force pencil, drop lightly near the mouth of a drain; to dart suddenly and swiftly upward towards the rooftops – but not suddenly or swiftly enough; to sense the angel banking upward with him and just above him; to feel its impact – stunning even though almost parallel to his own upward course; to feel, through his repulsor field, the cruel clutch of its mechanical arms, that were its grapples.

One whirling instant to think a command, with all the intensity he could summon, "The drain, Dickon, the drain! Make for the Sanctuary! Keep in contact – unconscious minds!" to sense in a dark corner of his mind the beginning of a ghostly answer, to see loom suddenly ahead a roof edge which the angel did not wholly avoid.

Then – one crashing, lasting, final instant of unconsciousness and darkness.

## CHAPTER TEN

DOWN a grey corridor in the crypts beneath the Sanctuary, two deacons escorted Jarles. This was a region shrouded in mystery, a region from which lower-ranking priests were normally barred. All elevator shafts save one stopped two levels above. It was said that a great research of some sort, involving human beings, was conducted here. It was said that a new batch of commoners was sent down here every day, and that each batch contained a high percentage of mentally defective and psychotic individuals. It was also said that most of them came up madder than when they descended.

That more than research might be involved was hinted by the rumour that recalcitrant and criminal priests were sometimes sent here, too.

Jarles tried to keep his mind from dwelling on the cruelly tantalizing mischance of his recapture by the Hierarchy at the very moment when he had become reconciled to the Witchcraft and was eagerly setting out to seek to join forces with it.

Had the Hierarchy known all along that he was hidden at Mother Jujy's, and waited all that time before it struck?

Or had Mother Jujy betrayed him? Or someone in the New Witchcraft, perhaps the Black Man? He must not even think of such a possibility! He had decided once and for all that the new witches were on the side of good, that they represented the forces with which he had resolved to ally himself. He must not, dare not, suspect them.

One of the deacons pacing beside him spoke. Both men he knew to be underlings of Cousin Deth.

"I wonder how this one will be when he comes out?" the deacon asked speculatively.

His companion was not much interested. "Who knows? I've seen them all ways and every one a bit different. Only one thing I'm sure of – Brother Dhomas will be glad to see this one. Brother Dhomas is always happy when we bring him a new mind."

"Yes, the old putterer!"

They approached an open door. Emanating from it, as chemical odours from a chemist's laboratory, Jarles sensed traces of various radiations affecting the human nervous system. Like tiny ghostly hands, they tugged at his emotions – alarming, reassuring, angering, soothing.

Nervously his eyes swept the room. They were first drawn, as to a focus, to a padded chair, provided with clamps. That was bad. But the mechanisms and instruments around about were those of a psychological laboratory. That was good.

"That's right. You needn't be alarmed. We won't torture you physically. And as for mental torture, there's no such thing! There is only – experience."

It was the strangest voice, rapid yet deep, and lacking individuality. Human – but generalized. As if many people were speaking the same words in perfect rhythm with each other.

The eyes of Jarles went to the speaker. A quakingly fat priest whose baggy, dirty robe was emblazoned with the human brain and arabesque of equations in psycho-sociology that distinguished the Sixth Circle.

From the emblazonment he looked up at the face. Strangely, the face was like the voice – generalized, despite the seemingly sharp individuality of double chins, thick, mobile lips, and scanty eyebrows. As if the solidographs of a dozen facially similiar priests – but each a distinct person – had been projected into the same space, with a resultant cancelling out of much of their individuality.

If any feature had more individuality than the rest, it was the eyes. They dwelt on Jarles engulfingly, thirstily, almost lovingly, as if he were the most interesting thing in the world. But not exactly because he was Armon Jarles, not exactly because he was an individual.

Those eyes held Jarles, so that it was with an effort that he looked away from them to the small man in black. Odd, that he had been able to look at the Sixth Circle priest without first noticing that Cousin Deth stood beside him.

"There he is, all ready for you, Brother Dhomas," said Cousin Deth. "And his archpriestship Goniface requests me to warn you that this one must not be botched. He was too hard to get. There will be unpleasant consequences if you turn up a gibbering failure."

Without taking his eyes off Jarles, Brother Dhomas answered swiftly.

"You can't scare me, little man. You know as well as I that my methods are still empirical, the results unpredictable. If a man is botched, he's botched! That is the agreement. I guarantee nothing."

"I have warned you," said Deth.

Brother Dhomas approached Jarles, moving rather easily for one so abnormally fat.

"I have been studying your unabridged dossier and listening to the speech you made in the Great Square." He indicated the solidograph projector in front of the central chair, but his eyes never left Jarles. "You have a very interesting idealism – very interesting."

His tone was that of a surgeon commenting on an unusual tumour.

"I will leave you now," said Deth. "And I will inform his archpriestship of your intention to treat this case merely as an experiment."

Brother Dhomas looked back at him. "Spiteful little reptile, aren't you? Your tight, self-infatuated mind interests me. I would like to get my fingers into it. Or your master, Goniface. There's a mind for you! What wouldn't I give to work on a mind like that!"

Cousin Deth's face froze.

"Masks! Masks!" rumbled Brother Dhomas, with a hint of laughter. "Don't you know I like best of all men who can mask their thoughts? It gives me something to work against."

Cousin Deth walked out, followed by the two deacons who had come with Jarles.

Instantly the eyes were back on Jarles. And now they studied him with such intensity, seeming wholly to lose themselves in him, that they appeared almost vacuous.

"A great sincerity, too," continued Brother Dhomas, nodding his head, as if he saw it through the pupils of Jarles' eyes. "Oh, yes, and negativism. Very well developed negativism."

With a sharp effort Jarles looked away.

"No, I'm not trying to hypnotize you," said Brother Dhomas, without interrupting his inspection. "Hypnotism would hinder my work, like a bad anæsthetic – deaden the reactions which I need to guide me."

His silent inspection of Jarles eventually ended.

"And now – if you will seat yourself." He indicated the central chair.

Jarles noticed then that several priests had unobtrusively drawn close to him after the departure of the deacons. Emblems intertwining diagrams of the nervous and circulatory systems proclaimed them to be priests of the Third Circle, the circle of doctors and lesser psychiatrists.

Two of them grasped his elbows and turned him towards the chair. Wildly, violently, he began to struggle – but more to convince himself that he was still a man than because he had any hope of escape. His flailing fists knocked down one priest, but two others seized the arm and bore it down. Inexorably he was drawn to the central chair, forced down in it, the clamps fastened.

And all the while Brother Dhomas kept calling to him, "That's right! That's right! Struggle now. Get it over with. It will make it easier for me afterward."

The Third Circle priests stepped back. The chair was luxuriously comfortable. But Jarles could not even turn his head.

Electrical and pneumatic recording instruments were attached to his body. Something was injected into his arm. Again Brother Dhomas read his suspicions.

"No, it's not a truth serum. Extracting the information you possess is merely a side issue. We want much more than the truth from you."

Brother Dhomas moved to a position directly in front of him, beyond the control bank of the solidograph.

"What is personality?" he said, in a new tone. "Merely a viewpoint, or a system of viewpoints. Nothing more.

"Viewpoints change. Why does not personality then change? The answer, of course, is that it does – but usually so gradually that the change is not sensed. *Your* viewpoints have changed. Your dossier shows that they have changed more often, and to a much greater degree, than those of the average. Yet you think of yourself as essentially the same person. That raises a perplexing question."

He might have been speaking in a schoolroom of the novices.

"For the thoughtful person, there is no more baffling sensation than that called up by memory of viewpoints he has discarded. He remembers, perhaps in great detail, how he entertained those discarded viewpoints. But the old arguments no longer appeal to him – he has a new viewpoint which perhaps completely contradicts the old. And yet memory and a kind of intuition tell him that he was the same person then as now. And so we come back to the perplexing question.

"The answer is rather obvious. Memory is the only link between past and present viewpoints.

"But memory can link – anything. Memory is cold and dispassionate. Memory is without morality. Think of the person that you most admire and the person you most detest. Imagine them as two stages in the life of one person. Imagine memory as linking those two stages. You see, even that is possible.

"Yes, personality changes. The problem is – to accelerate the change.

"You begin to see what we intend with regard to yourself? That's right! That's right!"

Any mental barrier Jarles might have managed to set up was insufficient to prevent Brother Dhomas from reading – or guessing – his fear.

"No, no, your present consciousness won't be snuffed out and replaced by another. That would be like killing you. You forget what I told you about memory. Personality will change, but memory – individual consciousness – will continue unbroken."

Almost, Jarles felt relief. At last he knew where the attack was coming and could marshal his forces. His hatred of the Hierarchy. His new-found loyalty to the Witchcraft – only it gave him a queer shiver to think that he could call it "new found." His love of Naurya. His detestation of creatures like Cousin Deth. But, much more important than any of those, his firm belief in the right of every commoner to freedom, equality, and a fair share in the world's riches – and his unswerving enmity to any group or

92

individual who sought to tyrannize over the commoners. Surely beliefs like that couldn't be changed. Other beliefs – about particular organizations or individuals – might change, according to what one knew about them. But a belief in human freedom was basic. It couldn't be changed. Brother Dhomas was bluffing.

"That's right," said Brother Dhomas, "it does seem impossible. But look at my face. Is it not that of a man who has transformed his own personality many times? Didn't you sense that as soon as you looked at me? As soon as you heard my voice? How else could I have gained the needful direct experience and skill, amounting in fanciful terms to a sixth sense, except by experimenting on myself? I haven't discovered telepathy, you know. My knowledge of the human mind – of your mind – is based on deductive skill and vast empirical knowledge, gained from – experience.

"I did not shrink from experimenting on my own mind. My sole regret is that I dare not change my personality sufficiently to interfere with my basic orientation as a research psychologist, that I can enjoy only the fringes of insanity – "

Those ceaselessly probing eyes had become, for Jarles, infinite abysses in which anything might lurk. But whatever Brother Dhomas said, he was bluffing. He admittedly hadn't changed his own basic personality. He couldn't change that of Jarles.

"That's right," said Brother Dhomas. "Be overconfident. It will make you more vulnerable when you begin to wonder. And now – action!"

Slowly, one by one at first, then more swiftly and many together, the various instruments in the room revealed their functions. Jarles was assaulted by sights, sounds, tastes, smells, touches, inward tensions. And by emotions. Emotions far more specific and intense than those produced by the sympathetics and parasympathetics with which he was familiar. Perhaps the injection accounted for his greater susceptibility. He fought against them all. Locked his jaw, compressed his lips, to hold back a laughter that bore no relation to his thoughts. But it broke all barriers and burst forth in convulsive peals. Steeled himself against the reasonless tears that next began to flow. But they still flowed, and still he sobbed like one broken-hearted by some great grief. Fought the anger that tightened to a sickening knot beneath his chest, fought the fear that made his flesh prickle and teeth chatter, fought them all, but vainly. It was as if he had been dispossessed from his body and must impotently look on, tormented by a wholly mental desperation and a kind of mental shame, while Brother Dhomas elicited from his body all the responses of which it was capable, like an expert musician testing the range and capacities of an unfamiliar instrument.

For now the room was in semi-darkness, and from a panel beside Brother Dhomas rose more than a dozen stubby pillars of different coloured light, constantly fluctuating in rhythm with Jarles' physiological and neurophysiological reactions. Ceaselessly Brother Dhomas' eyes went from the pillars to Jarles and back again, while his pudgy fingers squirmed like white worms over the control panel, slowly, tentatively.

From emotion to thought, from body to mind, the invasion progressed. Jarles felt that his mind was like a planet, with consciousness the illuminated side, and an inexorable force was rotating it. Ideas he tried to grasp, to hold firm, abruptly slid into darkness and were gone, beyond thought's reach, like a word that is on the tip of the tongue yet cannot be remembered. And from the other side of his mind – the night side – emerged a host of things forgotten and undreamed of. Petty hates and envies that had once flickered for an instant in his mind and then been repressed. And memories. Memories of childhood. His first confession. Sharlson Naurya – a stranger girl who had just come to Megatheopolis from another city. Fear of a bully. Fight with a bully. Work in the fields. Chores. Memories that went *too far back* into childhood. Himself lying in some box and goggling up at a world of giants. His mother's face – a young woman's face – bending over him. Then a fearful twilight realm, in which all inanimate things had life and were symbols of unseen powers, and words were magical formulas to control them. And then there were no words, and the unseen powers became sentient writhings, and there was no distinction between himself and the rest of the cosmos.

Slowly the dark memories retreated. Slowly the alien emotions ebbed from his flesh. For a while he was aware only of exhaustion, limpness. Then a growing jubilant relief. He was still Armon Jarles. He still believed as before. Brother Dhomas had failed.

"No," said Brother Dhomas, "that was merely exploratory. A random groping for weak points in the armour of your personality. The stimulus tapes are now being automatically correlated with the tapes recording your reactions. The results will be illuminating. Though, to be honest with you, I work more by feel.

"Also, it was necessary that you gain experience. A knowledge of your mind's hidden potentialities. Then you'll be able to work with me better. Against your own will, of course – resistance can be very helpful.

"The radiations, you see, change your neuronic gradients and potentials over neural areas whose limits and extent I can know only empirically. As a result, certain thoughts and memories are raised above, or depressed below, the threshold of consciousness, as the case may be.

"Your experience has shown you that any human mind has the wherewithal – if only in minutest traces – from which any kind of personality can be fabricated. Every person has experienced at one time or another fugitive flashes of hate and cruelty, which, if only sufficiently magnified and strengthened, would make him a monster. Every person has, at least for one split second in his life, wanted to destroy the whole world. You see?

"It is only necessary to manoeuvre your mind into the desired state – that's where my maximum judgement and penetration are required – and then freeze your mind by a sudden intensification of the radiations, sufficient to change the neuronic gradients and potentials *permanently*. If I misjudge and freeze your mind while it is in a state of temporary insanity, that is unfortunate.

"Our next exploration will be as purposive as the first was random. Action!"

Again the sensory bombardment, the emotional wrenching, the mental rotation. But because they were not so chaotic as the first time, they were not so instantly unnerving. In particular, the induced emotion was hardly troublesome at all – an odd mixture of fear and pleasure, promoting a watchful self-regard, so that for a moment he could smile with guarded contempt at Brother Dhomas.

But the sensations rapidly acquired a very specific and disturbing quality, though the induced emotions tended to make that disturbance chiefly mental. Where they had got that moving solidograph of himself, he could not say, but it was talking to him – himself to himself – and he heard his own voice repeating:

"Armon Jarles, there is only the cosmos and the electronic entities that constitute it, without soul or purpose, save so far as neuronic mind impose purpose upon it.

"Armon Jarles, the Hierarchy embodies the highest form of such purpose.

"Armon Jarles, the supernatural and the idealized have one trait in common. They are not. There is only reality."

Endlessly. Such statements, though, might have been patched up from recordings of his classroom recitations, his oral examinations. But then it dropped – still his own voice and image – into a more intimate key:

"Look at me, Armon Jarles. I am yourself as you will be when you have learned to see reality squarely and to disregard sentimental dreams. Look at me! I, Armon Jarles, laugh at you, Armon Jarles, for what you are now."

They must somehow have patched up even that, taking a word here and phrase there, blending them with diabolic skill. He could never have said that! Or could he?

And now the solidographic Armon Jarles began to grimace at him with cruel cynicism. It must be – could only be – a prolonging of some fleeting expression they had searched out in some moving solidograph of him. But he hated it. He closed his eyes against it.

Swiftly an instrument was adjusted around his head. He felt a moderate, adhesive pressure on his eyelids. They were gently forced open. At regular intervals the instrument imposed upon his eyelids a slow mechanical wink.

"We have no desire to torture you," came Brother

Dhomas' voice across a lull in the auditory sensations. "Pain would provide a core round which you could concentrate your personality. We desire to disperse it."

Jarles could still look away from the hated portrait of himself, but that did not keep him from seeing it dimly in the periphery of the retina – laughing, grimacing at him, and always talking.

And then once again repressed thoughts and memories began to slide from the inner darkness. And now they were all of a sort – anti-idealistic. They seemed to be marshalled like an army. The thoughts he clutched at, to use against them, melted away. Until he found the master thought – his belief in freedom and equal sharing, his hatred of all tyranny. And that thought, though its particular form of expression kept changing, did not vanish. It held the others at bay.

Again a lull in the sensory barrage, and Brother Dhomas speaking over it.

"What is idealism? It is distortion. A giving of false values to things which in reality do not possess those values. Personalities differ chiefly in their pattern of values. When the values are largely false, the personality is unstable."

Back then, into the churning inward darkness. Back once again, to the struggle against the forces of anti-idealism. Freedom and equality were right! But why? Why did man deserve them more than any other animal? Because man was a higher form of life? But to be higher only meant to be more complex, and what virtues was there in complexity? Why should all men deserve freedom and equality? Why not just a few? It was wholly arbitrary. The whole concept of deserving was an idealistic fiction. One either had something or hadn't it. One either wanted something or didn't want it. There was no such thing as deserving something.

Frantically Jarles strove to reanimate the concepts in which he had always believed. When this type of reasoning had perplexed him before, he had always sought refuge in anger – in hatred of oppression. But now his emotions were no longer his own. The cleansing flood of anger would not come. And a dry, dead world of facts and forces confronted him.

With an effort he called to mind individual commoners whom he had seen suffer, whom he had sympathized with, whom he had yearned to help. But now they seemed merely grotesque physiological machines. They did not move him.

Like a retreating soldier, then, he dashed from point of cover to point of cover, only to see each protection dissolve as he reached it.

His mother and father. They were heartless beasts who had betrayed him. It would be pleasant to watch them die.

Cousin Deth. He hated Cousin Deth desperately. But why? Cousin Deth was a sensible man, ever obedient to reality, ever solicitous about his own appetites. True, Cousin Deth did not like you. But no one liked you. There was no such thing as disinterested affection. Only hungry self-interest.

The New Witchcraft. Yes, it would be well to be in with them – if they won out. But they were warped with idealism. They wouldn't win out.

Sharlson Naurya. He loved her. That love couldn't be destroyed. It was something he could cling to. Almost he could see her. He loved her. He wanted her. And if she could be persuaded, or forced, to enter the sisterhood, he'd be able to have her.

The Hierarchy. There, at last, was real security. But for some reason he should consider it the wrong sort of security. What was the reason? He couldn't remember.

The Hierarchy. Like some great golden sun it rose in his mind, dazzling him.

Then that golden light become a blinding, searing flame. There was an ear-splitting, deafening roar of sound. As if he had become the centre of an explosion that shook the whole cosmos. An explosion that roared down every channel of sensation in his body, ripping his nerves with its awful intensity, destroying him.

Then, utter darkness of all senses.

Then, return from darkness.

He was still in the same room. Still in the same padded chair. Brother Dhomas was still staring at him.

Nothing had changed.

What had Brother Dhomas been going to do? Change his personality? But he hadn't! He was still Brother Jarles. The old fool had failed!

Of course he was Brother Jarles, priest of the First Circle – but he wouldn't stay there long! Let's see, the Fourth Circle was the one to aim at – the circle of promotion. The Third and Fifth were largely blind alleys.

Of course he was Brother Jarles. Faithful servant of the Hierarchy, because any fool knew that was the best way to feather your own nest. Cousin Deth was his friend – that is, Cousin Deth was willing to favour him. And anyone whom Deth favoured would go far.

Then came memory, like a blow. Incredulously, painfully, he remembered.

So Brother Dhomas hadn't really failed. His personality had been changed.

Unwillingly, with the acutest shame and embarrassment, he recalled that other, former Armon Jarles.

What an utter – what a contemptible, namby-pamby, sugary fool that other Armon Jarles had been!


CHAPTER ELEVEN

BROTHER CHULIAN was afraid of the man on the bed. He watched him with an almost painful intensity.

True, the man was presumably unconscious, had been since his capture. And so badly injured that an artificial heart was needed to supplement his own. Chulian could watch the blood coursing through the transparent tubes.

Hierarchic medical science was able to accelerate the process of healing to an amazing degree, but not by any stretch of sane possibility could that man move from his couch for many hours.

Still Chulian was afraid of him. For the man was a witch – or should one say warlock? At all events, a potent somebody in the Inner Witchcraft. And Chulian had had too many recent experiences with the powers of the Witchcraft. That abominable couch! He still couldn't sleep decently.

Those powers were outside the bounds of sane possibility.

Of course, the higher priests said they weren't. The majority of the higher priests maintained that those powers were just clever scientific trickery, engineered by an enemy of the Hierarchy. That point of view was being constantly dinned into the lesser priests these days. There were special meetings devoted to the subject. The higher priests promised that the Hierarchy would soon destroy the enemy. It only delayed to study the enemy and perfect preparations. Meanwhile the lesser priests should look on all phantasms with complete scepticism – and turn in detailed reports of them.

How much more helpful, wistfully mused Chulian, if the Hierarchy could announce that the Great God, in his supernatural omnipotence, had decided to smite the hosts of Sathanas. Only there wasn't any Great God. But how comforting it would be if there were!

A priest of the Third Circle came in, examined the man on the bed, took readings from indicators attached to the artificial extension of his circulatory system, and left without speaking to Chulian.

How mean of Cousin Deth to have given him this job!

But what could Brother Chulian do? By gradual stages, quite against his will, he had became a member of the entourage of Cousin Deth. And behind Cousin Deth loomed the awesomely powerful archpriest Goniface. After always having tried to avoid it, Chulian had became enmeshed in Hierarchic politics.

Temperamentally Chulian was with the Moderates. He once had heard the archpriest Frejeris speak, and he had never forgotten the experience. A large handsome man, calm as a statue. He had given Chulian a very comfortable and safe feeling.

Still, Chulian had to admit he didn't find the present policy of the Moderates very satisfying, with its minimizing of the danger represented by the Witchcraft. If they'd gone through what he had, they wouldn't minimize that danger! The Realists had the right idea there!

There was a faint sound, as if someone were clearing his throat. The man on the bed had opened his eyes, and was watching Chulian.

As consciousness ebbed back into the Black Man, his first thought was one that eddied up on the tide of consciousness from the depths of the subconscious – anxiety for Dickon. Without fresh blood, his little brother could survive for three days at the most.

Anxiously, he thought a message: "Are you there, Dickon?" Then he blanked his mind and waited.

Slowly, on the blank, a reply etched itself.

"Dickon is in the wind tubes. Dickon is very weak. Poor Dickon. But Dickon can see you."

Wind tubes? Ventilators! There must be an outlet in this room.

He thought: "Why can't you come to me?"

Hesitatingly – he could tell that his little brother's brain was dizzy with fatigue poisons – the reply came through.

"Dickon would like to come. He is in the mouth of a wind tube leading into your room. But there is always a priest in the room. It would be wrong for Dickon to take the slightest chance of a priest seeing him. You know that, brother.

"Dickon has been waiting here for a whole day. Poor, poor Dickon. He had a hard time getting here. He lost touch with his brother's mind more than once. Dickon wants you to tell him what to do, brother."

The Black Man thought: "Where is the priest?"

"If you turn a little to the left, you will see him. He is not looking at Dickon's brother now."

Carefully, very carefully, and noiselessly, the Black Man rotated his head until he could see Brother Chulian. The fat priest seemed lost in some worried mournful meditation.

He thought: "Have you enough energy to move swiftly for a little while, Dickon?"

"Dickon has still a few suppets of fresh blood in his sac. By sitting very quietly, Dickon has husbanded them."

"Good! This priest is an easy one to scare. Without showing yourself, scare him so that he runs out of the room. I will hold his attention while you slip in."

"Afterward may Dickon come to his brother?"

"Yes."

The Black Man cleared his throat. He did not know yet

if he could speak. One lung seemed wholly out of commission.

With a start, Brother Chulian looked up at him.

"I am a servant of Sathanas," said the Black Man. He spoke in a feeble, wheezy whisper.

"You are an enemy of the Great God," Chulian finally replied, with a kind of uneasy diplomacy.

The Black Man twisted his numb lips into what he hoped was a wicked smile.

"Who fears the Great God?" he whispered. "The Great God is without authority. He was created by Sathanas in order that men might have hope and so struggle more amusingly against evil and terror and death."

"Nevertheless, you are a prisoner of the Hierarchy," Chulian finally asserted, unconsciously flicking his robe, as if something had lightly touched his thigh.

"Yes," whispered the Black Man ominously. "And I am amazed that you have dared to offer me indignity. Release me at once, or I will do you an injury."

Again Chulian flicked unconsciously at his robe, all his attention momentarily concentrated on the Black Man.

"You can't move from that bed," he said with an uneasy insistence. "You can't leave this room. And you can't possibly hurt me."

"So?" whispered the Black Man, smiling, for the first smile had seemed to bother Chulian. "Even now I stretch forth invisible hands towards you. Even now they are upon you."

With a squeal, Chulian shot up from the stool.

Chulian rubbed his thigh, staring with a frightened suspiciousness first at the Black Man and then at the stool. Abruptly, as though he knew he would lose his nerve if he hesitated, he picked up the stool and turned it over.

Reassured in one sense, Chulian replaced the stool and seated himself.

Instantly the pinch was repeated.

With a squeal that was now one of terror, Chulian sprang up, crazily waving his arms about to fend off the invisible hands. Darting one last terrified glance at the Black Man, he fled the room.

The Black Man heard Dickon pattering towards the bed. Over the edge appeared a red-furred paw, the fingers clawed, the palm suctorial. (It was those palms which had enabled Dickon to cling always to the opposite side when Chulian had turned over the stool.)

Slowly and laboriously now, for the familiar had suddenly come to the end of its strength – the Black Man could sense dazed exhaustion in the quality of the vague tele-pathic impulses – the little creature pulled itself up into view.

It was like a spider monkey, but with a much smaller torso and far skinnier. Downy, reddish fur covered what seemed the merest outline or sketch of an animal – a tracery of pipestem bones and ribbonlike muscles. The incarnation of fragile nimbleness, though at the moment sluggish with exhaustion. The head was more like a lemur's, with large, peering eyes, now filmed and groggy.

A wraithlike, elfish thing.

But for the Black Man, the sight of it woke a pang of deep affection and kinship. He knew why its reddish fur was the same shade as his own hair, why its high-fore-headed, noseless face looked like a caricature of his own.

He knew it, loved it, as his brother. More than his brother. Flesh of his flesh.

He welcomed it as it crept feebly to his side and applied its strange mouth to his skin. And as he felt the suction and faint pricking, and knew it was drawing fresh blood from him and simultaneously discharging vitiated blood into his venous capillaries, he experienced a dreamy gratification.

"Drink deep, little brother," he thought. "This is on the Hierarchy, little brother. They must have transfused a lot of blood into me to maintain that artificial heart. So drink especially deep."

He felt suddenly very sleepy and weak. The discharge of deoxygenated blood from Dickon aggravated his faint-ness.

As in a dream he sensed Dickon's thought: "Dickon grows strong now, brother. Dickon feels strong enough to take a message to the end of the world, if Dickon's brother desires him to."

Good Dickon.

There were hurrying footsteps outside. But before the Black Man could think the warning thought, Dickon sprang swiftly away and out of sight.

"Dickon returns to the wind tubes, brother. Think out the message you want Dickon to take. Dickon will listen for it."

Through a haze of weariness, the Black Man heard the sneering voice of Cousin Deth inquire, "And just where are the hands that clutched you so irreverently, your reverence? Would you take the trouble to show them to me? Oh, but I was forgetting – you said they were invisible. Are they still pinching you, your reverence? I am all solicitude."

Then Brother Chulian's shrill reply. "I tell you, he touched me! He looked at me, he spoke to me, and then invisibly touched me!"

"How rude of him!" observed the sarcastic voice. "I fear I shall have to give the job of watching him to a less sensitive person. Oh, I believe he touched you invisibly all right. He touched your mind – with suggestion, hypnotism. The witches are very clever with such things."

The voice grew louder, until the Black Man, in his semiconscious daze, realized that Cousin Deth must be looking down at him.

"But I wonder how much his cleverness will count when he is well enough to go to Brother Dhomas."


CHAPTER TWELVE

It had been market day in Megatheopolis, and usually on market day the Great Square did not empty until almost curfew. But now the commoners were packing up and hurrying home before sunset. Business had gone halfheartedly. Thought of the coming night had taken the zest out of trading.

There had been an invisible merchant moving among them, who gave away his wares free. His name was Terror.

Who dared go home by twilight and risk meeting one of those great, grey, red-eyed beasts which last night had prowled and snuffed through all the alleyways? Or chance having his home cut off by such a creeping darkness as had driven a patrol of deacons to seek refuge in the dwelling of a commoner? Umder Chohn the Smith, at whose home it had happened, said the deacons had been more frightened than himself.

Everyone had some horror or wonder to tell and whispers had passed more swiftly than trade goods. Several swore they had seen angels – "great winged ones with glowing faces" – indicating that the Great God was at last taking some interest in the trials and tribulations of his creatures. But this reassurance was more than counterbalanced by a set of ugly and disturbing rumours which hinted that the priests themselves were not immune to the general terror.

These latter rumours penetrated everywhere, though whispered with sidewise glances to make sure no priest or deacon was in earshot. How a priest had fled screaming from a service in one of the lesser chapels because something invisible had clutched his throat as he preached. How a group of commoners, returning at night from their work in the fields, had been deserted by the priest who was supposed to escort them and protect them from the forces of evil. How a child had died of the Choking Sickness before dawn, because no Third Circle priest would come from the Sanctuary.

There were other indications that the Hierarchy itself was afraid. For two days now bands of rural priests had been trickling into Megatheopolis. Some said they were come for a religious festival. But others maintained in guarded whispers that they were seeking the protection afforded by the Grand Sanctuary. This was confirmed by the farmers who came to market. The farmers asserted – they were a little more outspoken than townsfolk – that many of the rural sanctuaries were deserted and that work in the fields was coming to a standstill.

Traders come by muleback or cart from the nearer cities said that the minions of Sathanas were at work in those cities, too. They were not a little disconcerted to find Megatheopolis similarly besieged.

Sathanas laughed. Earth shook. And the Great God took no heed.

So it came that an argument circulated with the tales of priestly cowardice.

It ran this way: "Why don't the priests protect us? We have confessed our sins twice over. We have reformed. We have been good. Then why don't they protect us from further terror? They tell us it's a test, but surely the test has lasted long enough. They've always said they could smite down Sathanas whenever they wanted to. Then why don't they?"

So Sharlson Naurya, slipping into the Great Square, sensed surliness as well as fear in the commoners leaving it. To her it was apparent in the readiness with which they quarrelled over right of way and other trifles, exchanged accusations of pilfering, and cuffed their children for loitering.

For her purposes, the bickering confusion was an advantage, since it occupied the attention of the few priests and deacons on hand.

She knew she was taking chances and disobeying the instructions of Asmodeus. But the disappearance of the Black Man and Jarles had altered circumstances. Jarles had been on his way to recontact the Witchcraft. The Black Man had gone to meet him. That was all Drick had been able to discover.

So, garbed as a commoner, with shawl drawn close to her cheeks, Sharlson Naurya threaded through the sullen crowd in the Great Square, like a young mother searching for lost children.

And she felt rather like one. True, she might love one of the two men. But they seemed more like her children. The Black Man the slightly spoiled darling – clever and good-natured, but impudent and mischievous and harum-scarum, too. Jarles the serious one, stubborn, beset by moral problems.

There was a commoner about Jarles' build slouching at the next corner. Instinctively she hurried her pace. He had a stubbly growth of beard, and wore a hood – perhaps to conceal a recent priestly tonsure?

She came closer. It looked like Jarles. It was Jarles. The emotion she felt was mixed with a certain tart self-satisfaction. So Drick had said it would be futile to keep the rendezvous? For that she'd take Jarles direct to the Coven meeting tonight. Drick would find out soon enough that she had gained a very able convert for the Witchcraft.

She caught his eye. With the barest nod in his direction, she turned into the side street. After a moment he followed her.

The elation Jarles felt was not unmixed with apprehension. He had hardly hoped to contact the Witchcraft so smoothly and so soon, but he knew that ahead lay many perils – threats to his bodily welfare. And recently Jarles had come to have a great respect for that bag of flesh and bones which contained his ego. Once let that bag be seriously ruptured and you could whistle through all eternity for another.

Why he had ever before taken such desperate risks – and not for personal gain! – was mixed up with the greater mystery of why he had ever been such an idealistic weakling as he remembered. He disliked thinking about it. It was all too cheap and puerile.

Of course, to achieve personal gain and ego-satisfaction, it was necessary to run risks. You never get anything for nothing. Obviously, Goniface wouldn't make him a Fourth Circle priest – the reward he had dangled before Jarles – unless there was something in it for Goniface. So it was necessary that Jarles embark on the ticklish job of betraying the Witchcraft.

Goniface! There was a man for you! Jarles never remembered envying anyone so acutely or admiring anyone so utterly, though grudgingly. Not even Cousin Deth. For the archpriest had the breadth of vision and capacity for power – and enjoyment of it – that the deacon lacked.

Elevation to the Fourth Circle – and all that went with it, even a little more besides – was a reward that justified taking risks. Anything was better than to grub along with the timid little minds down in the first two circles. But it was only common sense to minimize risks and stretch margins of safety as wide as possible.

So it was with alert senses and active mind that Jarles

followed Sharlson Naurya into the commoner's section. With a certain pleasure he noted the rich tones the sunset glow elicited from the crude masonry. Life had opened up for him in these last days and become infinitely more satisfying. Tasting, sniffing, touching – and all the other sensations – brought a keener delight. For now he clearly understood that he was nothing but an independent ego, free for a term to savour the pleasures of the world and impose his will upon it. Once you understood that, everything was clear as day and every moment was precious.

Foggy idealism had blinded that other Jarles to the possibilities of enjoyment right under his nose. But that other Jarles could no longer bother him now – except when he slept.

Now that they had left the Great Square behind, Jarles caught up with Sharlson Naurya and walked beside her. He judged it wise to say, in a low voice, "I'm with you people to the finish now. I thought it all through at Mother Jujy's."

For answer there came the warm, friendly pressure of her hand, bringing to his mind the special problem that had been nagging it ever since he had spoken with Goniface.

Goniface had given very explicit directions about Sharlson Naurya, to Cousin Deth as well as to Jarles. If she chanced to be caught in the coming raid, she must instantly be killed.

Of course, if it came to an issue, he would have to sacrifice her – even destroy her himself if it were absolutely unavoidable. But if, without drawing too much suspicion to himself, he could manage to spirit her away, that would be the ideal solution.

After all, why was Goniface so interested in her? She must know a secret or two that would be very helpful in speeding up Jarles' promotion. So he had a double reason for preserving her life, if opportunity offered.

Sunset had paled to twilight. His guide turned suddenly into a tiny shrine where commoners might come to pray. In the gloom he could make out the image of the Great God, the altar, and the few small benches. The place was empty. Sharlson Naurya advanced to the wall at one side of the altar and felt along the ornate plastic moulding.

A heavy panel slid aside. She stepped through. Jarles paused for a moment in the doorway, so that the bulb of radioactive tracers strapped to his left forearm would leave a heavier spoor at this point to guide Cousin Deth. Impatiently, she motioned him in.

The panel closed. They were in the interior twilight of a narrow passageway, lit by infrequent, tiny lamps. Again she felt along the moulding – plain here – beside the doorway. Evidently reactivating an alarm system that had been turned off while they entered. As she started down the passageway he took a chance, felt for the button, found it, depressed it, then quickly followed her.

At the end of the corridor they descended a flight of stairs. Another corridor. More stairs, Jarles' senses were strainingly alert.

"These passages date back to the Golden Age," Naurya explained to him.

She stopped.

"The entrance to the Coven Chamber is just ahead, beyond a zigzag," she said. "I'm going to take you in and immediately propose you for membership. They are meeting now. Here" – her hand touched the wall – "is one of the extra entrances. We use them only in emergencies."

Her finger touched a spot and a panel slid open.

Jarles' new personality thought and acted swiftly. Adjusting the controls on the wrath ray strapped to his right forearm to paralyzer quality, he directed its now-invisible, faintly hissing beam at her waist. She stiffened. There was a convulsive retraction of the diaphragm. Her mouth opened spasmodically but she made no sound.

Catching her arm, he let her fall gently into the side passageway she had just uncovered. Then, counting seconds, he coolly played the ray against her skull. When he was satisfied that she would remain unconscious for a sufficient period, he shut the panel, and proceeded towards the Coven Chamber.

Purple tinged darkness, and a voice speaking masterfully through it. Silhouetted against the lesser darkness of the far wall, a crowded ring of human forms, listening to the voice. A phosphorescent throne against the far wall, and in it a dead-black manlike shape, and the voice coming from the shape.

Vividly the remembrance came to Jarles of the first time he had been in this chamber. So vividly that for a moment the two experiences were mixed, although then he had been a different person. Memory could bridge any gap.

Silently he donned the ultraviolet transformer goggles, which Cousin Deth had provided for him at his own suggestion. It was as if a sickly yellow light had suddenly illuminated the whole room. Instantly mysteriousness vanished from the scene. With two exceptions it became very ordinary. Just a long, low room and a group of people listening absorbedly to a speaker who sat in an unadorned and unimpressive throne. Jarles experienced a pleasant feeling of superiority.

The two exceptions were the speaker and a tall something beside the throne.

The speaker was still only a manlike shape, not one whit less black than before. The field he wore drank *all* radiations.

The tall something so puzzled Jarles and distracted his attention that he still had not time to catch the drift of what the speaker was saying. Certainly the object had not been in the room on that other occasion. It was very like an angel, of about the same height and general conformation. But the broad, dusky, lifeless face was incredibly ugly, with wicked horns sprouting from the forehead, and the forearms were reptilian and clawed. A demon monolith, it stood there rigidly, twice as tall as a man and a little taller than the room, so that its horns extended upward into a large circular recess or orifice in the ceiling.

Some piece of ritual sculpture, Jarles decided. These people were very imaginative, yes, and very clever – perhaps. But they were children in true craft, giants in carelessness. How else could they permit him to penetrate so easily their secret councils!

Oddly the speaker was now expressing much the same thought. Jarles listened to the masterful voice.

"Thus far you have only played at being witches. It has

110

been a hard and dangerous game, but, to most of you, only a game. Most of you were drawn into the Witchcraft by a rebellious and mischievous desire to exercise secret power in a world where the Hierarchy has a monopoly of power.

"I and my co-workers recognized this when we devised the Witchcraft. We knew that a great cause and a worthy purpose would be insufficient to attract a following. We knew that you would obey our instructions only so long as they were sufficiently amusing. And when you embarked on private pranks, we did not interfere."

The voice paused. One of the circle of listeners eagerly interjected a question.

"What you say is true. But what would you have us do now, O Asmodeus?"

Jarles' heart pounded. Asmodeus! He had heard that name given to the leader of the Witchcraft. The coming captures would be of vast importance. Elevation to the Fourth Circle was no longer sufficient compensation. The Seventh Circle, at the least! lucky he had Sharlson Naurya to use against Goniface, if the archpriest balked.

"Now," continued the masterful voice, "the game is over. Or rather, it enters a more serious stage. Thus far you have been amazingly successful despite frequent fool-hardiness and carelessness. Most important, the Hierarchy has been slow to act. A conservative organization, it has never since its establishment faced any opposition worth the name. And it is at present troubled by internal dissensions. So, partly from conservatism, partly from cunning, partly as a compromise, it has adopted a waiting policy.

"But do not underestimate the Hierarchy! It is awakening – has almost awakened – to its danger. More and more, its vast spy system is being devoted to the work of tracking us down. In a thousand sanctuaries, research priests of the Fifth Circle are close to discovering and duplicating the scientific secrets of the Witchcraft. And there are signs that the internal dissension in the Hierarchy will soon be healed – by drastic surgery.

"Do not underestimate the Hierarchy! It is so powerful that it can afford delay. It is no empty priestly boast, when they threaten to call down help from heaven!"

Soon now, thought Jarles, Cousin Deth must strike. According to his calculations, the deacon must already be past the panel in the shrine. And still no alarm. That was good. Yet he felt a sudden pang of fear. Not fear for his own safety – he felt that to be sure, constantly, and it kept him painfully alert. But that fear was clear and sharp. The other was vague, formless. He tried in vain to grasp its nature.

"In warfare, time is all-essential," came the voice from the throne. It was a voice that gave the impression of wickedly bright eyes, not without humour and compassion. "How much more then, is time essential in the psychological warfare we are waging! Fear is our only weapon, and it has one great limitation – it swiftly loses its effectiveness. By a carefully plotted rising tide of terror we have badly shaken the lesser priesthood and planted the seeds of supernatural panic in the higher circles. But if we pause now, our advantage evaporates. We must create a stampede.

"It is for that reason that I have summoned you leaders and taken the unprecedented step of appearing before you in person."

Better and better, thought Jarles. All their leaders bagged at once. And Asmodeus! But the murky, undefinable fear still oppressed him. If only Deth would strike!

"I have come to discuss with you the plans for our final operations. Instructions conveyed on reading tapes are no longer sufficient or safe. I will handle those matters with you individually, after this meeting.

"But first I must warn you of a vast responsibility that may fall to your lot. It concerns myself and my co-workers. We, your leaders, are in a peculiarly vulnerable position. It may very well happen that, before the crisis comes, we will be found out and destroyed. In that case, you chief agents of the Witchcraft in the key city of Megatheopolis will have to take over."

Jarles clenched his fists in nervous impatience. His murky fear had now become something strange and unpleasant. He had the feeling that something was going to happen to thwart him, and that he could easily prevent it – if only he knew what it was. It made his head feel heavy and hot, as if he had a fever.

"Plans for such an eventuality have long been in existence. But they were intrusted to one of you who has since disappeared – presumably dead or the Hierarchy's prisoner. Therefore, it will be necessary to make new arrangements."

This reference to the Black Man ought to have interested Jarles, but he had almost ceased to listen to Asmodeus, the strange fear was affecting him so. It was making his throat dry and numb. When he raised his hand to his lips they were no longer sensitive to touch.

And yet, if he only knew what it was that was coming, he could prevent it. Maddening. If it got any worse, he would have to activate his tracers and summon Deth, though he was not supposed to do that unless he was apprehended.

" – critical moment approaches." He was only vaguely aware of Asmodeus' words. " – every move you make from now on . . . freighted with significance – Not only your own safety . . . fate of the world – This city . . . crucial – Future of mankind – "

At that instant a painfully convulsive spasm seized Jarles' vocal organs, and, to his intensest horror and dismay, he heard himself cry out, "You are betrayed! This is the Hierarchy's trap! Escape while you can!"

Then control over his muscles came back to him. With a snarl of rage and shame – for the moment he was beside himself with hatred of that other Jarles who had spoken – he activated the tracers strapped to his left arm to a maximum intensity which would jolt Deth's instruments if he were anywhere near.

And Deth must have been very near, for before the semi-circle of witches and warlocks could more than rise to their feet, deacons bearing wrath rods and other weapons poured into the room.

Out from the semi-circle of witches and warlocks, a shadowy scurrying went along the floor, like rats running for their holes. Before Jarles could get his own wrath ray into action, they had vanished.

Asmodeus was the only human being who had reacted swiftly to the warning. He sprang for the demonlike sculpture beside the throne. The thick violet gout of a wrath rod cut down a witch and impinged upon him. For a moment his blackness glowed eerily, as the absorbent field strained to drink the power. But before the field collapsed, he was behind the sculpture, which seemed resistant to the ray.

Jarles circled forward, hoping to get a shot at him from the side. Asmodeus was too greatly outnumbered. He had managed to reach a point of cover, but he couldn't hold out long.

Not behind the sculpture, though. In it.

A solid blow – fringe of a repulsor field – sent Jarles reeling. The demon figure moved, lifted, and, the focus of a dozen tongues of violet incandescence, shot upward through the orifice in the ceiling.

Sprawled on the floor, Jarles realized bitterly that his first impression had been right. The thing was like an angel – mobile. And the shaft into which it had vanished must lead to the surface. It was probably disguised as a chimney.

Deth had said there would be angels patrolling overhead. They were the last, slim hope of catching Asmodeus.


CHAPTER THIRTEEN

IN the pearly grey chamber of the Apex Council Goniface watched Brother Frejeris rise to accuse him. The Moderate's voice had a silky note. "Do I rightly understand your purpose in having your servant Cousin Deth bring those instruments here?"

With a wave of his hand, he indicated an arrangement of gleaming apparatus before the Council table. A chair, with attachments for confining the sitter, was a chief feature. Engaged in testing the apparatus was a group of Fourth Circle technicians, under the direction of Cousin Deth.

Goniface nodded.

"Torture!" Frejeris enunciated the word with indignation. "Have we become barbarians, as threatened in the Golden Age, that we stoop to such brutality?"

The idea of brutality actually shocks him, thought Goniface amusedly. I wonder what name he has for the toil we exact of the commoners, and the penances we impose on them?

Frejeris continued, "Our Brother Goniface all of a sudden informs us that his agents have apprehended a group of individuals who, he tells us, are dangerous to the Hierarchy. His agents have done this without the knowledge or consent of the Apex Council, in direct violation of all procedures. Now he tells us that these private captives of his are members of the New Witchcraft. On top of all that, disregarding the scientific methods we have at hand for extracting truth, he proposes that they be questioned under physical torture and – again secretly – makes arrangements for it. Why, I ask the Council, this reversion to barbarism?

"I will tell you why," Frejeris continued after a dramatic pause. His magnificent voice deepened in timbre and grew more vibrant. "And in so doing I will reveal Goniface as a ruthless upstart, seeking to seize absolute power. I will show you that he has organized a hierarchy within the Hierarchy, a clique of deacons and priests loyal only to himself. I will prove to you that he is taking advantage of this matter of the Witchcraft and exaggerating the danger it represents, in order to foment a world-wide crisis and seize power in defiance of precedent, with the excuse that he does it to save the Hierarchy!"

With a sweeping glance up and down the table, Frejeris prepared to launch into a detailed accusation.

He never began it. The archpriest Jomald, bellwether of the Realists, rose and said simply, as if it were a very ordinary matter, "The archpriest Frejeris has placed the Hierarchy in grave danger by obstructing and delaying action against the Witchcraft. If left free to his own devices, he will continue to do so. His motives are highly suspect. I ask for his immediate excommunication for the space of a year. I further ask that the matter be brought at once to a vote."

Frejeris glared at him with a cold and supercilious disdain, as if outraged merely by the unprecedented discourtesy of the interruption.

"I second that!" lean Brother Sercival snapped unexpectedly, from where he sat beside Goniface.

Even the old Fanatic plays along with us, thought Goniface.

And still Frejeris stood there uncomprehending, as if waiting for the rude interruptions to come to an end, so he could get on with his oration. He was a magnificently stately man.

His own Moderates understood what was happening before he did. Ominously for him, they looked more frightened than indignant.

"Are there any objections to bringing the matter to a vote?" asked Jomald. His voice was like the rap of a gavel.

Very slowly, very hesitatingly, one of the Moderates started to rise to his feet, glancing uneasily up and down the table. What he saw there caused him to change his mind. He sank back, avoiding Frejeris' eyes.

Only then did Frejeris understand. To his credit, it did not break his calm. His large, handsome face lost nothing of its statuesque quality.

One after another, clenched fists were laid on the gleaming table. Frejeris glanced haughtily at the archpriests who thus voted against him, but more with the air of a man who rebukes discourtesy than that of a priest facing excommunication.

At the end, not one hand had been laid palm downward to indicate a negative vote, and only two Moderates had abstained – and they looked acutely uncomfortable.

"Execute the sentence!" cried Jomald to the group of Fourth Circle technicians.

Several archpriests betrayed surprise, only now realizing how closely everything had been planned.

But still Frejeris preserved his calm. The Moderates to either side of him shrank away, but he did not flinch. Like a marble statue he stood there.

And like a marble statue he was toppled down. Invisible emanations played upon him, establishing blocks in his sensory nerves. The optical nerves were the first to be affected. Gropingly, he raised his hands to his blinded eyes, but before they could reach them, his tactual sense was gone. Equilibrium went with the rest. He swayed forward and fell heavily across the table – a table he could no longer feel.

More helpless than a baby he sprawled there, an insensate ruin, excommunicated from the universe as well as from the Hierarchy, shut off from all sensory contact, doomed for a year to the private hell of his own thoughts – a year that would be an eternity, for there would be in it no way to measure time.

And even as lesser priests were stepping forward to remove the fallen leader, Brother Jomald spoke again.

"I further ask that power to use all our resources against the common enemy be vested in the archpriest Goniface, that he be declared World Hierarch, until the Witchcraft is no longer a menace to us. During this period the Apex Council will function as his chief advisory board."

That motion, too, was passed without a single dissenting vote. Even old Sercival, who might have been expected to cling grimly to independence, went with the rest. Goniface, who had not spoken a word all this time, made no comment. He simply rose and said: "Bring in our prisoners. Let the questioning begin."

This brought an unanticipated objection from the Fanatic Sercival. His parchment face was the incarnation of zealous hatred.

"I beg you, your supreme eminence, let us have no traffic of any sort with the agents of Sathanas! If you certify that they are witches, let them instantly be slain! They are too foul a blemish on creation to let exist.

"I voted to give you supreme power," continued Sercival, "because I consider you a strong man, willing and able to fight ruthlessly against the Lord of Evil. No quarter to his witches, I say!"

"I have heard you," Goniface told Sercival coolly. "You will not find me sparing the enemy. But it is necessary to question them."

Reluctantly Sercival sat down. "I still say they should be slain," he muttered doggedly.

But attention shifted away from him to the captured witches being escorted into the Chamber under a heavy guard of deacons. With feigned casualness the archpriests made the most of their first opportunity to study the enemy face to face.

117

The first impression was reassuring. The prisoners were all dressed alike in coarse-woven, scanty tunics. And they actually seemed dirty! Moreover, the fact that they did not struggle at all or resist in any way the ungentle and unnecessary shoving and jerking to which the deacons subjected them, had the appearance of servility. There could be nothing to fear from such a ragamuffin crew as these! Why, they looked like a road gang – except that most of them were women. A few of the women seemed moderately pretty – might even be rather fetching if decently groomed and clothed in the appealing garb of the sisterhood. But as they were now, these supposedly potent enemies resembled nothing so much as a crew of the humblest menials.

The second impression was not so reassuring. The individual faces were obviously more sensitive and intelligent than those of the average run of commoners. What had passed at first glance for oafishness became on close inspection a brooding thoughtfulness. And there was a subtle air of solidarity, of mutual loyalty, about them, so that they seemed to stand firmly together as a group – and this impression was only heightened by their garb. Likewise, it became apparent that they did not so much submit frightenedly to the rough handling they were getting, as ignore it because their minds were concentrated on other matters.

That impression of brooding thoughtfulness was the most intangibly disturbing. One got the feeling that they were communing with powers outside the Council Chamber.

On the whole, however, it was the first impression that predominated. The other was only a lurking afterthought.

With a toss of his dwarfishly large head, Cousin Deth signed to a Second Circle clerk to begin the proceedings. From the very instant that Goniface had been granted dictatorial powers, the little deacon had dropped the mask from his features, so that all his emotions registered there in naked ugliness. His bold glances toward the Apex Council said more plainly than words, "I am the second man in the Hierarchy now."

From the luminous face of a reading-tape projector, the clerk recited to the prisoners a brief indictment that was also a conviction.

"You have been apprehended while conspiring against the Hierarchy, under the guise and pretence of witchcraft. If any one of you will stand forward now and make a full confession of guilt, holding back nothing, that one will be spared the torture."

Abruptly one of the women began to tremble and shake spasmodically, her head thrown sharply back, her eyes closed. Swiftly her movements became more violent. Her neck muscles stood out sharply, and her knees were bent as if she were bracing herself with a great effort. It was as if something invisible were shaking her. Suddenly she fell down and frothed at the mouth like an epileptic.

"Lord, protect us!" she screamed, writhing convulsively on the floor. "Sathanas, aid thy servants!"

A vast wolfish shape materialized from the misty grey of the walls at the other end of the Chamber. Its eyes were like two sooty hearths filled with dying embers. Towards the Council table it stalked, big as a house, the very incarnation of skulking, slavering destruction.

The archpriests had risen. Several of them could not conceal their emotions. The lesser priests also shrank back involuntarily.

"Dissolve it!" Goniface called sharply to Cousin Deth. Then he rose, too. "The thing is only a telesolidographic projection -- as all of you must realize!" The last phrase was directed bitingly at his fellow archpriests. Almost he wished Frejeris were still among them. The pompous Moderate at least knew how to put up a front.

Partially reassured, the archpriests noted that there was indeed a certain transparency to the advancing monster, so you could dimly see through it to the wall beyond; and it was a ghostly slaver that dripped in ropes from the gigantic jaws. Moreover, the great paws with their foot-long nails seemed sometimes to step a little above the floor and sometimes a little below.

Then Deth's technicians got the range of it and it began swiftly to melt away. Whole sections of the body disappeared instantaneously, leaving only a few remnants which their instruments had not caught at the first focusing. True, there was something hellishly suggestive, almost worse than the original, about those remnants – an ear tuft here, a paw there, a patch of dirty fur coarser than grass, and the smoky hellhole of an eye. But in the main the results were very helpful to priestly morale.

"There was, of course, no need to dissolve it," said Goniface coldly. "I merely wished to demonstrate conclusively its solidographic nature. Our Fourth Circle brethren were able to dissipate it with the recently invented polyfrequency neutralizer. The thing was purely photonic in nature and yielded quickly to an application of the principle of interference. All phantasms employed by the so-called New Witchcraft are of a similar sort. To put a complete stop to them, it will only be necessary to discover and destroy the hidden projectors – merely a matter of time, even without the information that will soon be at our disposal." He glanced significantly at the group of witches. "We could with the greatest ease insulate this chamber – or the whole Sanctuary – from such projections. But there is no need. Our research scientists are sure that it is impossible to transmit physically injurious frequencies and intensities. Should we insulate the Sanctuary, it would give the false impression that we are afraid." His next words were very definite. "I command every priest and deacon here to take no notice whatever of any projections directed into this chamber."

And he sat down – instantly to become aware of a slight sultriness and of the fact that everything in the Chamber had turned bright-red and become exceedingly foggy and indistinct.

Disobeying the command they had just been given, most of the archpriests sprang up and crowded to either end of the table, away from Goniface. For where their World Hierarch had been sitting, there now sat a huge red devil, whose shaggy red legs seemed poked through the table itself, and whose great horned head swung from side to side, grinning down at them with fiendish mirth. Coiled up monkeylike over his shoulder was a thick red tail ending in a vicious barb.

In the interior of the redness, the figure of Goniface could be made out hazily, like an insect embedded in cloudy amber.

He stood up and for a moment his head emerged from the redness. Then the devil stood up, too.

There was a commotion among the witches. They had dropped to their knees and many of them were calling out adoringly, "Master! Master!"

Old Sercival raised a shaky hand. His glittering eyes rolled confusedly. He seemed not so much frightened as indignant.

"What does this mean?" he cried. "Have we voted for Sathanas himself?"

Deth's technicians also disobeyed the command, Swinging their projector around, they stripped the solidographic projection from Goniface. First his head emerged, then the rest of his body. He looked very grim.

But even as that happened, there came a startled cry from the deacons. An inky cloud of darkness had suddenly engulfed the kneeling witches, billowing ever wider threatening to fill the whole chamber. From the cloud emerged deacon guards, hands stretched ahead of them, hastily groping their way.

"Wrath rods!" called Goniface, even as the black cloud lapped dangerously close to the technicians and their instruments. "Swing them into the darkness at waist level. If it doesn't dissipate, keep going all the way through. No neutralizer can counteract *their* energy!"

Beams of violet flame spattered against the grey walls of the Chamber, swinging in towards the darkness. The cloud seemed to make a last despairing effort, thrusting out an inky pseudopod towards the door of the chamber. But the wrath rays touched it, cut into it. Abruptly the cloud vanished and the wrath rays halted.

"If any further solidographic projections are introduced into the Chamber, witches will be slain!" Goniface announced harshly. "For every such projection, five witches!"

"Are you not going to slay them all, immediately?" demanded old Sercival. "I only now heard you order that they be slain with rods of wrath, as I advised from the first."

"It was merely a device on my part, your reverence," Goniface answered curtly. "These are worldly matters which it is doubtless difficult for your saintly nature to comprehend!"

At this rebuke, Sercival subsided, though muttering and shaking his head. It was apparent that several other arch-priests would have been relieved to see the Fanatic's advice followed.

"Begin the questioning!" ordered Goniface.

Two deacons singled out one of the witches and led her towards the chair by which Cousin Deth was standing. She was a fair young woman, but very frailly built for a commoner. Her skin had a waxy quality and her features were peaked.

She went quietly until they reached the chair. Then she struggled like a wild animal, biting and scratching. But as soon as she had been secured, this spasm left her.

The clerk read out: "Mewdon Chemmy – for that, although you deny it, is the name by which you have been identified – it is my duty to advise you to answer all questions truthfully and satisfactorily. Otherwise you will put us to the unpleasant necessity of influencing you to make an answer. Past cultures have used all manner of devices to induce pain – the rack, the wheel, the boot, the dental drill and a host of others. But the Hierarchy is merciful and is not pleased by mutilation. Therefore its priests have devised a means of producing all the same sensations of those varied tortures by direct stimulation of the nerves that transmit the sensation of pain. Thus the same results are achieved without any injury to the bodily organism, save it come through shock or convulsion. There is this further advantage – the torture need not be interrupted for fear that injury to the tissues will result in death."

The clerk sat down.

Leisurely Cousin Deth walked forward a few paces, then suddenly turned on the witch.

"What is your name?" he asked.

There was a pause. Then, faintly, the voice of the witch, "The servants of Sathanas are nameless.'

Cousin Deth laughed. It was unpleasant to think that he had been repressing such a laughter for many years. He said, "You have been identified as Meadon Chemmy, commoner of the Eleventh Ward, trained in the colouring of pottery, wife of Meadon Rijard. Do you deny this?"

No answer.

"Very well, Meadon Chemmy. You are accused of conspiring to overthrow the Hierarchy."

"Your clerk said more than that." The voice was faint, but very clear. "He said that I – all of us – already stood convicted."

"True, Mewdon Chemmy. But if your answers are satisfactory, it will save you pain. Precisely in what ways have you conspired against the Hierarchy?"

"I have followed the instructions of Sathanas."

Deth laughed. "What instructions?"

"To make myself a vehicle for his supernatural volitions. To practise the lore taught me. To curse and cast spells. To vex and torment those whom Sathanas points out to me."

For a third time Cousin Deth made the sound that passed with him for laughter. "It may be that you are accustomed to use a nonsensical jargon to describe your activities. Understand, then, that it does not interest us. We want only material facts. What scientific procedures have you been taught?"

"I know nothing of such procedures. Being omnipotent, Sathanas has no need of them."

Deth looked up from her to his chief technician. "Are you ready?" he asked.

The priest nodded. A thick metallic canopy had been moved forward behind the chair. It fitted around the witch's head like a cowl. Curving flanges followed the lines of her body.

Deth looked again at the witch. "Thus far, in view of your tenderness and sex, we have been lenient with you, Mewdon Chemmy. That leniency will be cut short if you persist in childish evasions. Understand once and for all, we will waste no further time listening to meaningless babbling of Sathanas and other supernatural unrealities. I hardly need remind you that you are not dealing with credulous commoners."

There was a stir at the Council Table. Such blunt, unsubtle talk was highly irregular. Old Sercival muttered indignantly. Several archpriests glanced questioningly at Goniface, but failed to catch his eye.

"However, Mewdon Chemmy, you still have a chance," Deth continued. "If you will give us the material facts, and if they are subsequently verified, we will deal mercifully with you."

The witch's face, shadowed by the metal hood, looked small as a child's, pale as a ghost's.

"How can you deal mercifully with me? You have admitted that the Hierarchy has no faith in the Great God. Could you loose me to tell that to commoners? Could you take the slightest risk of any of us revealing your shams?"

Deth triumphantly whipped his reply at her. "Now we are getting somewhere! At last you admit that all is scientific mummery?"

The silence in the Council Chamber was such that her whisper was plainly audible.

"Not so. For more than a century Sathanas has let you believe that, in order that your downfall may be the more complete and your torment the more tantalizing. Sathanas is! He rules supreme in the hell you call the cosmos!"

There was a stir at the Council Table. Goniface ignored it. He motioned to Deth.

"Mewdon Chemmy, we want facts!" cried the deacon harshly. "First, who is your real leader?"

"Sathanas."

"Evasive babble! Let the pain enter the fingers of the left hand."

With the words came an increase in the tension pervading the grey chamber. Rods of wrath were lifted warningly against the witches. But, eyes closed, they seemed to be repeating inaudible prayers to their dark divinity.

Then, from the metal shroud, came the faint sound of air sucked suddenly between teeth and tongue.

But Goniface, World Hierarch, did not hear it, although he was listening intently. For, at the same instant, he felt that the fingers of his left hand, hanging at his side, had been dipped in molten metal.

With a sudden and supreme effort of will he checked the impulse to jerk his hand upward, to writhe and cry out. With a continuation of the effort that was only less than the first effort itself, he glanced up and down the table. If he had made a betraying movement, none of the archpriests had noticed it.

"Mewdon Chemmy, who is your real leader?"

"Sathanas. Sathanas." Rapid, breathy whispers.

Goniface let his glance slip downward. There was nothing unnatural about his hand, except the white knuckles and taut tendons. Slowly he moved it until it rested on the table. The searing pain was unabated.

"Let the pain creep into the wrist. Who, leaving aside the one you call Sathanas, is your leader?"

"He is – Give me strength, Sathanas!" A whimpering gasp. "He is Asmodeus!"

To Goniface, it was as if he had drawn on a red-hot gauntlet.

"Who is Asmodeus?"

"Sathanas, aid me! He is King of the Demons."

"Into the arm! Who is Asmodeus?"

"King . . . of the Demons."

"We know that Asmodeus is a man. What is his real name?"

"King – " a choked scream. "May Sathanas burn you forever! I don't know. I don't know."

"Then Asmodeus is a man?"

"Yes. No. I don't know. I don't know! Sathanas, burn them as they burn your servant!"

Goniface felt beads of sweat pricking his forehead, as the invisible incandescence lapped higher, and higher still.

He must think. Think!

"Mewdon Chemmy, who is Asmodeus? What is his name?"

"Don't know . . . don't know!"

"Have you ever seen him?"

"Yes. No! Yes! Mewdon Chemmy, Sathanas! Your faithful servant."

"What did he look like?"

"I don't know. A blackness! A blackness . . . and a voice."

The beads of sweat were trickling down Goniface's forehead in nervous little rushes. Only a little longer and the witch would break. And this impossible pain must have a source. Think!

"Very well, Mewdon Chemmy. We will leave Asmodeus for the moment. Where in Megatheopolis are the headquarters of the Witchcraft?"

"I don't – Where you captured us."

"That was only a meeting place. You know I don't mean that. Where are the real headquarters?"

"I don't – There are none."

"A lie! You know something, for you twice started to conceal it. Where are the real headquarters? Where is the scientific armament kept?"

"In the – There is no such armament. Sathanas does not need –"

"Into the shoulder!"

Agony groping upward, scalding. Think! Think! A commotion of some sort at the far end of the chamber. The high doors opening. And from the kneeling witches, a low, murmuring supplication, rhythmic, intense, like the beat of a muffled drum. "Sathanas, aid us. Sathanas, aid us."

"Mewdon Chemmy, where are the headquarters? You are in the Great Square. You are going to the headquarters. You are walking towards a street. You are entering it. What street is it?"

"Of the Wea – No! No!" A whimpering scream.

"You are walking along the Street of the Weavers, Mewdon Chemmy. You smell wool. You hear the sound of the shuttle. You are walking. Now you are no longer in the Street of the Weavers. You have turned. Where?"

"No! No! It's Mewdon Chemmy calling you, Sathanas!"

A group of priests were hurrying from the great door towards the council table, scarlet robes flapping. Slowly, effortfully, Goniface rose, his left arm rigid at his side, the left shoulder stooped, as if he lifted a great weight.

"From the shoulder then –"

"Stop the questioning!" ordered Goniface loudly, and with such a strained, mechanical enunciation that all stared at him.

Deth waited a moment, then shrugged his shoulders and motioned to the technicians.

Relief came to Goniface with dizzying suddenness. An invisible torrent of ice water took his breath away. The whole chamber seemed to rock, and he gripped the table to keep from staggering.

"What is the matter?" he asked the newcomers, the laboriousness fading from his enunciation as he spoke. "Only the most urgent reason could justify your interruption."

"The commoners are marching on the Sanctuary!" cried one. "They have left their work. All attempts to halt them have failed. Two deacons opened up with wrath rods in the Street of the Smithies, but were overwhelmed and torn to pieces. A priest of the First Circle who ordered them back was captured and mistreated. He is still in their power. Already they fill the Great Square. They demand to know why we do not smite down Sathanas and end the reign of terror. They cry, 'What about the Witchcraft? What about the Witchcraft?' They shout down any priest who seeks to reason with them."

An alarmed murmuring flurried along the Council Table. Goniface heard an archpriest mutter, "Warblasts! Sweep the Square!" He recognized one of the newcomers as being from Web Centre and bid him speak.

"News of similar rioting is pouring in from half Earth's cities. It looks like prearrangement. A mob broke into the Sanctuary of Neodelos. They were driven out, leaving many dead behind. From everywhere come pleas for instructions."

Goniface spoke rapidly. "Unship the parasympathetics in the Cathedral and play them on the Square. By amplifier, proclaim tomorrow a holiday and announce that a Grand Revival will be held. There will be solemn supplications to the Great God, miracles will occur, and the Great God will vouchsafe a sure and infallible sign of the coming victory over Sathanas."

To the priest from Web Centre: "Relay the same instructions to all sanctuaries. Tell them to use all available parasympathetics, including the hand models in the confessional booths. If the crowds do not disperse after the announcement, deluge them with music. In no event must force be employed! If any sanctuary is mobbed, I will count it as a black mark against the incumbent priesthood. Instruct Neodelos, on pain of general excommunication, to hold solemn funeral for all slain commoners and convey home their bodies with the greatest pomp. Contact all sanctuaries, even those not asking instructions, and ascertain conditions. Inform them that detailed instructions for conducting the Grand Revival will be on their way by nightfall, Megatheopolis time. In two hours return me here a complete survey of the general situation."

To a clerk: "Fetch me the records of all previous Grand Revivals, including moving solidographs of the last two."

To another clerk: "Summon the Sixth Circle Faculty of Social control. The Apex Council desires their advice. Send to the crypts and ask Brother Dhomas to attend me at his earliest convenience."

To a third: "Inform the Fifth Circle Faculty of Physicists that a telesolidograph shield must be set up around the Great Square. All technical resources are placed at their command. They may requisition any and all apparatus. But the shield must be complete by dawn tomorrow."

To a fourth: "Make further effort to contact the ship bringing reinforcements from Luciferopolis. If successful, inform it to make full speed.

To Cousin Deth: "Return our prisoners to their cells. Confine them individually. Each must be watched continuously by at least two guards, and the guards watched in turn. Be prepared for the most fantastic attempts at rescue you can conceive. I hold you solely responsible.

"There will be a private session of the Apex Council. Clear the Chamber!'

"Can you still intend not to slay the witches, your supreme eminence?" There was a fierce, though quavering note in the harsh voice of old Sercival. "The testimony of that wicked woman proved conclusively that they are agents of Sathanas. It is dangerous and foolhardy – and an offence against the Great God – to let them live longer."

"It is essential that we obtain information from them," Goniface answered sharply. "I only interrupted the questioning because there are weightier matters at hand. We must plan the Grand Revival."

Sercival shook his head. A mad – or prophetic – glint seemed to enter his hawklike eyes. "It were better that we fall on our knees and ask pardon of the Great God for our long years of unbelief, and beg his mercy. Else I see darkness loom before us and doom for all!"

There was grim finality in Goniface's reply. "Your reverence's mind is tired and confused. But I shall excommunicate the next priest who talks of failure or implies that there is any supernatural reality in Sathanas."

From the witches departing under their doubled guards came a monotonous, murmurous chanting, faint yet seeming to fill the whole chamber.

"Thanks be to Sathanas. Thanks be to Sathanas. Thanks be to Sathanas."

## CHAPTER FOURTEEN

As Jarles activated the door of his private apartment in the crypts, he frowned at the Fourth Circle emblazonment mistily reflected in its gleaming surface. Goniface had rewarded him insufficiently, considering the importance of the service he had rendered. Still, Asmodeus had escaped. As always, it caused him a bitter pang to remember that Asmodeus would not have escaped had not that other, puerile Jarles managed to seize control of his body and bleat out a warning. But he should consider himself lucky that his hideous slip had not been brought to light.

Having entered the apartment, his first concern was to reactivate the lock. It irked him somewhat that Cousin Deth had been given sole credit, in public, for capturing the witches. However, as Goniface had told him, it was undoubtedly best that he work in secret for the present. Save for Goniface's private following, no priest had any inkling of his return to the Hierarchy, let alone the awakening of his true personality.

In any case he had some compensations for this temporary obscurity, he decided, glancing around him. He passed through a second room, as sumptuously furnished as the first, and entered a third, reactivating all locks behind him.

On a couch, pale face upturned, eyes closed, hands folded as in death, lay Sharlson Naurya.

He looked at her for a while. Then, with a mild, stimulative beam of antiparalysis quality he dispelled her unconsciousness. Her eyes opened. He read in them a hate that he interpreted half as a compliment.

She sensed the interpretation. She said, slowly and distinctly, "You incredible, disgusting egotist."

He smiled. "Not egotist. Realist."

"Realist!" Contempt gave strength to her utterance. "You're no more a realist now than when you were a blind and stubborn idealist. You're a fiction villain! I suppose that every blundering idealist who hasn't been brought face to face with the hard facts of life carries, at the back of his mind, a sneaking suspicion that villainy is a very dashing and romantic thing. When your mind turned turtle, or when they turned it for you, your new personality was necessarily fabricated out of all your fragmentary romantic notions of villainy – unlimited ambition and conceit, absolute lack of emotion, and all the rest of the super-villain ideology!"

She paused. Her eyes opened wider, in incredulous loathing. "You like me to talk about you that way, don't you?"

He nodded. "Certainly. Because I'm a realist. Experience has taught me how close hate is to love."

"Another cheap romantic fallacy!" Anger made her tremble. "Realist! Can't you understand that you're behaving like a book? Have you no conception of the risks you are running in this game you're trying to play, according to some romantic code of villainy, with men like Goniface? Realist! Look at your insane recklessness in bringing me here. What will happen to you when Goniface finds out?"

He smiled. "It was necessary to bring you here. There was no one to whom I could intrust you. And who would think of looking for you here? Moreover Goniface trusts me. He doesn't dream that, while serving him, I plot against him."

She glared at him. "What if I should reveal myself?"

"You won't be able to. And even if you could, you wouldn't. Because you'd know it meant instant death for you, by order of the World Hierarch. That's the beauty of the arrangement.

"Speaking of Goniface," he continued, "why don't you tell me why he wants you killed? You must know something about him that would endanger his position if revealed. Why not tell me what is is? Then we'll be able to drag him down together, after the present emergency is past."

She looked away from him.

"Come now, you're being very unrealistic," he continued, persuasively. "Don't you realize what I'm offering you? In any case, you should be a little grateful to me for saving you from so many unpleasantnesses. This morning your former associates were put to the torture."

He nodded confirmingly. "Oh, yes, and you may expect a bit of a change in your friend the Black Man if you ever happen to see him again. Today he was well enough to be taken to Brother Dhomas."

"You mean they intend to –" She tried to push herself up.

"To awaken him to a state of realistic self-interest? Yes. So you see, Naurya, the Witchcraft is done for. Just a matter of time. And that means there's no longer any point in your remaining loyal to it. Surely that must be obvious to you.

For a long time she just looked at him. Then she asked him, in a strange voice, "Do you ever dream now?"

For once he did not smile. "No," he said flatly.

Slowly she shook her head, keeping her eyes fixed on him. "Oh, yes, you do."

"Dreams mean nothing," he said coldly. "They are unreal."

"They're as real as anything else," she shot back at him. "And they merely mean conscience."

For a fraction of a second her gaze slipped past him. Suspiciously he turned. Nothing there but the locked door.

"Conscience is only social pressure," he told her, tense without quite knowing why, "the impulse to submerge your ego in that of the herd, and do what other people want you to because you're afraid of their censure. Realistic self-interest frees a person from the childish restrictions of conscience."

"Are you sure of that, Jarles? What about your dreams? Conscience may be partly what you say it is, but it's more than that. It's hearkening to the wisest thoughts that have occurred to minds of the human race."

"Do you seek to persuade me to that shadowy unreality called virtue? Next you'll be talking of ideals!"

"Certainly I'll talk about ideals! For it's ideals that torment you when you dream. I saw you grow, Jarles. I saw your ideals grow. Maybe they grew too fast for their roots. But though they've been toppled and broken up and shoved down into the depths of your subconscious mind, they're still there, Jarles – a private hell in your own mind, and just a door between it and your consciousness. And at night the door opens."

In the nick of time, an involuntary sideways wavering of her vision warned him. He dodged and struck out as the little furred horror struck suddenly at him – from nowhere, it seemed. The razor claws slashed his cheek instead of the throat beneath the ear. His flailing arm chanced to catch the thing and hurl it across the room. In the moment before it recovered itself, his wrath ray blasted out and almost cut it in two. There was a great splatter of blood, much more than could have been expected from such a creature.

He darted over to it, then recoiled from the incredibly frail monster whose big eyes, glazed by death, goggled up at him. For a moment he had the incredible conviction that he had somehow killed Sharlson Naurya.

He looked back at her. She had struggled up into a sitting position, but there further strength failed her. She was not crying, but her shoulders were racked by an emotion that seemed mingled of unappeasable hate and a dry, anguished grief.

"This creature meant that much to you?" he asked sharply. He glanced quickly back at it. A look of sudden, almost incredulous understanding tightened his features. "I think I've got it," he said slowly, more to himself than to her. "Although I'm no biologist, I think I've realized the secret of the familiars. And that will be very welcome news to the World Hierarch."

"You've killed Puss," he heard her say. The words were like little stones.

"Your sister, in a sense, I believe?" He smiled. "Well, she tried to kill me, while you held my attention, so that's all square. Don't think I harbour resentment. This discovery will put a new emblazonment on my robe – and another shovel of earth from the grave we're digging for the Witchcraft."

He looked at her, blood dripping from his cheek. "I rather like your nerve and your ruthlessness," he said. "We'll get along very well together after you've been fixed. Oh, haven't I mentioned that? Well, after the present emergency is passed and we've attended to Goniface one way or another, I'll have Brother Dhomas turn your mind right side up."

She made one more attempt to rise, and failed. She could only say, each word seeming to choke her, "You dirty, little storybook villain."

He nodded, smiling. "That's right," he said, and turned the paralysis beam on her.


## CHAPTER FIFTEEN

DICKON had been gone four days. Wearily, again and again, the Black Man blanked his mind for the message that never came. It was laborious work, for the recent session with Brother Dhomas had made his mind a quasi-chaos, like a planet riven by catastrophic volcanic activity, so that new continents and archipelagoes rise everywhere from the steamy sea, and all the coastlines are changed.

In a way, his session in the crypts had been a hunt, with Brother Dhomas the hunter and his personality the quarry. And he had won out. His still-weakened physical condition had necessitated a return to his cell to recuperate, before Brother Dhomas had achieved his purpose. But soon the hunt would begin again.

And if he somehow managed to win out a second time, the hunt would begin a third time.

And then – well, he had seen what had happened to Jarles. The renegade priest now seemed to be in high favour with the Hierarchy and to enjoy the confidence of Cousin Deth, for he had twice come to visit the Black Man in his cell.

Doggedly, each time with greater difficulty, he blanked

his mind for Dickon's questing thoughts. No question here of the familiar reaching him through the ventilators. This was no hospital chamber but a metallic cell under the constant surveillance of two guards. Nothing but telepathy could get through. Moreover, Dickon did not know its location. He would have to cast around for it at random and in great peril.

Once again the Black Man blanked his mind. Once again no answer came. Once again his own fantastic thoughts, distorted by the session with Dhomas, scribbled themselves on the blank.

Through the narrow, circular darkness Dickon quested, guided only by the vivid tactual sense that edged his suctorial paws when his claws were retracted.

Dickon was not worried. Such emotions were much too elaborate for his clear-cut, highly simplified mind. Even his frequent self-pity was matter-of-fact. But he knew that his fresh blood was running low, and waste blood piling up, even under the slight demands of his ribbonlike muscles. He had gorged himself at the Breeding Place, but it wouldn't last forever. Eventually he would have to stop moving.

But before that happened he would be able to explore a few more branches of the huge inside-out tree which was Dickon's mental diagram of the ventilation system of the crypts.

It was very windy in the tunnels. He had to buck a constant gale. If he ever let go at all four suctorial paws at once, he would be whisked like a bit of waste for an indeterminate distance before he managed to bring himself to a stop with his claws – if he could. For Dickon, as he often told himself, was a mere diagram of a man. His bones were lighter than a monkey's, his body had not a genuine fat cell in it, and his internal organs were reduced to a single compartmentalized cavity which served both as blood pump and blood-storage chamber. All physiological substances for the production or conditioning of which other organs were necessary, he sucked in along with the blood he drew from his symbiotic partner through his wizened little mouth. He neither digested nor eliminated. He did not breathe, although he could make feeble sounds and even talk sketchily by drawing air into his mouth cavity and expelling it between taut lips. His bones were hollow, since he needed no marrow for producing blood corpuscles. He was without ductless glands and had no sex. His fine, short fur insulated him against loss of body heat.

Just a skeleton, muscles, tendons, skin, fur, heart, simplified circulatory system, nervous system, twitching ears, peering eyes – and a personality as queerly simple as his physiology.

One of the aims of the original makers of his artificial species had been to devise an extremely swift and nimble organism by eliminating as much weight and as many functions as possible. This aim they had achieved, but at the inescapable cost of making the creature absolutely dependent on its symbiotic partner or some other blood supply, and strictly limiting the extent of its activity before return to such blood supply became imperative.

These various limitations and his general fragileness did not bother Dickon in the least. Like all his kind, Dickon took a fatalistic and gently stoical view of things.

So it was without fear that Dickon negotiated the windy tubes. If there had been light, and anyone to see him, he might have been mistaken for a huge, reddish, furry spider, scuttling rapidly – for Dickon's most efficient speed was considerably higher proportionately than that of a man.

"Must find brother. Must find brother." The words repeated themselves in his mind with an unemotional, almost soothing insistence. Not only did he long for the warmth of his brother's side, flatly curled against which he had spent most of his days. He also wished to unburden his mind of certain facts, which he knew would greatly interest his brother, and which now filled his mind to bursting, like a box stuffed very full. That was very much how Dickon thought of his mind – as a little room behind his eyes, lined with boxes of memories, and in the middle of it a very little Dickon, who was his real self and peered out through the eye windows, and listened through the trumpets of his ears. In the room were two blackboards, one of them headed

"Rules" and closely filled with writing; the other was blank. It was for his brother's thoughts.

Dickon's brother was the cardinal fact of his life. He was so close to him that at times Dickon felt himself to be nothing more than an extension of his brother's personality. There was good reason for this. Dickon absorbed his brother's emotions with the hormones of his brother's blood – indeed the familiars spoke to one another of "frightened blood," "angry blood," "loving blood," and the like. Though such emotions were on the whole fleeting and did not greatly disturb the even tenor of Dickon's thoughts.

More important, Dickon was in every part of him a simplified version of his brother. In short, his brother's identical twin, developed from a cell of his brother's body that had undergone a process known as chromosome-stripping, a technique of microbiology discovered in the Golden Age and then supposedly lost. The stripping technique removed from his brother's chromosomes the determinants of sex, alimentation, and many other functions. But in all that remained, Dickon was his brother's identical twin. And this accounted for their telepathic contact.

When brain waves were first discovered by the Dawn Civilization, it was realized that, if telepathy did ever occur, it would most likely be between identical twins, since similarity of brain structure would mean similarity of brain waves – putting the two minds in tune. But this idea had lain dormant until almost the end of the Golden Age, when it had been discovered that telepathy could only occur in such cases where one of the two stations was of a much simpler pattern than the other, thus doing away with otherwise unsurmountable interferences.

Production of simplified, symbiotic identical twins by the stripped-chromosome process had provided the solution. Briefly, the Golden Age had dreamed of extending the personality of every individual by furnishing him with such a symbiotic partner. Then, in swift succession, had come darkened times, cessation of the research, more than worldwide chaos, establishment of the Hierarchy. Until, when the New Witchcraft first began, vastly detailed instructions had come from Asmodeus for the setting up of a breeding place and the creation of symbiotic identical twins, in imitation of the familiars of the ancient witchcraft.

From his birth, from his first conscious moment after being taken from the breeding tank, Dickon's thoughts had been immersed in those of his brother – so that in a sense he had had no babyhood or childhood, but had thought adult thoughts from the start. Direct contact with his brother's mind had enabled him to reach full mental maturity within a few hours, and had also made it possible for him to achieve insights and understandings beyond the unaided capacities of his simplified nervous system. The chief other influence on his development was provided by his fellow familiars, his social equals, with those minds he had telepathic contact of lesser degree and shorter range.

But his brother was much closer to him than any of them. So, as Dickon scuttled through the black branches of the wind tunnels seeking his brother, he came as close as he could, lacking a glandular system, to experiencing an emotion of his own.

Five more branches at the most, he told himself, before he would have to stop and be still. Then suddenly there appeared the dimmest trace of a picture on the blank blackboard of his mind.

He stopped. It began to fade. He moved forward. It faded all away. Back again then, and wait. After a while another picture started to appear, like a photograph developing – a photograph that moved and changed even as it developed. A feeling that, had Dickon possessed emotion, would have been akin to fear, filled the familiar's mind. He had never seen quite that sort of mental landscape before. And yet he was certain it was his brother's.

Without warning the picture disappeared. Rapidly the tiny Dickon behind his eyes ran to the blackboard and wrote a message.

"Dickon is here, brother. Dickon writes on your mind."

His message vanished and instantly the blackboard became choked with such a hurly-burly of thoughts that Dickon knew his brother must be very startled and excited. And most of the thoughts had that odd alien tinge. Quickly, they were wiped away, as if his brother had realized they were too confused to be helpful, and a concise questtion replaced them.

"Can you understand me clearly, Dickon? Is contact sufficient?"

"Yes, but your thoughts are strange. And some of them seem hurt. Has someone injured your thoughts, brother?"

"A little, but I haven't time to explain." Here, Dickon got a fragmentary glimpse of Brother Dhomas and his laboratory in the crypts. "Except for the strangers, present contact is sufficient?" the Black Man continued.

"Yes. But Dickon would like to come to you. Will you help Dickon find the way?"

"Sorry, Dickon, but it can't be done. They've got your brother locked up tight. Did you deliver my message?"

"No. Dickon could not. He found things very different from what they should be. He has much news for you."

"Tell it."

At that the little Dickon behind his eyes began to yank open the memory boxes.

"After Dickon left you in the room of sickness – do you still have that queer outside heart, brother?"

"No, I'm better now. You've been gone four days. Go on."

"Dickon went by the tunnels. First the little, then by a narrow burrowing into the big, then into the little again. But he did not find Drick or Drick's familiar at the place where Drick should be. So Dickon started for the Coven Chamber. But in the tunnels below the chamber he found many familiars, Drick's among them – Jock, Meg, Mysie, Jill, Seth, and many more. Those familiars told Dickon he must not go to the Chamber for there were priests in it. There had been a meeting, they said, and all their Big People had been betrayed. Deacons had burst into the Chamber and captured their Big People. They were in bad shape, those familiars. They had lost contact with their Big People, and they did not know what to do. Many of them stood in need of blood.

"Dickon remembered that stores of blood for the embryonic familiars are kept at the Breeding Place. So he gathered the lost familiars into a band, bidding the stronger help the weaker, and led them down, down through the tunnel to the Breeding Place. It was a hard trip. Towards the end many had to be carried. And if they had not known they were returning to their birthplace, I do not believe they would have made it.

"When Dickon and the other familiars finally arrived, they found there were no Big People in the Breeding Place either. It was deserted. The other familiars would have drunk the first ampules of blood they found, for they were famished. But Dickon held them back and would let none drink, until he found the case where is kept the blood-that-all-may-drink-in-safety.

"So Dickon left them gorging themselves with blood and returned by the way he had come, for he knew his brother would want news of all these happenings, and he wished to know what his brother would want him to do now. But when he had retraced his path, he found that his brother was no longer where he had left him. He searched, but could not find his brother or his brother's thoughts. So he returned to the Breeding Place for fresh blood and came back to search again. This happened many times. Until at last he decided he must return no more, but find his brother or else stop moving. So he searched farther than ever before. And here he is."

Then Dickon wiped clean the blackboard in his mind, but no answer came – only a confusion of thoughts which told him that his brother was much disheartened by the news he had brought – a jerky, wordless, mental landscape, tinged more than ever by the mood Dickon found so alien.

Suddenly the tiny Dickon behind his eyes caught sight of a small memory box that had not been opened.

"There is one thing I have not told you, brother.

"Dickon said that the Breeding Place was deserted when we reached it. That is true, so far as Big People are concerned. But there were two newborn familiars there, whom the Breeders must have left behind. They were two strange familiars – not of witches or warlocks."

"What do you mean?"

"You must know the one of them, brother. The familiar of that priest who was to be one of us, and who stayed at Mother Jujy's and who – "

"What does he look like?"

Rapidly, Dickon sketched on his mental blackboard the portrait of a dark-furred familiar.

"And the other one?"

Dickon sketched a mental portrait of a sallowy-skinned familiar, whose black fur had a blue-steel tone to it.

For a time then there came no further message, but Dickon sensed that his brother's mind was furiously plotting in the old way he knew so well. When words finally came, they were sharp and clear.

"Listen, Dickon. Those two newborn familiars. Did you touch minds with them?"

"Yes, a little. They are very stupid, since they have never been with their big twins. But some of the other familiars have been communing with them, seeking half in sport to teach them. They are making some progress."

"Do you think, if they were with you now, I could touch minds with them, through yours?"

"I think so, brother."

"Good. Listen carefully now. I want you to return to the Breeding Place and bring back those two newborn familiars. Each of you can carry an ampule of blood, so you will have a reserve supply – "

"Dickon never thought of that. It would have made everything so much easier. Poor, stupid Dickon! "

"No, no. You've done more than I ever hoped. But to continue, you are to bring the two others to the place where you are now, and seek to contact my mind. Do you understand?"

"Yes," Dickon answered gravely.

"Can you do it?" came the anxious message. "Return to the Breeding Place, I mean? Have you enough blood left for that?"

"I do not know," replied Dickon simply. "I came farther this time, hoping to draw blood from my brother when I found him."

"Sathanas!" Dickon sensed his brother's dismay. "Listen, Dickon, it is essential that you carry out my orders. Therefore I release you from the rule that forbids you to take blood from any other person but your brother. Take blood when and where you can get it!"

Dickon caught the afterthought and remarked quietly, "Dickon understands the peril to which his brother is referring. That was why he insisted the other familiars wait until he found the case of blood-that-all-may-drink-in-safety. He knows that if he takes a stranger's blood there is a chance he will die in swift convulsions. But life is a little thing – as little as Dickon – and Dickon does not mind."

He could not wholly comprehend the emotion that rose up then in his brother's mind, but it heartened him.

"You'd better be starting, Dickon," came the final words from his brother. "It's a small hope that you're carrying – as small as you are. But it may be the only one for the whole world of Big People."

"Dickon will do what he can. Good-bye, brother."


## CHAPTER SIXTEEN

SINCE the dawn the mighty carillon of the Cathedral had been deluging Megatheopolis at intervals with an excited and joyous pealing of bells, and before the first burst had ended the Great Square had begun to fill. If the darkness had not been so full of the terrors of Sathanas, the commoners would have started coming at midnight.

"Awake! Awake!" the bells seemed to ring out. "Wonders. Wonders untold. Hurry! Hurry!"

Many had come fasting and brought no food. For was not this to be a Grand Revival? It was the Great God's turn to provide.

From every corner of Megatheopolis they came, and from miles out in the surrounding countryside. By an hour after midmorning, the Square was packed up to the double line of deacons, who kept clear a considerable space in front of the Cathedral steps. The surrounding rooftops were thronged, boys had climbed the chimneys. A little earlier a small, overcrowded balcony had collapsed, injuring several and creating a minor panic that was quickly hushed by the deacons scattered throughout the crowd. The surrounding streets were crowded with late comers. Everywhere were jostlings, elbowings, disputes as to who had first claim to the best places, shouting for lost children, and a ceaseless hum of conversation which the clangor of the bells periodically drowned out.

It was not exactly a happy crowd or even a pleasant one. It was the same crowd that yesterday had stormed halfway up the Cathedral steps, screaming insults at the Hierarchy because it could not defend them from Sathanas. The same crowd that had killed two deacons, manhandled a priest of the First Circle, and flatly demanded that the Hierarchy prove itself. But now the commoners were observing a kind of truce. Yesterday the priests had promised them that the Great God would give them a sign of his favour and of his mastery over Sathanas by performing miracles at the Grand Revival. And last night, as if in token of this, there had seemed to be a decrease in hauntings and other satanic eeriness.

Moreover, it was hard to maintain anger in the face of the soothing effect of the parasympathetic emanations which drenched the Square.

The parasympathetics had one other effect. They stimulated the nerves controlling the digestive tract and thereby greatly increased the hunger of a crowd which had for the most part not yet eaten today. A hundred thousand mouths filled with saliva. A hundred thousand throats swallowed, swallowed, swallowed.

Finally, at high noon, the carillon broke off in the middle of the loudest and most clangorous burst it had yet pealed forth. For a moment there was silence, and a sensation of tremendous pressures as a hundred thousand commoners held their breath. Then, from the Sanctuary, came the deep organ notes of a solemn march, sombre and rolling, yet full of mystery and majesty and power, like distant thunder become harmonious – such a music as must have sounded when the Great God first imposed his will upon black chaos and created the Earth.

Slowly, in step with this titan melody, the reviewing stand which had been raised overnight beside the Cathedral door, began to fill with priests whose scarlet robes were agleam with gold. The nearest commoners could make out the emblazonment on their breasts – a triangle at whose vertex glittered a great jewel – and word was breathlessly whispered back that no less than the Apex Council itself would preside over the Grand Revival. There were few enough commoners who could boast of ever having seen an archpriest. To glimpse the whole Council was like getting a peek at Heaven.

Wonder began to crowd out surliness. The music quickened. The high doors of the Cathedral swung outward, and there issued forth, four abreast, a procession which incarnated the pomp and power of the Hierarchy. Priests of all circles – magnificent men, handsome as demigods. They circled the space the deacons had kept clear before drawing up in ranks around the reviewing stand.

And as the priests marched, as the music grew ever more rich and warm and dazzling – as it climbed like the sun to the top of the sky – they seemed to tread under their feet all evil, all darkness, all rebellion, any and everything that presumed to lift its head against the Hierarchy.

On the reviewing stand, Goniface wrinkled his nostrils and turned to one of the lesser priests standing in attendance behind him.

"Whence comes that odour?" he inquired.

There was no longer any disregarding it. Mingled with the cloying sweetness that was diffusing through the Square, came ever stronger and stronger whiffs of a pungent, goaty stench.

The attendant priest indicated that he would find out. Leaning forward, Goniface glanced thoughtfully at the two priests bearing censers. But he recognized them both. One was a staunch Realist, the other a stern-faced Fanatic.

He touched a switch on the portable televisor set up in front of him, and there sprang into view the features of the chief technician at Cathedral Control Centre.

"No, your supreme eminence, there is no possibility of the Witchcraft hocussing any of our apparatus," he explained in answer to Goniface's question. "We have a comprehensive warning system set up, which will instantly inform us if force pencils or any similar manipulatory fields are introduced into the Square, and we have countermeasures ready. The telesolidograph shield is, as you know, completely adequate. In short, the Great Square and the Cathedral, and a considerable region around them, are isolated. You can rest assured of that.

"The odour? Oh, we know about that already. A most unfortunate, though unavoidable accident in the mechanism of one of the odour projectors. It has been rectified."

As Goniface reprimanded him, he scanned the faces of the other priests in the control centre. All loyal Realists, except two of the Fifth Circle physicists. And they were Fanatics. Good.

"Yes, your supreme eminence," the chief technician assured him in answer to a final question, "we can at an instant's notice throw up a repulsor dome over the reviewing stand. And the squadron of angels you desired us to hold in readiness can get into the air almost as quickly."

Satisfied in the main, Goniface switched off the televisor. True to what the chief technician had told him, the goaty odour had almost faded out, though a few wrinkled noses were to be seen here and there. He would have liked to have Cousin Deth beside him at the moment, but the little deacon couldn't be spared from the witch hunt. Jarles, however, made a fair substitute.

The march had finished in a great, triumphal burst of sound that seemed to signify the Great God's final and most important act of creation, when, after the catastrophic experiment of the Golden Age, he had brought into being the crowning glory of the Hierarchy.

The crowd, eager with hours of waiting, but soothed by the parasympathetics, fell easy prey to the revivalistic preachers, whose mightily amplified voices thundered one after another through the Square. Strains of a softer music than the march subtly emphasized the rhythm of the preacher's fervent chanting, while the parasympathetic emanations were artfully varied to increase the effects of their exhortations, with sympathetics occasionally mixed in.

The emotional resistances of the crowd gave way. Whole sections began to sway from side to side, until the movement had spread through the whole Square, and all the commoners, including those on the rooftops, were swaying like a single organism. And from a hundred thousand throats came a wordless sound that intensified the preacher's rhythmic emphases – a profoundly stirring yet disgusting animal sound midway between a grunt of pleasure and a sob.

Here and there were symptoms of even more violent emotional release – ecstatic wails, screams, wildly flailing arms, tiny holes in the crowd where someone had dropped to his knees. It would have been easy to throw them all into a state of crazy and utter abandon, but that was not the intention. As it was, deviations to a wilder behaviour could make no progress against the general chanting sway, and were quickly re-engulfed in it.

"Great God, hurl down Sathanas, hurl down the Lord of Evil!" Grunt and sway. "He caught us in snares, but we struggled against them!" Grunt and sway. "He raised terrors by darkness, but we called upon you!" Grunt and sway. "He sent horrors against us, but we clung to our faith!" Grunt and sway. "Send him back to Hell, send him back to his sinners!" Grunt and sway. "Let him root in filth, let him swill with the damned!" Grunt and sway.

Then, with a thrilling display of mob-mastery, the last and ablest of the preachers stilled the swaying and hushed the sound – not by calming it, but by transforming it into motionless tension, an almost unbearably poignant anticipation.

All eyes turned towards the preacher, who stood alone on a rostrum in front of the reviewing stand. He dropped to his knees then, and cried out, in a voice vibrant with compassion. "Great God, your people ache for your loving kindness. Long have they gone without the milk of your infinite mercy, the food of your infinite strength. They thirst. They hunger."

This was no more than literally true. Kept waiting until midafternoon, ceaselessly bombarded by parasympathetics, the crowd was ravenous.

Turning on his knees, the preacher lifted his hands in supplication to the massive, all-dominating image that formed the upper half of the Cathedral.

"Great God," he cried, "your people have passed the test! In terror and suffering, they have maintained their faith. They have torn out Sathanas from their hearts. Be good to them, Great God. Tilt for them your horn of plenty. Animate with your divine presence the cold, lifeless stone and let ambrosia drop from your hands and nectar stream from your fingertips. They have hungered long enough, Great God. Give them food and drink!''

Mentally stupefied and emotionally taut as they were, the crowd realized what must be coming and prepared for it. The older knew from experience, and the younger had been told, what wondrous dainties would soon come spilling down. Wooden bowls and copper pitchers appeared suddenly. Other commoners stretched small sheets between them to catch the miraculous cakes. Tubs and buckets showed up on the rooftops, while a few frantic souls climbed on their neighbour's shoulders and teetered there precariously, holding containers of one sort or another.

But the majority just stood with heads thrown back, mouths open, and hands upstretched.

There was a faint shudder of movement in the gigantic image, sudden silence in the Square. Slowly then the vast, awesome face looked down. Slowly the harsh lines softened, to be replaced by an indulgent and benignant smile – like a stern and preoccupied but withal loving father who finally remembers the obedient children crowding around his feet.

Slowly the gargantuan hands stretched out over the Square in a gesture of titan generosity. Then, from the right hand, ten thousand tiny fountains suddenly sprayed, while from the left cascaded down, blossoming outward like an inverted flower, a rain of crusty flakes and tiny cubes.

A greedy cry rose from the crowd, as the food and drink began to sprinkle them.

One second. Two. Three. And then the cry changed abruptly to a strangled spewing, and there swept through the massed ranks of the priests and across the reviewing stand a hideous stench that seemed compounded equally of putrid meat, rancid butter, mouldy bread, and embalming fluid.

As from one giant throat, the crowd gargled, retched and spat. And still the noisome nectar and noxious ambrosia continued irrevocably to fall, drenching them, plastering them. Heads were ducked, hoods pulled up. Those who had spread sheets crowded under them, while a few of those who had held up bowls now inverted them and clapped them on their heads. And still the dreadful stuff rained down, so thickly that the farther side of the Square was murkily obscured.

Snarls then, and angry cries. First a few, then more. Here and there the fringes of the crowd surged forward against the double line of deacons.

The preacher on the rostrum rose to the emergency. Stepped-up amplification enabled him to outroar the crowd.

"The Great God is only testing you!" he bellowed. "Some of you must lack faith! That is why the miracle-food does not taste like ambrosia and nectar!

"But the Great God is now satisfied of your faith!" he continued, not caring how illogical he sounded so long as he got to his main point, which was, "The Great God will now perform the true miracle! Behold how he rewards you!"

The stinking rain ceased.

On the reviewing stand Goniface thundered at the televisor, "Stop that second miracle!"

From the panel the chief technician stared back blankly at him. He gave no sign that he had heard the order. He seemed stunned, bemused. "But we're isolated," he was repeating dully. "We haven't got a quiver out of any of the warning systems."

"And someone has turned on the sympathetics!" Goniface continued rapidly. "Attend to it! And stop that second miracle!"

The chief technician came to life with a jerk and quickly signed to one of his assistants, who almost immediately answered with frantic gestures of impotence.

For the first moment it seemed that Goniface's fears were groundless. From the Great God's outstretched hands there began to sprinkle a shower of tiny golden coins.

The forward movement of the crowd checked. Again they looked upward. The ingrained habits of a lifetime were not easily overcome. It was second nature to believe what a priest said. And the descending shower did have a true golden glint.

But after the first sprinkle, it changed from gold to red

– too bright a red. Screams and yells of sudden pain mingled with the renewed snarls as tiny red-hot discs spattered against tender flesh, or were greedily caught out of the air and as quickly hurled away, or chanced to drop inside clothing or were trodden by bare feet.

With a roar that muffled the cries of pain, the crowd surged ponderously forward in a ragged wave, partly to escape the red-hot shower, which stopped just short of the double line of deacons. But that was not the main reason, for the shower stopped and the forward surging continued, strengthened, and the roar became louder and uglier. Fists were raised. Deacons went down. Here and there the double line bent backward, broke.

To avoid any chance of such a stupid tragedy as had occurred yesterday at Neodelos, Goniface had forbidden the cordon of deacons to carry wrath rods. Now at his rapidly transmitted command, the First and Second Circle priests in front of the reviewing stand marched forward to support the deacons, hurrying in either direction to form a long-enough line, and switching on the repulsor fields of their inviolability as they went, so that their robes puffed out tautly. Across the dissolving line of deacons, the crowd hurled filthily smeared pots and pitchers at the advancing priests, but they rebounded harmlessly from the individual repulsor fields.

Something was wrong with their halos, though. They were flashing on and off.

Suddenly there was confusion in their ranks. The first impression was that those in the centre had simultaneously hurled themselves at each other and then neglected to break apart. Swiftly others catapulted themselves at the original group and stuck to it. The ends of the hurrying line were jerked suddenly backward, some of the priests falling, yet still skidding along, until all of them were jammed together in one helpless, roughly circular, scarlet clump.

To Goniface, it was apparent almost immediately that some unaccountable influence had changed their repulsor fields to attractors, with a simultaneous increase in range and power.

But most of the archpriests could only stare helplessly at

the ever-mounting chaos around the reviewing stand. Long habit had taught them to preserve inscrutable expressions, but now their facial masks concealed nothing but empty stupefaction. It was not physical fear that froze them. They felt that the whole materialistic world on which they based their security was going to pieces before their eyes. Physical science, which had been their obedient servant, had suddenly become a toy in the hands of a dark power that could make or break scientific laws at pleasure. Something had scratched out the first principle of their thinking: "There is only the cosmos and the electronic entities that constitute it, without soul or purpose –" and scribbled over it, in broad black strokes, "The whim of Sathanas."

The high-ranking priests massed around the reviewing stand were in no better shape. They stood there, doing nothing, as the stinking wave of the garbage-drenched crowd surged forward, engulfing the struggling deacons like a row of black pebbles, breaking around the helpless clump of the lower-ranking priests as around a red rock and roaring up the steps of the Cathedral.

A stone, its momentum almost spent, lobbed into the reviewing stand. It brought no reaction. With three exceptions, the archpriests and their attendants were like scarlet-gowned dolls.

The three exceptions were Goniface, Jarles and the old Fanatic Sercival.

Goniface had at last managed to get an order through the minor chaos of Cathedral Control Centre. Down over the Cathedral, swerving around the still-forward-bending image of the Great God, swooping a bare few yards above the reviewing stand, dove a squadron of angels – a sight fantastically grotesque, as if a score of flaxen-haired demi-gods had swan-dived from the cloudless sky.

They flattened out where the forward edge of the crowd was hurling itself on the ranks of the higher priesthood, and skimmed across the Square – so low that they brained a few unfortunates.

The attractor field of the clumped lower-ranking priests interfered catastrophically with the course of the centre angel. It nosed downward and crashed, crushing priests and commoners alike. It crumpled, revealing its metallic construction. Through a gaping rent there showed the body of its priestly pilot, killed in the crash.

But the other angels banked sharply upward, just missing the rooftops across the Square, and looped back for another dive.

There were ghastly screams from those who had felt the mangling force of the downward-directed propulsion jets.

Insane terror began to replace the insane anger of the crowd. Like some helpless beast, it floundered senselessly. Some in the forward fringe still grappled with the higher-ranking priests. Others, attempting to flee, only added to the confusion of the trapped, milling central mass. All street mouths were hopelessly choked.

Then, when the angels had momentarily become tiny shapes against the blue of the zenith, there came hurtling from the commoners' section, over the horizon of roofs, six black forms trailing like cuttlefishes a dense, inky smoke behind them. Straight for the Cathedral they came, like bats out of hell. And that hell was their most likely source, was soon apparent, for as they hurled closer well above the mob, they were seen to have misshapen and taloned arms, furry nether limbs rigidly extended, and short black tails. While horned black fiend-faces grew, grew, grew.

The first went whipping in close circles around the rostrum on which the preacher cowered, wreathing him with black fumes until he was completely obscured.

The next two banked upward and executed intricate loops around the head, body and arms of the Great God, festooning him inkily. His vast face still wore the original indulgent smile, now imbecile. Then, from the mightiest amplifier of them all, that located behind his own idiot-grinning mouth, the Great God began to bleat thunderously, "Mercy! Mercy, master! Do not hurt me! I will tell everyone the truth! I am the slave of Sathanas! My priests have lied! The Lord of Evil rules us all!"

The last three devils shot straight at the reviewing stand. White-faced archpriests, at last springing up, stared at them horrifiedly. Then, when they were hardly yards away, there was a cutting-off of sound and a wavering in the scene before the archpriests. In response to Goniface's frantically repeated commands, Cathedral Control Centre had finally thrown up the heavy repulsor dome to shield the Apex Council. The three approaching devils careened away wildly.

In that pocket of sudden silence in the midst of visible chaos, it was startling how clearly the doomful voice of old Sercival rang out. All through the Grand Revival, the lean and aged Fanatic had not spoken a word, only gazed before him with a sombre displeasure, occasionally shaking his head and seeming to mutter to himself.

Now he cried, in a voice that smote like an icy dagger, "Who, I ask, has performed the miracles today? At long last the Great God sickens of our unbelief. He deserts us. He leaves us to Hell's mercy. Prayer alone – and faith absolute – can save us, if it be not too late even for prayer."

The other archpriests did not look at him, but the impression they gave was that someone was speaking their inmost thoughts. They stood motionless – lonely men communing with terror. Even Goniface's exasperation and contempt were sullied with the faintest trace of the poisoning corruption of doubt and fear.

But into the hard, watchful eyes of Jarles, standing sideways behind Sercival, there crept a look of incredulous realization. Today was the first time he had ever seen the leader of the Fanatics. Now, for the first time, he heard him speak.

Memory and the unerring sense of recognition that came with memory, fought with incredulity and conquered. Instantly his new personality made one of those hairline decisions which were its chiefest pride.

Conscience smote him as he did the deed. Black, agonizing waves of guilt washed through his mind, telling him this was a crime beyond forgiveness, a nefarious action from which the universe turned aside in loathing. Yet he choked down conscience, as a sick man subdues his retching.

He pointed the Finger of Wrath, full power, at the back of the gorgeously gold-worked robe, a foot below the silver-touched parchment skull, until a tiny patch of daylight showed raggedly through.

As Goniface wheeled towards him, as the other archpriests cringed dazedly from this new menace, as the grimly erect form of the mortally wounded Fanatic swayed before it fell, Jarles cried out, "His was the voice I heard in the Coven Chamber! He is Asmodeus, leader of the Witchcraft!"

And springing forward, he caught the toppling body, let it down smoothly, and slitted open the scarlet-stained, scarlet robe, with its ray-charred hole. Clinging in death to the skinny, rib-ridged torso, slain by the same blast that had mangled the Fanatic, its age-silvered fur drenched in its own blood, was a gaunt familiar whose wizened face was a grim travesty of the pain-racked features of his twin.

The archpriests stared as if at the impossible, their masks of inscrutability torn away at last.

Goniface looked down at the two. It was as if the dome-sealed reviewing stand had become for a space of time the silent centre of the universe, where all secrets are laid bare, the tense and motionless core round which all action wheels and swirls. Outside the dome, a mad conflict was progressing through momently altering phases. The crowd, saved from a second onslaught by the angels, heartened as well as dumfounded by the appearance of its demon allies, had once again come to grips with the higher-ranking priesthood, who were withdrawing into the Cathedral. The angels had swooped back into the fight, violet wrath rays blazing from their eyes, three or four to each devil, and there resulted a giddy, whirling combat, in which black fumes were employed as smoke screens.

But, for the moment, that wild, silent commotion seemed no more to Goniface than a strange, savage mural on the repulsor dome – a painting of a battle – a background for true crisis.

So overpowering was his urge to question the dying Fanatic, that he grudged the moment he had to spare in contacting Cathedral Control Centre and making the chief technician understand his command: "Seize the two Fifth Circle Fanatics! They are the ones who confused and interfered with your controls! Slay them if need be!" He did not pause to watch the outcome of the struggle between the outnumbered traitors and his loyal Realists.

He grudged, too, the moments lost in ordering his lieutenants: "Descend at once into the Sanctuary. Organize raiding groups. Seize all Fanatics. Slay them if they resist. Close the Sanctuary, both to prevent their escape and to stand off the crowd. Inform Cousin Deth in the crypts of the new situation. Have Web Centre transmit similar instructions to all sanctuaries. Take all obvious auxiliary measures. Move!"

Then, stony-faced, yet terribly eager, he turned to the old Fanatic.

Sercival smiled with pain-drawn lips through which shallow breaths went quickly.

"You sat beside me when they put the witches to the torture," Goniface began – it was not the question he had intended. "You used a short-range pain gun on me, I believe?"

With difficulty Sercival smiled again. His voice was like a something from the tomb – windy, faint, laboured.

"Perhaps. Perhaps not. The strategems of Sathanas . . . are varied." The eyes of the archpriests widened. Almost a shudder went through their crowded, scarlet-and-gold ranks.

"Sathanas? Rot!" Goniface contradicted. "You wanted power, just like all of us. The Witchcraft was your trick to get it. You –"

But Sercival did not seem to hear. Feebly he moved his hand until it touched the blood-matted, silvery fur of the stiffening familiar.

"Dead, too, Tobit, oldest of your short-lived brethren?" He breathed. "I shall be with you . . . in Hell. We will wear fine new forms . . . and be true brothers."

"The curtain's down. No need to keep on acting," Goniface interrupted harshly.

Old Sercival lifted his head a little and thick sounds came from his throat, as if he sought to speak. The fingers of his left hand moved feebly, tracing the beginnings of some ritual gesture.

"Sathanas," he whispered, "receive . . . my . . . spirit –"

The archpriests were like so many scarlet images. Outside a scene of continued tumult was illumined by a red sun already close to the western horizon. From the east, darkness was creeping.

"You were very clever," Goniface continued, bending even nearer to the dying leader of the Witchcraft, driven against

153

his will to ask a final question, "but you made one strange mistake. Why did you always support me in the Apex Council? Why were you so quick to vote for the excommunication of Frejeris? Why did you offer no opposition when the most realistic of the priests, the one most dangerous to the Witchcraft – myself – was made World Hierarch?"

There was silence in the isolated hemisphere under the repulsor dome. The archpriest leaned forward, bent close to catch the answer. But it never came.

Asmodeus was dead.


## CHAPTER SEVENTEEN


CANE in one shrivelled hand, candle in the other, Mother Jujy hobbled through the ancient tunnel. Occasionally she muttered to herself venomously.

"Won't let an old witch spend her dying years in peace! Won't even let her live under the ground like a mole! Oh, no! The deacons must come down and muck up her tunnels and chevy her deeper and deeper. Not that it's Mother Jujy they're after. Oh, no! Brain Mother Jujy and leave her in the corner! We don't want her. It's the new witches they want. The young witches. The pretty witches. Mother Jujy was pretty once. These new ones wouldn't have had a chance with her! But now they've gone and jiggered the whole world with their craziness, turned it topsy-turvy, so there's no place left for an old witch! May they prance on red plates in Hell for it!"

In her vehemence, she had stopped and was shaking her cane at the low, rounded ceiling. A black cat, which had been scouting ahead by the wavering candlelight, came back and mewed at Mother Jujy inquiringly.

"No Grimalkin, it's not a mouse, and I've got no food for you! But never mind, Mother Jujy'll starve down here, and you'll be able to pick her bones – unless she picks yours first! And you may thank the new witches for it, who ruined the trade!"

Grimalkin resumed her scouting. Hobbling along, Mother

Jujy continued her savage grumbling. Then from ahead came a terrific spitting and squalling. Mother Jujy hurried forward, the long shadows limping and reeling wildly with her as the candle bobbed and flickered.

"What have you found, Grimalkin – a rat, a roach or a dead deacon? Whichever it is, it's not worth the rumpus you're making."

Grimalkin, a black arch of swollen cat, had retreated from a little copper-touched huddle of shadows and was hissing dreadfully at it.

Mother Jujy advanced towards it, bending and squinting. "What is it? A red rat? No, a red monkey. No, by the stench of Sathanas! A familiar! A dirty, dead familiar!" And she raised her cane to hit it.

From the huddle of shadows came a feeble, piping voice.

"Aye, kill me. Slay Dickon. Dickon is weary of waiting for death in the chilly dark."

Mother Jujy paused with uplifted cane.

"What's that? Be quiet, Grimalkin! I can't hear what this morsel of foulness is lisping at me."

"Slay Dickon, I said. Shatter his brittle bones with your huge stick, Mother Jujy. Give your manslaying cat leave to rend him with her claws and drink his cold, worn-out blood. Dickon's ghost will thank you for it."

"What makes you think we'll do you any favours, snivelling puppet?" Mother Jujy inquired acidly. "I know your voice. You are the foul pet of that jigging trickster, the Black Man."

"Aye, but now Dickon's big brother languishes in the cells of the Sanctuary, where cruel priests torture his very thoughts. He cannot protect Dickon now. You can slay Dickon in safety."

"It's useless to beg, filthy manikin, for we won't oblige you. Back, Grimalkin!" The cat had pranced forward stiff-legged and was making threatening swipes at Dickon with rigid forepaw. "So your cocky master finally fell off the fence he capered atop, eh?"

"Aye, Mother Jujy, and the whole New Witchcraft goes swiftly to ruin with him. Many others have been captured and imprisoned. There was one slender hope. If Dickon had been able to run an errand his brother sent him on, something might have been accomplished. But now Dickon lies helpless in subterranean darkness. Slay Dickon before his misery slays him."

"Speak louder, filthy manikin, I can't half hear you!" said Mother Jujy, bending closer. "Why, ungrateful, disobedient skin-and-bones, can't you run the errand? Why have you stopped here like a lazy apprentice to snivel and whine?" and she prodded the familiar with her cane.

"Dickon's blood has given out. The little suppet he has left would not carry him a hundred paces, and it grows swiftly cold. If Dickon had fresh blood, he would go skipping like the wind. But there is no fresh blood here."

"Insult us, filthy manikin?" cried Mother Jujy angrily, raising her cane. "Grimalkin and I have blood, and withered though we be, I'll have you know it's fresh enough!"

"Your pardon, Mother Jujy. Dickon meant no insult. Dickon was referring only to blood that he might drink."

"Conceited tatter of fur! What makes you think you have the right to decide what blood you'll drink and what you won't?"

The familar looked up at her with big, reproachful eyes. "Do not tease Dickon so cruelly. You hate Dickon. As soon as you have finished tormenting him, you and your fierce cat will slay him."

"Chittering little know-it-all!" hissed Mother Jujy, so furiously that the familiar shrank from the sound. "Do you presume to dictate the actions of your betters? You'll drink Grimalkin's blood and like it!"

And she snatched up the almost weightless familiar by the scruff of the neck. Grimalkin, however, as if sensing that her mistress intended to involve her in something unpleasant, retreated along the tunnel. And at the same time the familiar piped shrilly, "A cat's blood would slay Dickon as surely as a cat's claws. Even your blood, Mother Jujy, might slay him."

For a moment it appeared that Mother Jujy was going to use her cane to bat the limp familiar down the tunnel after the cat.

"Not good enough for you? Not good enough for you?" she screamed in a voice strangled by indignation. "Mother Jujy's blood not good enough for a filthy, shrivelled manikin? Here quickly now, before Mother Jujy beats you to a pulp and makes Grimalkin a red jacket of your fur!"

And she jerked at her neck, exposing a sallow, bony shoulder.

"Mother Jujy means it?" asked the familiar faintly, peering at her from where he dangled helpless in her hand. "She is not deceiving Dickon?"

"Call me a liar now?" screeched the old witch. "One more such question, and I will deceive you! I'll deceive your head in with my cane! Feed, filthy manikin!"

And she applied the familiar to her bare shoulder.

For a few seconds there was silence. Then Mother Jujy jerked nervously. "You tickle," she said.

"Your skin is tough, Mother Jujy," the familiar paused to explain apologetically.

Again it appeared that Mother Jujy was going to hurl him down the tunnel. She almost danced with rage.

"Tough? Tough? When she was a girl, Mother Jujy had the softest skin in all Megatheopolis! Obscene, sexless puppet! Merely to touch it honours your degraded mouth!"

Her furiously scathing comments died to a muttering, which stopped. For a long time the chill, dank silence was broken only by the low, jealous mews of Grimalkin, who paced in the shadows, lashing her tail, murderously eyeing her mistress' new pet.

At last the familiar lifted his head. Now all his motions were rapidly and curiously sprightly.

"Dickon feels light as air," he chattered shrilly. "No task is too difficult for him." His tone grew respectful. "It was very, very good blood, though seething with strange emotions. It did not hurt Dickon at all. Oh, Mother Jujy, how will Dickon ever repay you? How will his brother and his brother's companions ever discharge their debt? It is far beyond Dickon's calculating what your kindness may have accomplished. Dickon has no words to describe —"

"What? Wasting time on palaver and flattery while the world waits on your errand?" interrupted Mother Jujy.

"Begone!" And she brushed at him, albeit a little weakly now, with her free hand.

One puckering smile he gave her. Then, with a gust of motion that set Grimalkin rearing back on her hind legs, hissing and clawing at the empty air, he was gone down the tunnel in the direction from which they had come.

Long after his wraithlike shadow had sped into the darkness, Mother Jujy stood there watching after him, leaning heavily on her cane, droplets of wax dripping from the slackly held candle to harden and whiten instantly as they hit the cold floor.

"They might be able to do it," she muttered to herself, her voice heavy with an emotion she would have repudiated before anyone but Grimalkin. "Sathanas help them, but they just might be able to."

## CHAPTER EIGHTEEN

SLOWLY and with leaden steps, as if the very air had thickened to impede him, Jarles made his way towards his private apartment in the crypts. His mind was fogged by a black guilt which was all the more intolerable because he loathed and detested himself for feeling it.

In every corridor he was met or overtaken by hurrying, panic-eyed priests. One stopped and tried to engage him in speech, a fat and ineffectual little priest of the Second Circle.

"I wish to congratulate you on your elevation to the Fourth Circle," he said swiftly, twisting his chubby hands in a nervous and apologetic way. "Surely you remember me, your eminence. I am Brother Chulian – your old guide –"

The fellow sounded as if he were screwing up courage to ask some favour. Or, perhaps, in the general flood of insecurity and fear, he was merely trying to assure himself of as many points of support as possible.

Jarles glared unpleasantly at his former companion and pushed past him without answering.

The crypts were almost deserted. The raiding parties, which had combed the entire Sanctuary in search of Fanatics, had now departed with their captives, to lock them away in the general prison of the Sanctuary – unconnected with the subsidiary prison used by Goniface for his captives before he had become World Hierarch.

As Jarles neared his apartment, his wretchedness abruptly increased, becoming stingingly acute. To his horror, the black fog of guilt oppressing his thoughts suddenly came alive, whispering into his ear – closer even than that – "Do you hear me, Armon Jarles? Do you hear me? I am yourself. Run. Shut your ears. It will do no good. You cannot lock me out. You cannot keep from listening to me. For I am yourself. I am the Armon Jarles you have maimed and imprisoned, the Armon Jarles you have trampled and denied. Yet, in the end, I am stronger than you are."

And – crowning horror – it was not his own voice, though much like it. He was denied even the resource – horrible enough in itself – of explaining it away as an hallucination, a projection from his own subconscious. It was too real, too individual, for that. It was like the voice of some close kin, the voice of some brother who had never been born.

As if all Hell were at his heels, he dashed into his apartment and, with hands that fumbled in their haste, reactivated the lock.

But inside it was worse.

"You cannot escape me, Armon Jarles. Where you are, there I am also. You will hear me until you die, and not even the cremator's flame will end your hearing."

Never had he hated anything like that sourceless voice. Never had he so desired to crush, to tear apart, utterly to destroy something. Yet never had he felt so helpless to accomplish an aim.

Pictures began to form in his mind. He was stumbling through the ruins, Mother Jujy's bony hand clasping his wrist. He wanted to cry out to the pursuers, to strangle her, to beat in her skull with her own cane. But he could not.

He was sitting at a rudely hewn table, sharing a humble dinner with his family. He had poisoned their food. Interminably he waited for them to take the first mouthful, but they were dawdling unaccountably.

He was in the laboratory of Brother Dhomas, but now everything was reversed. A man-shaped blackness sat in Brother Dhomas' seat. Evilly grinning witches and chattering familiars manned the various instruments.

Suddenly then he was looking into a mirror, but instead of himself he saw the reanimated corpse of Asmodeus standing there. And Asmodeus was explaining something by gestures, first pointing at Jarles, then at the charred gaping hole in his robe, over and over again. And when Jarles felt he could bear it no longer, Asmodeus stopped – but then the tiny head of a bloodstained, gaunt, and greyed familiar thrust itself out of the charred hole and began to repeat his master's gestures.

Jarles' hatred of life, of everything, rose to a peak. It occurred to him that it would be possible for a single man, if he worked subtly enough and unswervingly, to destroy the whole human race except for himself. It could be done. There were ways.

With a tremendous effort he looked around the room. For a moment he thought it was empty. Then he saw, squatting on the gleaming desk, between the projector and the scattered spools of reading tape, a loathsome beast, a dark-furred, peering familiar, whose face was a tiny, tapering, noseless copy of his own.

Instantly he sensed that this was the creature who was thinking the thoughts that were torturing him, whose telepathically transmitted words were resounding unstoppably in his skull.

And instantly he determined to slay it. Not by wrath ray – his mental processes had already reached too primeval a level for that. He would strangle it with his bare hands.

It did not stir as he walked towards the table. But his progress was nightmarishly slow, as if the air had become gelatinous. And as he walked, step by laboured step, a final vision formed in his mind.

He was utterly alone, his fingers on the controls of a mighty war blast, at the summit of a little hill in the midst of a flat, grey wasteland. There was no life whatsoever, save his own. As far as eye could see – and it seemed he could see around the curve of the Earth – were the graves of the species he had annihilated, or perhaps the graves of all men and women, of all ages, who had suffered and fought and died seeking freedom, seeking something more than a jealous, conservative, senselessly ordered society could provide for them.

And he was very much afraid, although there was nothing left to threaten him. And he kept wondering if his war blast were sufficiently powerful.

Only a few steps separated him from the desk. His hands were outstretched like talons of marble. The hateful thing was peering at him. But the vision kept coming between them.

Suddenly the wasteland began to ripple and shake. Like an earthquake, except the motion was more general and less violent. As if a million moles were tunnelling. Then, here and there, the grey earth cracked and parted and there rose up skeletal forms, clad in mouldering flesh and tattered cerements. More and more of them until, like an army, they marshalled themselves and advanced from all sides upon the hillock, shaking grey earth from them as they came.

Round and round he slewed his ravening war blast. Down they went, by scores, by hundreds, like rotten grain, collapsing into a second death. But over them, through the smoke of their burning, stepped hundreds more. And he knew that thousands of miles away still others had risen and were marching towards him up around the Earth.

One step more now and he could lean forward. His hands would close around the scrawny throat. Only one step.

Still they came, marching in perfect order, and the stench of their burning obscured the leaden sky and choked him. Now their fallen made a great ring higher than the hillock, and he had to swivel his war blast upwards to cut down the figures who came lightly stepping over the crest – except when he must sweep it briefly downward to finish off a charred skeleton crawling or hitching itself towards him from the heap.

He was at the desk. His marble hands were closing in on the black caricature of himself.

But on him the others were closing. Waves and waves of them. He was sweating, panting, choking. Each time he frantically slewed round his war blast, the ranks he mowed down were a little closer. And one blackened skeleton had got inside his range and was weakly clawing at his ankle with charred phalanges.

His hands closed around the throat of the furry abomination. But it was as if it wore a collar of transparent plastic. He could not quite touch the black fur. One supreme effort –

Then, even as a skeletal phalanx dissolved at the muzzle of his war blast, hands of bone seized him from behind. In a paroxysm of terror, surrender, and ultimate guilt, he screamed, "I give up! I give up!"

At that instant a shock more profound than any electrical one tortured his nerves. In his mind there was a pounding and wrenching and shaking, as of machines broken loose from their moorings. With sickening suddenness his mind spun, then came to rest with the impact of a concussion.

Consciousness darkened, but did not quite fade. Memory strands were strained to the breaking point, but held. His eyes, screwed shut at the final moment, opened.

He was Jarles. He was the old Jarles. The Jarles who had defied the Hierarchy singlehanded.

But that realization brought no relief. On the contrary, it was the beginning of a new agony, less endurable even than that which he had just undergone. For memory was intact. He remembered every action of the secondary personality – the betrayal of the Witchcraft, the kidnapping of Sharlson Naurya, the taunting of the Black Man, and, above all, the murder of Asmodeus. Those were his actions. He was responsible for them.

With a tortured, incredulous gasp he snatched away his hands from the familiar's throat and slitted open his robe, preparing to turn the Finger of Wrath upon himself.

But that release was denied him.

"Expiation, Armon Jarles! Expiation!" sternly resounded the inner voice. "You must first make atonement for your guilt."

At the same moment there scrambled lightly up from behind the desk a second familiar. Coppery fur and a distorted facial resemblance proclaimed him the Black Man's twin. Even his voice was a squeaky echo of the Black Man's. "I am Dickon, Armon Jarles. It is I who have spoken to you through the mind of your little brother, just as my big brother instructed me. But my words were shaped in your little brother's brain to a resemblance of your own. All three of us have touched minds.

"There is no time to lose. You must rescue my big brother. You must release him from his cell."

A third familiar sprang up from behind the desk. Jarles' dumbfoundment was complete. The inky creature bore an unmistakable, eerily hideous resemblance to the World Hierarch Goniface.

For a moment he felt that by some incredible sorcery every human being in the whole world had been transformed into a chattering puppet, and that he, the only man left, was their prisoner and slave, a giant constrained to do their bidding.

"Haste! Haste!" cried Dickon, tugging at his robe.

Jarles obeyed. Soon he was striding hurriedly through the gloomy grey corridors of the crypts. The superstitious of an earlier age might have believed him to be a zombie, so white was his face, so set was his expression, so stiff and mechanical his strides.

Through the ponderous metallic doorway of the subsidiary prison, the turnkey viewed him, satisfying himself that this was one of Goniface's principal agents.

The doorway slid aside, then swiftly closed behind Jarles. He turned towards the booth. The turnkey started to question him about his business. Jarles' hand came up and he directed at the turnkey and his assistant a paralysis beam.

Then he reached forward and withdrew the activator of the locks from the little square box at the turnkey's waist.

Like a figure of wax the turnkey stood there, his open lips forming a question that was never uttered. While behind him sat his assistant, one eyebrow raised in an unchanging expression of casual curiosity.

Down the prison corridor Jarles strode to the single cell in view of the booth. The two deacons guarding it had noticed, but had misinterpreted, the action which had taken place at the booth. They recognized the Fourth Circle priest who was approaching. More than once he had come here to conduct ironic and rather unpleasant conversations with their prisoner. So with looks of obsequious and respectful recognition on their faces, they were frozen by the paralysis beam.

Then the electrical emanations from the activator in Jarles' hand played on the lock.

Slowly the cell door slid aside. At first only a hand could be seen – a hand that groped unsteadily at the wall of the cell, as if its owner were steeling himself to face and endure a terrible disappointment. Then the entire figure came into view.

Physical injury and psychological strain had taken their toll of the Black Man. He appeared pale and dwarfed in his grey prison tunic.

And his thoughts were dwarfed and pale. Jarles, he decided, had only come to taunt him once more. The cold, wooden look in Jarles' eyes seemed to confirm this. Besides, the guards were sitting there as if nothing had happened.

"I have murdered Asmodeus," he heard Jarles say, and it was to the Black Man a final confirmation of his worst fears. Despairingly, he gathered himself for a lunge into the corridor. Knock down Jarles – try to seize a wrath rod.

Then – rush of a coppery shadow, and before he knew how it had happened, Dickon was clinging to the breast of his tunic and plucking gently at his face.

"Brother, oh brother," the tiny voice piped. "Dickon has done what you commanded. Dickon's brother is free, free!"

And even as he sought to grasp the simple meaning of those words, he heard Jarles repeat, in the same formal tone as if he were making a statement before a Hierarchic court of law. "I have murdered Asmodeus –"

The Black Man could not understand. For a moment he wondered crazily if this were some stratagem of Brother Dhomas to unseat his reason. Then Jarles added – "who, as you know, was the Fanatic archpriest Sercival."

As if at some stupid, pointless, yet unbearably ludicrous joke, the Black Man began to laugh. Then suddenly he clapped his hand to his mouth, hardly realizing that Dickon's had already been laid there, warning him to be silent. Incredulously, he stared at Jarles.

"The other captive witches –" he asked.

" – are still imprisoned here," Jarles answered.

A few moments more and Jarles was again striding down the prison corridor. Beside him walked a figure draped in a deacon's robe, face shadowed by black hood, hands gripping a wrath rod.

The corridor made a right-angle turn. Before them stretched a block of cells, two deacons stationed at each door. Down that corridor they paced, and the almost inaudible hissing of a paralysis beam accompanied them. The last three pairs sensed danger, but too late. They were frozen in the act of reaching for their wrath rods, stacked frozen against the wall. The last pair were actually lifting theirs to take aim, but in that position they remained.

The Black Man threw back his hood.

A door across the corridor opened and through it stepped Cousin Deth. With a swiftness almost incredible for a man he directed his wrath rod at the Black Man and Jarles.

But a familiar's reactions are swifter than a man's. In a blur of movement Dickon scuttled at him across the floor.

Deth's sallow face was contorted suddenly with a fear that had only been there once before – when he fled panic-stricken from the haunted house.

"The thing in the hole!" he cried hollowly. "The spider!"

A moment more and he had realized his misapprehension, and the violet needle of his wrath ray was swinging down at Dickon.

But the Black Man had gained time to act. His own wrath ray lashed out, swished into that of Cousin Deth's. Since the two rays were mutually impenetrable, unable to cut through each other, Deth's was fended off from Dickon.

Like two ancient swordsmen, then, the warlock and the deacon duelled together. Their weapons were two endless blades of violet incandescence, but their tactics were those of sabreurs – feint, cut, parry, swift riposte. Ceiling, walls and floor were traced with redly glowing curlicues. Paralysed deacons, seeming like spectators frozen in amazement, were burned down where they stood or stooped or sat.

The end came swiftly. On a whirling disengagement, Deth's blade ripped burningly through the slack of the Black Man's robe, under his arm. But he parried in time. Instantly he feinted one riposte, made another, and the sallow face and swollen forehead of Cousin Deth ceased to exist.

Fending off the beam of the wrath rod that slipped from Deth's fingers, the Black Man hurried forward and switched off both weapons.

Then he turned to Jarles, who had stood motionless against the wall all through the fight, inviting destruction. He ordered Jarles to activate the locks.

But he wasted not a word on his captive fellow witches, as they emerged wonderingly from their cells, like ghosts summoned from the Underworld. Even Drick he turned away with a quick headshake. His every effort was concentrated on drawing from the seemingly hypnotized Jarles a terse account of the recent events which had shaken Megatheopolis.

Jarles was activating the last lock. The Black Man noted that the hitherto set expression on the face of the twice-renegade priest was beginning to cloud a little, like a man recovering from the actions of a narcotic drug.

Haltingly, with the effortfulness of a man who begins to realize what enormous crimes he must make amends for, Jarles said, "I can take you to where the Fanatic priests are imprisoned. We can attempt to release them and to seize the Sanctuary."

Almost, the Black Man was tempted. His duel with Deth had put him in the mood for such a venture.

But wrath rods were not witches' weapons, he reminded himself. Asmodeus had wagered everything on fear. And, so, it was by fear alone that the wager could be won.

Again Jarles spoke. He seemed to the Black Man to be groping for the solution of some profound inward problem. "If you desire it," he said, "I will attempt to assassinate the World Hierarch Goniface."

"By no means!" the Black Man answered, hardly certain yet whether or not he should treat Jarles as a sane man. "Operations of a very different sort are intended against Goniface. If only I knew what has happened to Sharlson Naurya –"

"She lies in my apartment," said Jarles dully, "under the influence of a paralysis beam."

The Black Man stared at him. He was only now beginning to realize what an utterly incredible accomplice he had in Jarles. Then he laughed, the brief laugh of a man who suddenly understands that the incredible and the inevitable are sometimes the same thing. He had to trust Jarles, for tonight Jarles was blind destiny personified.

"Return to your apartment," he ordered Jarles. "Rouse Sharlson Naurya. Tell her we proceed with the operations against Goniface as planned. Aid her in reaching the vicinity of his apartment without being detected. Take with you Goniface's familiar and your own."

Then he turned and motioned to his witches and warlocks to follow him.

## CHAPTER NINETEEN

WITH a small escort, Goniface was returning to Web Centre, having completed a hurried tour of the principal control points in the Sanctuary. Tonight the Apex Council was sitting at Web Centre. His place was there. But to maintain some direct touch with local developments was one of the World Hierarch's cardinal principles of action.

From Chief Observation Post, high above the other structures of the Sanctuary, he had watched a small black shape – apparently one of those devil constructions which had appeared at the Grand Revival – dart waspishly around the image of the Great God above the Cathedral, like a tiny, frail aircraft attacking a giant. Again and again he watched it evade, by unexpected twists and turns, the blue war blast beam projected from the Great God's hand.

That flitting shadow was a black flag of revolt for the commoners, who tonight were defying the age-old curfew regulations. The great mob which had rioted at the Grand Revival had broken up into gangs which roamed the narrow streets, attacking Hierarchic patrols or setting traps for them. Their peasant brutality, repressed for generations, had a peculiar ghastliness, which was only augmented by their belief that they had joined forces with the Lord of Evil and were thereby released from all restraint. The few priests or deacons they caught died hideously. One of their unsuccessful stratagems was an attempt to lure a patrol into a house packed with combustibles and to shut them in and burn them. Showing surprising ingenuity, another gang, composed of members of the mechanical trades, had managed to construct and set up a catapult in the Street of the Smithies. They actually succeeded in lobbing a few paving stones into the Sanctuary, one of which brained a First Circle priest, before an angel discovered and destroyed their crude artillery.

A little later Goniface had seen the devil construction attempt too close a turn, fail to escape the blue beam, flare into incandescence, and crash in the Square. But as he was leaving Chief Observation Post he noted that another bat-flitting shape had taken its place.

Power Centre reported all well. The atomic batteries which served the whole Sanctuary were easily handling the increasing energy demands of the emergency. The morale of the Fourth Circle priests on duty there, and of their Seventh Circle supervisor, seemed good.

Cathedral Control Centre, where the Fanatics had sabotaged the Grand Revival a few hours earlier, also seemed to be functioning adequately.

At Sanctuary Control Centre, adjoining Web Centre, an unpleasant incident occurred. In a queer mental seizure that was all the more disturbing because at first it had no outward symptoms, the Master of Locks and Guards began to activate open all main gateways leading to the Sanctuary. His action might readily have escaped detection. It was Goniface himself who first noticed the telltale configuration of lights on the Locks-and-Guards control panel. When the priest realized that he had been detected, he babbled wildly of some hideous doom with which Sathanas had threatened him if he did not obey certain commands. Apparently he was in no sense a real traitor. As far as could be made out from his confused story, he had been terrorized for weeks by strange manifestations which appeared to him when he was alone. He claimed that since childhood he had been vaguely haunted by a fantastic fear – that floating globes of fire would burn his skull and destroy his brain. This fear had been a shadowy thing, and in later years he had forgotten it – but then small floating globes of fire had manifested themselves to him, moving purposefully through the air and speaking to him in human voices, threatening to burn his brain if he did not perform certain actions.

Goniface saw his place taken by a competent-looking substitute, but the incident left an unpleasant taste. It typified all too well the intimate and insidious strategy of the Witchcraft. The Fanatics had moved freely among the loyal priesthood, and had had access to the dossiers of practically all members of the Hierarchy – two of the clerks in Personnel Control had been Fanatics. As a result they had been in a position to discover the secret, deep-buried fears of individual priests. And the telesolidograph and similar instruments gave them the means to manifest those fears.

Yes, thought Goniface, fear was the Witchcraft's secret weapon, and the only one spelling real danger. All other threats were distinctly subordinate. Direct attack on the Sanctuaries would fail, since the Hierarchy held more than the balance of military power. Rousing the commoners to revolt had achieved considerable confusion; but the commoners could no more overrun the Sanctuaries than a band of apes could take a walled city.

But fear – that was a different matter. Goniface conned the faces around him for signs of it. It was impossible that the Witchcraft could be victimizing all members of the Hierarchy with individual terrors – to do that would take an organization as large as the Hierarchy itself. If there were only some swift and sure way of determining which priests had been specially victimized. It could be done, given time. Tomorrow – But first the Hierarchy must survive tonight.

Dismissing his escort, Goniface entered Web Centre by way of the gallery. He did not at once take his seat, but tarried just inside the gallery door, watching. In the absorbing and ceaseless surge of activity, his return was not immediately noticed.

Web Centre was like a brain. The floor space was occupied by communication panels, at each of which sat a priest. One section of these co-ordinated and verified the information pouring in from the world network of Sanctuaries. This information then appeared on the world map which took up the entire wall, slightly concave, opposite the gallery. From the gallery the members of the Apex Council conned the world map, received additional information through secretaries and runners and individual televisor panels, and made their decisions. Each archpriest was responsible for a definite sector of the Earth. Their orders were handed down to the priests of the Web Centre Staff, who sat directly in front of the gallery. They checked the orders and passed them on to the section of priests handling out-going messages.

Apex Council and Web Centre Staff co-operated admirably. There was a minimum of friction. Some of the archpriests were serving on the Staff. Tonight Brother Jomald was Chief of Communications and, in Goniface's absence, exercised supreme authority.

There was almost no noise or bustle. This was made possible by an elaborate code of gestures, amounting almost to a language, and the general use of earphones, whisper transmitters, and old-style written messages flashed by televisor.

At either end of the room were grouped large televisor panels, one for each key city.

But it was the huge world map that dominated Web Centre and gave it its special character. Projected in glowing colours from the other side of the translucent wall, it seemed almost a live thing. And, indeed, if one closely watched the region of faint shadow covering half the map, one could discern its very slow movement. That region of shadow represented night. Slowly its forward margin crept across ocean and land, engulfing the dots representing Sanctuaries. Slowly its rearward margin withdrew from others. Megatheopolis, at the centre of the map, was also at the present moment approximately at the centre of the creeping blanket of shadow.

Most of the dots on which the shadow encroached were scarlet. Many of those from which it withdrew were black. The change indicated that those Sanctuaries had stopped communicating, had presumably been deserted or fallen to the Witchcraft.

Fully half the tinier dots, which represented rural Sanctuaries, were black. All of the largest dots were still scarlet.

Goniface studied the map more closely, noting the disposition of the tiny blue-wing symbols representing squadrons of angels, the black batwing symbols that had been improvised to indicate devil constructions, the grey, wolflike diagrams marking regions troubled by enemy solidographs, and all the other meaningful pictorial hieroglyphs of the map.

As he studied it, he frowned. Indubitably the Witchcraft had been making progress – swifter progress. He sensed a better co-ordination of enemy forces, a more unified plan of campaign. They were taking clever advantage of the fact that the Hierarchy lacked sufficient angel squadrons to patrol all key cities.

Tomorrow the ship from Luciferopolis should land, carrying fifty angel squadrons, besides a number of archangels and seraphim, of which there were none here. But that was tomorrow.

He walked to the centre of the gallery and took his place, annoyed rather than flattered at the stir created by his arrival. They were all too conscious of him. They should be more completely absorbed in their work.

From the station of the Chief of Communications directly below the World Hierarch's box in the gallery, Brother Jomald started to recount recent developments. But Goniface, having discerned most of them from the map, signed Jomald to wait. He put a question to one of his secretaries.

"I sent for Deth. He should be here."

"We have been unable to contact him. We are checking all likely points."

"The Fourth Circle priest Jarles?" he continued. "I sent for him, too."

"We are checking."

But he had to dismiss the matter from his mind. Now that his return had been noticed, the archpriests and staff members were shunting over to Goniface reports on critical sectors with requests for advice. It kept his secretaries' hands full sorting them out and presenting them to him.

"Mesodelphi invaded by blackness. Shall detach half squadron angels from Archeodelphia to render assistance?"

"Eleusis reports telesolidograph discovered and seized.

Do you want details on construction?"

"Hieropolis – atomic batteries failing. Can spare power from elsewhere? Or send trained technicians to supervise repairs?"

"Sixth Circle Faculty of Olympia sends urgent message over private communication channel, warning that Olympia Control Staff is being mentally influenced by Witchcraft. Instructions?"

"Rural Sanctuary 127, East Asian Sector, reports mysterious crash of two angels. Glimpses of vast, batlike form. Shall warn all angels from sector?"

"Relief ship from Luciferopolis contacted. Will arrive approximately dawn, Megatheopolis Time. Shall land at usual port?"

Too many reports. Too many requests for advice. Time and again Goniface made, across the room or into the televisor, the curt palm-upward gesture which signified, "Handle at your own discretion. Use your own judgement." They ought to know better than to ask for advice on such matters. His being World Hierarch made them over-anxious for his approval. Even with highly capable men like Jomald it made a difference. They were taking too slavish an attitude towards Goniface and his judgements.

He did reply, however, to the last request.

"Instruct relief ship from Luciferopolis to land openly behind Megatheopolis Sanctuary on Blasted Heath, prepared to give instant assistance."

Was the Hierarchy growing old, Goniface wondered – while another part of his mind was immersed in the business of the moment. Was the priesthood losing its vigour, its stern strength of purpose, its cold joy in rulership? Everywhere he fancied he could detect an undercurrent of laxity, of weakness, of escapism – as if most of his companions were flogged on only by habit and social pressure.

Perversely, it irked him that he no longer sensed jealousy and bitter rivalry in those around him. The Apex Council was not as it had been in the old days, when every archpriest was grasping at prestige and increased authority, and when each session was a brilliant duel of wits. Gone was the keen yet realistic competition for personal power, which had been one of the chief driving forces of the Hierarchy. His chief rival, Frejeris, was out of the picture, as good as dead, and he knew that even the strongest of the Realist leaders besides himself had given up any plans they might have had for supplanting him. They were content to accept him as master. He sat alone on the World Hierarch's throne and no one wanted to push him out of it.

Oddly, it was in his traitorous agent Jarles that Goniface had last sensed a rapacity and driving force akin to his own – though cruder and more naïve. He wished Jarles would come. It would give him an obscure exhilaration to know that the cold, treacherous little cockerel was standing beside him, envying him. Perhaps, after the present crisis, Brother Dhomas could fabricate a few more such personalities to supply the animal vitality and ruthless self-interest which the Hierarchy had lost.

Morbid fancies! Ridiculous and suicidal, too, in the present crisis, when discipline and obedience were essential. Yet they kept troubling the under surface of his mind.

He noticed that the booth to his left, the one Sercival had always occupied, was empty, and he impatiently motioned the next archpriest to transfer to it. Bad for morale to have that reminder of the enemy who had so recently been discovered in their midst.

Yet as soon as the archpriest had obeyed his order, he wondered if he ought to have given it. Something in his mind kept wanting to transform the man's thickish face into Sercival's lean, hawklike one. And there was still an empty seat –

What had Sercival – Asmodeus – been after, really? Goniface would have given a great deal to have heard him answer that last question. Why had he wanted Goniface to achieve supreme authority? Had he foreseen the feeling of purposelessness that would trouble Goniface once his personal aims were achieved – the dry rot of slavish obedience that would begin to eat every other member of the Hierarchy?

Above all, why had Sercival died keeping up a silly pretence of believing in the supernatural? Could he have been a senile dodderer after all? Impossible! The leader of the

Witchcraft had proven himself a man of astonishing energy, daring, and resourcefulness. It must be assumed that Sercival had acted as he had in order to maintain the prestige of the Witchcraft, devoting his dying moments to a final effort to shake the scepticism of the Apex Council. But, according to Goniface's experience, dying men didn't do that sort of thing – or at least didn't do it so well.

The man had been so diabolically sincere! "Sathanas, receive . . . my . . . spirit," and all that! Was it possible that Sercival had believed his own words, *had had reason to believe them?* After all, to the truly sceptical mind, diabolic forces are just as reasonable building blocks for the cosmos as mindless electrons. No possibility, however seemingly fantastic, should revolt the truly sceptical mind. It all depends on the evidence. The evidence decides everything.

Suppose Sercival had had access to avenues of evidence which are denied most men? Suppose that, under the scientific mummery of the Witchcraft – seemingly identical with the scientific mummery of the Hierarchy – there was really something else? The mummery proved nothing. No reason why diabolic forces shouldn't sometimes make use of mummery to achieve their ends.

These dubious underthoughts were swept from Goniface's mind by the reports coming in from Neodelos. The situation there had reached a crisis. Half the priesthood of Neodelos was incapacitated by panic or by subtler manifestations of fear. Horrible phantoms stalked its corridors. Invisible voices made frightful threats.

Neodelos was the first of the key cities to come to final grips with the Witchcraft. It was also the first city where the countermeasures devised by Goniface would receive a thorough test. All the priests at Web Centre, over and above their own work, were conscious of the messages flashed at frequent intervals on the Neodelos televisor at the end of the room. Depending on the import of those messages, their feelings rose and fell.

"Neodelos Control Centre calling Web Centre. Power Centre here reports a disturbance. Two technicians incapacitated. Will ask for details.

"Report by runner – Cathedral Control Centre here in-

174

vaded by manifestations of some sort. Have no description except that manlike shapes accompany phantoms. Technicians have fled.

"Have ordered limited counter-attack, in accordance with your instructions. Cannot contact Power Centre. Deacons seeking to recharge wrath rods cannot reach armoury.

"Power failing. Have switched to reserves. Report by runner – devil constructions landing at Chief Observation Post.

"Still cannot contact Power Centre. Uneasiness at Control Centre. Three seizures.

"Lights failing. Anticipate general failure of power. Control Centre crowded by priests fleeing something in corridor outside.

"Darkness complete. Are working by pocket illuminators. Have ordered general counter-attack. Doors of Control Centre opening. Grey shapes – "

The Neodelos panel went dead.

The gloom that last message brought to Web Centre was something tangible. Goniface could sense a wave of fatalistic resignation. Though operations continued without interruption, there was a certain frantic haste apparent in them – an air of desperation.

"Neodelos Control Centre calling Web Centre! Counterattacks at Control Centre and Power Centre successful! Numerous witches slain. Others have retreated. Power Centre reports sabotage by witches, but one atomic battery still in order. No word as yet from Cathedral Control Centre or Chief Observation Post. Skirmishing continues. Will send further reports as they come in."

At Web Centre that message had the effect of a reprieve from a death sentence. It was as if parasympathetics were suddenly flooding the room. The large black dot which represented Neodelos on the world map blinked rapidly back to scarlet.

To a certain extent, Goniface was gratified. His countermeasures were proving satisfactory. They were very simple, being based on one hard fact. So long as the Hierarchy held the principal control points in the important sanctuaries, particularly the power sources, it could not be beaten. Likewise the Witchcraft, no matter how completely it depended on psychological weapons, must eventually attempt to take physical possession of those control points, after having terrorized the defending priests. At that moment the personnel of the Witchcraft became vulnerable to counter-attacks or ambuscades by *unsuspected secondary defenders*, for whom the Witchcraft had no terrors prepared.

The plan seemed to be working at Neodelos.

And yet, looking around him, conning the work-absorbed faces of the priests at Web Centre, Goniface had the feeling that something was lacking. Despite their obvious enheartenment at the outcome of the struggle at Neodelos, he had the feeling that deep in their minds was something that was disappointed, something that had wanted Neodelos to fall, something that wanted the whole Hierarchy to fall – a frightened, tired something.

Dimly – again in the under levels of his thinking – Goniface felt that he had just witnessed the last truly great triumph of the Hierarchy.

Everything seemed with them now – complete victory within their grasp – but that made no difference. After a hesitating and inauspicious beginning, the Hierarchy had finally risen to and met the challenge of the Witchcraft – but that made no difference either. Win or lose, the last great moment was past. Hereafter everything would be trifling. The Hierarchy, the most perfect form of government the world had ever known, had entered its old age. Ambitious men might come again, the rivalry for personal power revive. But they would be second-rate ambitions, a second-rate rivalry.

He had seen the last great moment fade, and even about that there had been something desperate and spasmodic, something that became unreal as soon as it was over, like the last rush of a dying carnivore or the last full exertion of physical strength a man makes before he becomes reconciled to old age and a thrifty husbanding of resources.

Irresistibly – though still in the under-levels of his thinking – Goniface was driven to a realization of the parallelism between his own career and the recent destiny of the Hierarchy. For his own career had surely been a spasmodic and desperate thing. And now, looking back, it began to seem fantastically unreal. A wretched boy, son of a Fallen Sister and a priest, forced to take his mother's family name of Knowles, forever barred from the Hierarchy, most despised of the despised. Knowles Satrick – a seeming weakling, who shut himself up from the world as much as a commoner's child could, hating with a terrible hate his family and especially the mother who had betrayed him by the very act of bringing him into the world, but getting only their contempt in return. Yet in that miserable boy had burned an ambition and a resentment so tremendous that they had worked like destiny. Again and again he had murdered to cover up his past, but they had been no ordinary crimes – it was rather as if fate itself had mixed the poison or wielded the knife. For his ambition had held true. Becoming a Hierarchic novice at Megatheopolis, he had climbed with phenomenal rapidity up the complacent ranks, from First to Second Circle, from Second to Fourth, from Fourth to Seventh, and thence to the Council. And with every upward step his flaming resentment and ambition had been eased a little, though in no way diminished.

That was not the way a man rose to power in a healthy, vigorous state. It was rather like the fulfilment of some dark prophecy, like the stealthy, fatalistic march of an assassin.

And now that he had reached the top, now that he had created a single peak for himself where none had existed before – the World Hierarchship – he still felt the undiminished impulse to climb upward; yet, where the next rung of the ladder should be, was only emptiness. He looked down and there were none who grasped upward at him, no ambitious successors to struggle with. Even the Witchcraft was being beaten.

Inevitably – still in that under level of thought, which was rising now to challenge his surface thoughts – Goniface was being turned back on himself, he was being driven back towards his own beginnings, as if to complete some mysterious circle. Irresistibly, his memories began to trend backward in time towards the carefully blotted-out period of his youth. He thought of the spiteful, irresponsible, grandiosely dreaming creature who had been his mother. Of his doltish half brother – But most of all of his younger sister Geryl. She had been the only one of them who had at all resembled him – in purposefulness and a certain sombreness of character. And she might very well be alive – it had been a very convincing resemblance he had noticed in the solidograph of the witch Sharlson Naurya. He gained a certain obscure satisfaction from thinking that she might miraculously have escaped from his murder trap and have devoted her life to accomplishing his downfall – the same sort of satisfaction he got from Jarles' jealousy and envy.

Knowles Satrick. Knowles Satrick. The name was repeating itself in his mind like a voice out of time's abyss. Come back, Knowles Satrick. You've gone as far as you can. Come back. Complete the cycle.

There was something very real about that voice. And something hypnotic about the name itself, like a winking point of light in utter darkness. It seemed to print itself on his mind in archaic black letters, over and over again. With a confused start, like a dozing man, he realized that his chief secretary was speaking to him.

"Sanctuary Control Centre here desires to contact you. There are two separate communications. I believe you will want to attend to them personally. Shall I put them on your televisor?"

Goniface nodded. The familiar face of the Sanctuary Control Chief flashed into view. He looked grim, shaken.

"We have contacted Cousin Deth. His body was discovered at the subsidiary prison. The face had been burned away, but identification is certain. Some of the guards there had also been slain by wrath ray. The rest were paralysed. The cells are empty. There is no sign of the prisoners."

For a moment Goniface felt only a kind of weariness, as if he had known about this long before. Deth's gone, Knowles Satrick, the voice seemed to say. The little deacon will smile no more on your enemies. But that's all right, he served his purpose. You don't need his help any more. You've got where you wanted and you can't go any further. It only remains to come back, Knowles Satrick. To come back.

The voice had the strangest effect, as if it were pulling at him, as if it were drawing him off in some undetermined direction – perhaps back across time. With an effort he half roused himself. So the prisoners had escaped from the Sanctuary? That would account for the better-co-ordinated plan of attack the Witchcraft had shown this last hour. They had got back a part of their leadership. But what did it matter? The Hierarchy was winning out at Neodelos. They were beating the Witchcraft despite its improved leadership.

He realized he was putting a question to the Sanctuary Control Chief. "Any news of the Fourth Circle priest Jarles?"

The face in the televisor grew more troubled. "Yes, your reverence, and in an unexpected connection. One of the guards has been revived. He asserts that it was none other than Jarles who engineered the escape! I will let you know what story the others tell."

The panel went blank as Goniface terminated the interview. He felt no resentment towards Jarles for his treachery, nor even towards himself for having trusted Brother Dhomas' handiwork too much – only a mild disappointment.

Jarles is gone, too, the voice was saying. But what's the difference? All of them are gone, or have ceased to matter. Nothing matters any longer. Come back, Knowles Satrick. Complete the cycle.

The under-thoughts had engulfed all except the most superficial portions of his mind, though he was still listening to reports, studying the world map, issuing orders, giving or refusing advice. The affairs of the Hierarchy seemed very far away – trivial, as though the Hierarchy were jog-trotting down some unimportant bypath in time. Only the mystery of his personal destiny seemed to have significance. Knowles Satrick – Knowles Satrick. He would eagerly follow that voice if he could ever discover in what direction it was calling him – and if it proved to be a direction a man could follow.

The face of a minor priest appeared in his televisor. Vaguely he remembered that his secretary had mentioned a second communication from Sanctuary Control Centre. At sight of Goniface, the minor priest drew back startledly. Then, apparently fearing that this might be interpreted as an affront, he grew haltingly apologetic.

"Your pardon, your supreme eminence. But I was sure, in spite of what they told me, that your supreme eminence could not be at Web Centre. I handle communications for the portion of the Sanctuary which contains your apartments, and for the past few minutes I have been receiving messages from them. I have previously had the honour of hearing your supreme eminence speak, and I was sure that I recognized your voice, although the connection was not wholly satisfactory –"

"What messages?" asked Goniface.

"That's the strangest part of it, your reverence. Just a name. Repeated over and over again. A commoner's name. Knowles Satrick."

To Goniface, in his present trancelike, visionary state of mind, this frightening coincidence seemed neither a coincidence nor frightening. It was something that, it seemed now, he had known would happen. So the voice was only calling him to his own apartments? He had expected a much longer journey.

What did surprise him a little was the casual sound of his own voice asking a question.

"You say you heard my voice coming from my apartments? You didn't see my face in the televisor panel there?"

"No, your supreme eminence, but I did see something else – something that perplexes me. I'll flash it on to you if it's still there."

The face of the minor priest disappeared. For a moment the panel was blank. Then Goniface was looking across his desk in his own apartment. Propped up so that its image filled the televisor panel, was a shadowy oblong of greyish paper, of the sort that commoners used. On it he could make out the same archaic black letters that he had already seen printed in his mind. Knowles Satrick.

Goniface stood up, signing to Brother Jomald to take control temporarily. He felt very calm. It seemed to him the most natural thing in the world that he should go to his apartments to see what was written on the other side of the paper. More than natural. Inevitable. Preordained.

Outside the gallery door his escort rose to accompany him,

but he shook his head. This was his journey – no one else's. As he walked the corridors unaccompanied, he felt that he was in an altogether different time-stream from that of the hurrying, taut-faced priests around him. A retrograde time-stream.

You're coming back, Knowles Satrick. You're completing the cycle. It's been a long journey, Knowles Satrick, but now you're coming home.

He entered his apartments. They were in semi-darkness. He picked up the oblong of grey paper in front of the tele-visor. The other side was blank.

He looked up. Standing in the doorway of the inner rooms was a woman clad in the drab homespun of a commoner. Despite the darkness he could see her plainly, as if she faintly glowed. It was the witch Sharlson Naurya. And – for now the conclusiveness of the resemblance could not be denied – it was also his sister Geryl.

For the moment his trancelike state vanished entirely, being replaced by an icy alertness. What, in the name of reason, had he been doing? He had walked into the Witch-craft's trap.

His old nature reasserted itself. Almost he smiled. So this was how the Witchcraft hoped to frighten and coerce him? A trap, indeed, a psychological trap, but not quite good enough.

Violet energy lashed from his outstretched hand. For a frightful moment it did not seem to affect the figure at all. Then the homespun flared, the face blackened. A disfigured, dissolving thing, it collapsed back into the inner room, out of his range of vision. In his nostrils was the odour of burned flesh.

For a moment he felt the surge of a great personal triumph. It was as if he had defeated his own past, come to engulf him. He had reaccomplished his last murder, tardily but once and for all. His past was dead forever. The voice which still seemed to be calling him back no longer had any hold over him.

But, almost in the same moment, he realized that this seeming victory was an unreal thing. That it was his Neo-delos – the last great flare-up of his old energy; and from

181

there the way went all downhill.

For out of the inner door, unsinged by the flames that had destroyed her, softly walked Geryl in the same drab homespun.

And behind her followed a queer procession. A gaunt old woman who limped on a crutch. A very old priest whose jowls, once fat, had now grown loose and flabby. A dull-faced, surly commoner a little older than himself. Another priest and several more commoners, most of them very old.

You've completed the cycle, Knowles Satrick. You're through with it. It's all over. It might as well never have happened.

For that silent procession was made up of the people he had murdered. But they were not as he remembered them, not as they were when they had died. Had they been, he might have suspected some guileful deception – and have had the strength to act on that suspicion.

Like Geryl, *they were as they would have been had they lived until today, ageing in normal fashion*. These were no thin ghosts, but the solid phantoms of a materialist's hell – the hell of an alternate time-stream which had swirled out to engulf him. He had not killed them at all. Everything had been cancelled out. Or he had killed them and they had continued to live – elsewhere.

Asmodeus had been right. There was more to it than mummery. And the more was horrible.

They circled him where he stood at the desk, eyeing him coldly, without hate.

He noted that the dark outlines of the room had changed. The shadow masses were different.

One last despairing flicker of scepticism – they might be telesolidographic projections of a diabolically artful sort. With an effort that he knew could not be repeated, he blindly groped outward, touched the nearest one – Geryl.

He touched substantial, living flesh.

Then Hell closed round him, like the clang of a prison door.

It was not so much terror he felt, or guilt – though in a sense he was enduring the extremes of both emotions – but an all-encompassing realization of doomful predestination, a complete surrender of will power because he was faced with forces which could nullify all the achievements of will power.

In front of him a little square of light leaped into being. It was a moment before he recognized Brother Jomald's face in the televisor panel, another moment before he remembered who Brother Jomald was. Even then it was as if he were looking at a picture which chanced to resemble someone he had known a long, long time ago, in another life.

"Your eminence. We have been deeply concerned for your safety. No one knew your whereabouts. You will return at once to Web Centre? There is an emergency."

"I will remain where I am," answered Goniface, almost with a touch of impatience. What a futile, chattery creature was this ghost! "Ask your questions."

"Very well, your eminence. The situation at Neodelos has again grown grave. It was not the clear victory it seemed at first. After the first successes there its priesthood has had no more. Power Centre there is again threatened. Meanwhile, Mesodelphi and Neotheopolis are both invaded. In view of what has happened at Neodelos, shall we order similar counter-attacks at both those Sanctuaries?"

With difficulty Goniface recalled some of the problems of that ghostly time-stream in which the Hierarchy was dying. They seemed as remote as the affairs of another cosmos.

He lifted his eyes to the circle of old faces around him. They spoke no word, but one and all shook their heads. He particularly noted the little toss, jerky now with age, of his mother's haggard features. He knew it so well.

They were right. The Hierarchy was fading from that other time-stream, even as he had faded. And it was best that it fade swiftly.

"Cancel all counter-attacks," he said, the words forming themselves effortlessly. "Suspend all such operations – until tomorrow.'

For that dying time-stream, tomorrow would never come.

There followed what seemed to Goniface a pointless and tedious argument with the ghost of Brother Jomald. Yet Goniface persisted, for he felt that the fading of the

Hierarchy was a necessary and essential consequence of his own fading. It, too, had a cycle to complete. It, too, must return to its beginnings.

And all the while, beneath Jomald's objections and oppositions, Goniface sensed – dimly, as if it were an emotion remembered from another incarnation – a frightened and tired willingness to terminate all struggles and tensions, a thankfulness that the end was at last in sight.

Finally, Jomald said, "I will obey your commands, but I cannot take sole responsibility. You must speak to the Apex Council and the Staff."

And now a little picture of Web Centre filled the square of light. Those pygmy ghosts seemed to be looking at him.

"Cancel all counter-attacks," he repeated. "Suspend all such operations – until tomorrow."

It was strange to think that that ghost world still had a dim existence, stranger still to think that the ghost name of Goniface should mean so much in it.

More words with Jomald then. With monotonous regularity, messages of Hierarchic defeat. Ever-deepening gloom. Tragedy of a time-stream dying.

Finally a note of frightened yet futile urgency.

"Cannot contact Cathedral Control Centre here at Megatheopolis. Chief Observation Post reports that Cathedral war blast no longer flares. Chief Observation Post cut off. Shall order counter-attack?"

For a last time Goniface raised his eyes. But he knew beforehand that the answer would be "No," and that he would give that answer to the frantic yet hopeless question. This time he particularly noted the senile, pendulum-like headshake of the old priest, his first confessor.

"Disturbance at Sanctuary Control Centre. Light failing. Priest fleeing into Web Centre report a blackness, with eyes, flowing down the corridors, engulfing them. No word from Power Centre. Counter-attack?"

But Goniface was thinking how like his own was the destiny of the whole Hierarchy and of every priest in it. Whether they murdered their families – and their own youth – actually or only in spirit, it amounted to the same thing. They betrayed and deserted them, left them for dead, to enjoy the power and pleasures of a sterile tyrant class.

"Doors burst open. Blackness. Shall order –"

Goniface made no answer. As the panel went black – but not because it had gone dead – as, to his seeming, the time-stream died, his feeling of resignation became complete.

He did not know that, in the under levels of his thinking, he was holding tight to one last defence against the forces which had engulfed him.

## CHAPTER TWENTY

DAYLIGHT had come back to Megatheopolis, bathing the terraces of the Sanctuary with a white splendour. There was a general feeling of emptiness and of dazed relief, as when, after a great hurricane, fisherfolk come out on the beach to talk in hushed voices of the might of the storm and of the damage it has wrought, to peer curiously at the wreckage washed ashore and incredulously at the highwater marks of last night's waves.

Such a feeling was apparent in the faces of the commoners who wandered about the terraces in small groups – and not too many of those, for the victors in last night's struggle were determined to keep matters well in hand. Later on the commoners would begin to talk in loud voices and poke at things and pry, but for the present they touched nothing, said little. Their eyes and their minds were too busy.

They kept meeting priests who were wandering about even more aimlessly than themselves. At such times they merely stepped aside to avoid each other, without comment. Most of the priests wore ragged black armbands, perhaps torn from the robe of a dead deacon, to indicate that they had changed sides, although no one as yet had asked them to.

Occasionally the terraces were crossed by a man or woman who walked briskly and obviously knew what he or she was doing. Most of these wore a simple black tunic, but a few were still clothed as commoners or even as priests. On the shoulders of some peering familiars perched, like trained monkeys.

Necks were craned as a faint hissing broke the silence. Looming over the intervening structures, the Great God's head was visible. A light scaffolding had been set up on the shoulders, and pygmy figures were setting to work in a businesslike way. There was the flicker of tiny blue flames.

Onto the topmost terrace four figures issued – one in the scarlet and gold of an archpriest; two in black tunics; one – a woman – in drab homespun.

"Yes, it was very simple," Sharlson Naurya was saying, and the after-the-storm emptiness was apparent in her words. "No alternate time-stream, no dead come alive, nothing like that. But it was what Asmodeus had devised for you long ago, and so it worked – though the emergency forced us to make some changes. It was your familiar who influenced your thoughts by telepathy. Likewise it was he who called your name from your apartments. With one exception, the ghostly figures that appeared to you were telesolidographic projections, reconstructed on the basis of old duplicate solidographs preserved in the Hierarchic Dossiers of Commoners, the effect of normal ageing achieved by painstaking retouching. Telesolidographic projections also accounted for the seeming change in your room.

"You would have known that they were solidographs, except that you touched me and found me real. I placed myself in such a way that it would be me you touched. My clothes were impregnated and my skin filmed with a faintly glowing preparation, so that I would resemble the others.

"You found I was real – and yet you knew I could not be real, for you had just destroyed me with your wrath beam. There lay Asmodeus' clinching sublety. When you first saw me in your apartments, you saw a telesolidographic projection. That was what you destroyed. A sequence showing its blackening and dissolving had been faked and was switched on by the operator as soon as you activated your wrath ray. You may remember the time lag.

"Had the scheme failed, as by some error in timing, you would instantly have been killed and an alternate plan adopted. But it was better to let you live and make use of your power over the Hierarchy, to defeat it, than to kill you and by that action perhaps jar your overawed subordinates into taking over your responsibilities and the supreme command. Asmodeus died, but the Witchcraft triumphed, because there were those who could and did succeed him. With you it was just the other way."

Goniface did not reply. Once again his face was a mask — to hide his bitter, nauseous self-contempt. But he was not altogether without consolation. For he knew that the Hierarchy would still win out, although with no credit to himself. Almost slyly, he turned his head and looked beyond the Sanctuary walls. On this side, away from the commoners' section, lay the Blasted Heath, an arid grey expanse of many acres, on which no vegetation grew. His gaze lingered there knowingly.

"All my life I have looked forward to this moment," he heard Sharlson Naurya say, and there was a weariness apparent in her voice. "As if all my life I had been falling from the bridge and looking up at your face and willing the miraculous moment to come when I would be able to reach up and pull you after me. Now the moment has come and it means very little."

The oddly distorted shadow of a man entered her field of vision. She looked up. The Black Man raised his hand in greeting. Dickon was responsible for the distortion. From his shoulder-perch he imitated his brother's greeting. His fur was a gorgeous golden red in the sunlight.

"I have just come from Web Centre," the Black Man explained. "We have established contact with our forces in most of the key cities. There only remains the mopping-up of a few small towns and rural sanctuaries."

Without any animosity, but with frank curiosity, he looked at Goniface, who slowly turned back from his contemplation of the Blasted Heath. The glances of the two leaders met.

At that instant there came a distant roaring that grew momently louder, a curiously profound throbbing and drumming that seemed to shake the ground. Those wandering on the terrace gazed quickly towards the head of the Great God and the workmen who were still busy around the neck. But the new sound was too big for that.

Its thundering filled the sky. Something was coming from the sun, darkening it.

There was a sluggish triumph, in Goniface's eyes, as he held those of the Black Man. "You've won," he said, "but now you've lost. Late but not too late comes the aid we summoned from Heaven, bringing enough military machines to turn the tide and win back the scantily armoured Earth."

The thunder rose to a shattering climax. A great shadow darkened the Sanctuary. A vast ellipsoid construction appeared overhead from the direction of the sun and came to rest above the Blasted Heath, its mighty repulsor beams ploughing like huge pillars into the grey soil, digging great pits. While it still rocked there aloft, circular ports began to open in its dully gleaming surface.

Goniface waited for the look of dismay to come over his adversary's face. But it never came.

As the thunder died the Black Man smiled in a friendly way and said casually, "Oh, I know all about the relief ship from Luciferopolis. I came out to see it land. What you say about it is largely true. I also know that Lucifer is the name of the Morning Star – Venus. Unfortunately for the Hierarchy, it's also one of the names of Satan. Of course, it's understandable that you wouldn't know about the recent turn of events there. Communications with Venus have been very bad, haven't they? And not altogether because she's moving towards opposition, I fancy. Still I would have thought that you'd have guessed that the Witchcraft was operating on Venus, too – and that it would work a little faster in the colonies than on the mother planet. I imagine it's been all over on Mars, too, for some time, but since Mars is on the other side of the Sun, it will be a couple of months before we find out for sure."

He turned and looked up. From the open ports of the spaceship, black squadrons were darting, to the amazement and awe of the wanderers on the terrace, who looked as if they might start a panicky flight.

"They'll be all angels, I imagine," he commented. "Just refinished in black and touched up a bit. Except the bigger ones. You call those archangels and seraphim, I believe?

"You see, it was really our relief ship," he went on reflectively. "I imagine that Asmodeus understood from the beginning that any revolt against the Hierarchy must be multi-planetary. Besides, the Hierarchy was always a bit more shaky in the two colonies. The colonies are supposed

188

to have been a bit more in the right, I'm told, in the inter-planetary war that paved the way for the Hierarchy. It would have taken a big war like the Interplanetary one to have shattered the Golden Age, wouldn't it now? The Blasted Heath itself is one of the scars of that war, isn't it? Devilish weapons they used in those days. Ours would seem puny to them by comparison."

He looked sideways at Goniface. With a certain malicious humour, he remarked, "Must have been rather comforting for you priests to know that you could always call for aid from Heaven, or escape there if need be – and an ironic pleasure in knowing that the myth of mankind storming Heaven was no more than literally true. Well, now we'll have a bit of Heaven on earth for a change."

Goniface no longer sought to conceal his sick self-contempt.

"I hardly need remind you," he said coldly, "that it would by just as well – indeed, very wise – to order my immediate execution. Unless you desire to enjoy further crude jibes at my expense."

The Black Man laughed heartily. "I do enjoy them," he said. "I seem to be one of the few who can enjoy that sort of thing." This with a quick glance at Sharlson Naurya. Then he looked at Goniface and his voice grew somewhat more serious. "No, I'm afraid we can't enjoy the luxury of that kind of revenge. We're too shorthanded to spare material. The Hierarchy had its hands full managing the commoners, so our difficulties must be very obvious to you. We can't spare a mind like yours. It occurs to me that Brother Dhomas would as soon remake personalities in one direction as another – all he cares about is the changing. Of course, it might not work, Jarles was rather a costly success, wasn't he? Still, with suitable precautions, it's worth a try."

After the former World Hierarch had been led away, the Black Man and Sharlson Naurya watched the jittery excitement of the crowd as some of the black devil squadrons landed on the lower terraces and their Venusian-colonist pilots emerged. Then they turned towards the Cathedral and noted that the workmen had almost completed their circuit of the Great God's neck.

He confided to her in an undertone. "I'm a lot more eager than I even admitted to put the best Hierarchic minds to work on our side. It's no joke about us being shorthanded – especially considering what we want to do. And Asmodeus dead – oblivion be good to him! When I think of what's coming! Things will be quiet for a few days, but after that – First of all, the commoners will want to kill off all the priests. There's a little of that sort of thing going on right now. We're their only protection. Next, the commoners are still thoroughly steeped in supernaturalism. They take it as a matter of course that the Witchcraft will be set up as a religion. They fully expect to go to church and find an image of Sathanas over the altar. They're probably already disappointed that there aren't a lot more satanic miracles going on. When they find that we consider the Witchcraft finished, some of them will want to revive it against us. Others, a little later, will decide to revive the cult of the Great God. On top of all that, Hierarchic counter-revolutions will be attempted! I fear that all of us will spend very busy old ages – if we live that long. When you think of the work that's going to be involved in educating the commoners and remaking their social system and gradually shifting them over to Hierarchic – I mean scientific – economy! For, of course, at the beginning we'll have to maintain both economies – feudal and Hierarchic – which will inevitably suggest to some of our none-too-well-balanced co-workers that it would be very convenient to revive the Hierarchy under a new name, with black robes instead of scarlet. Oh, things will be lively, never fear!"

As he broke off he noticed that a fat little priest with a black armband was peering at him and at Sharlson Naurya from a distance – timidly and nervously, as if debating whether to attempt to introduce himself and perhaps ask a favour. Apparently the looks he got in return frightened rather than encouraged him, for he turned and walked off rapidly.

"I know that priest," said Naurya. "He was the one who –"

"I know him even better," the Black Man interrupted. "Brother Chulian. Dear little Brother Chulian. Mild, soft, quite well-intentioned, but utterly selfish – and completely typical of the vast majority of them. When you think that we've got to integrate chaps like that back into their families, or at least back into the society of commoners, remembering – as you know well – that commoners are no paragons of loving kindness, but have been turned hard and cold by generations of useless, back-breaking toil – Oh, well, we've been over that before. But doesn't it suggest to you that I'll need someone to comfort me during the years of exasperation and thankless labour ahead?"

And he looked very frankly at Sharlson Naurya.

And she looked back at him as frankly. For a moment the grave, tired lines of her face softened into a smile. Then she slowly shook her head and looked away. The Black Man followed the direction of her gaze.

He was standing at the far end of the uppermost terrace, his back to them, looking out into space. He still wore the scarlet robe of a Fourth Circle priest.

"Oh, I suppose you're right," the Black Man admitted rather unwillingly after a moment. "I suppose he deserves something, too, after the rough time he's had. And I don't suppose the provisional government will want to execute him for the murder of Asmodeus. Yes, I see your point, all right!" he finished rather sourly.

She nodded. "I've lived for a thing like revenge," she said softly. "I've gone through something of the kind of hell he's going through. When it was over, this morning, he tried to kill himself. I made him promise – "

As he turned to go, she added, "After all, you at least have a sense of humour to comfort you."

"Yes," he admitted. "But there are some situations in which a sense of humour isn't very amusing."

And with that he turned to walk away. But a crooked figure in rags and a peaked hat, accompanied by a black cat and hurriedly hobbling up the terraces, waved her cane at him to wait. To either side the commoners made way for her, bowing low and making awed reverences. They seemed rather relieved to see someone who was obviously and undeniably a witch. It satisfied their sense of what was fitting in the situation.

"Silly ninnikins!" was the contemptuous term that Mother Jujy applied to them when she arrived, somewhat out of breath, on the topmost terrace. "Everywhere bobbing and scraping to me, as if I were an archpriest or some other monstrosity! A few days ago they wanted to burn Mother Jujy, but we don't hear any talk of that now!"

"Greetings, ancient and honourable one," said the Black Man. "Do you dislike the homage that is your due? Is there anything that you desire? You have only to ask."

"Maybe I've come for my pint of blood," she suggested darkly.

"Oh, Mother Jujy," replied the Black Man, cutting short Dickon's floridly piped gratitude, "that pint of blood is the most precious in the world. If we were going to put the Cathedral to its former use, I would have that pint of blood enshrined as the most sacred relic of them all."

"Stuff and nonsense!" said Mother Jujy. "I'm a wicked old woman and I like vile sensations. That's the only reason I let him play the vampire." She leered at Dickon. "No, I didn't come here to be buttered with praise. I want to know what's going to happen to me."

"I think you can be of very great help to us," said the Black Man thoughtfully. "We stand in need of your – er – no-nonsense point of view, and the commoners will want, even more than before, just that sort of counsel that you alone can give them. A kind of general liaison officer, perhaps – "

Mother Jujy emphatically shook her head. "No. A witch I am and a witch I remain! And I want to tell you I don't like what's going on! Why, your people are going around telling commoners that Sathanas doesn't exist!"

"That's right, Mother Jujy. The Hierarchy and the Witchcraft are both finished."

"I don't like it! You'll get into trouble if you start giving away your secrets. That always happens."

"I'm afraid you're right," he said.

With a hollow reverberation, as of departing thunder, the head of the Great God crashed in the Square.